LITTLE
MUSEUM
OF HOPE

A unique story full of hope.
Guaranteed to pull at the heartstrings

SALLY JENKINS

Choc Lit
A JOFFE BOOKS COMPANY

Choc Lit
A Joffe Books company
www.choc-lit.com

First published in Great Britain in 2023

ISBN: 978-1-912550-86-9

To my mum, who has cheered me all the way.

ACKNOWLEDGEMENTS

In 2013 I read a newspaper article about The Museum of Broken Relationships, based in Zagreb, and began to create stories around the donors to a fictional version of the museum. In 2016 'Maxine's Story' achieved a competition shortlisting and I realised readers loved the concept as much as I did. Vanessa came to the foreground and my ideas became a novel. I will be forever grateful to the Choc Lit Tasting Panel for giving *Little Museum of Hope* the thumbs up: Gill Leivers, Penny Crawley, Barbara Temple, Alan Roberton, Honor Gilbert, Shona Nicolson, Michele Rollins, Donna Morgan, Darcey Stickley and Jo Elliott. I am indebted to my editor for her wisdom and suggested improvements to the manuscript and I would like to thank the whole Choc Lit/Ruby Fiction team for their support, encouragement and belief in me as a writer. I am so lucky to have you as my publisher.

My real-life writer friends, Helen, Maddie, Lorraine and Marjorie deserve a mention for putting up with me talking constantly about this book for the last ten years. I'd also like to officially record my appreciation to all those who have supported me virtually via social media and by following and commenting on my blog — it helps morale a great deal.

Finally, to my husband, Paul: Thank you for everything!

CHAPTER ONE

September

Before he admitted adultery, Dave was predictable to the point of boredom. One teaspoon of sugar in coffee, only half in tea. BBC News over ITV. Holidays meant returning to the same, now slightly-dated, apartment in Funchal. On his birthday, only a home-made coffee cake with walnuts and copious amounts of buttercream to fill the sunken hole in its middle would do. The dubious results of my baking escapades were a standing joke between us: Presentation — Null Points; Sweetness — Dix Points.

Living with Dave was akin to burrowing down in a predictable but pleasant rut. A college maths lecturer, logic and common sense always took precedence over romance, excitement and roses — but we rubbed along OK for three decades. I loved him.

He fired the lightning bolt that split us asunder at the end of the first day back at work after the school summer holidays. When he came through the front door his face was contorted in the same way it had been at his father's grave-side. Something bad was coming and the important news I was due to announce disappeared from my head. Dave made me a cup of tea and we sat at the kitchen table.

''nessa, there's no easy way to say this, love.' He was holding my hand over the wooden tabletop. My heart pounded. 'Our marriage has been good but it's run its course.'

His words didn't make sense. He made us sound like a dried-up river. 'What do you mean — run its course?'

'I'd like us to go our separate ways.'

'What?'

'I've met someone else. I want a divorce.'

His words hung in the air, meaning nothing and then suddenly, meaning everything.

'A student?' It had to be a student. Dave didn't do anything apart from go to work and come home.

He nodded, stared at the table and had the decency to look ashamed. This had always been a danger. But Dave was fifty-five, the same age as me, and he was balding, with the beginnings of a beer belly. What could he offer a beautiful young thing a third his age? Money, status and possibly a fast track onto a degree course?

'Is it serious?' A fling would be forgivable. Or at least discussable.

'Yes.' Still he didn't look me in the eye. 'There's no going back. Never.'

I didn't cry. I gripped the wooden edges of my seat. I didn't get hysterical. I sat there and stared at him staring at the table. My world was tilting out of kilter. If I loosened my grip on the chair or moved my eye gaze, I would slide off the wooden seat into a black hole.

'I'll pack a few things,' he said.

'You're going now?' I clung tighter to the seat. Why was he leaving so suddenly? Shouldn't we talk, or argue or at least scream at each other first? Was there an etiquette for such a situation? 'You don't need to go now.'

'There's no point in dragging things out, 'nessa. The decision's been made. A clean break and all that.'

I wasn't aware I'd made a decision but the words of retaliation wouldn't form. Dave's announcement had winded me. He went upstairs. Slowly I uncurled my fingers from the edges of the chair and placed them on the tabletop. A sharp tug removed my wedding ring. My hands looked old and spinsterish. A bubble of panic grew in my chest, squashing the air from my lungs. I would die old, shrivelled . . . alone. Deep breaths. Focus on the everyday and take deep breaths.

The world had listed precariously to one side but my kitchen looked the same as it had fifteen minutes earlier. The faded wood-effect cupboard fronts still needed replacing, the black stain was as obvious as ever on the vinyl near the back door, where one of us had walked oil in on our shoes, and the old photo of Liam with his giant rucksack at the airport was still fastened to the fridge with a magnet bearing the red maple leaf of Canada.

I stood up slowly, keeping one hand on the table and the other on the chair back. My brain wasn't confident my body would react to orders. The slow walk to the sink was without mishap. I emptied the cold tea from our mugs and washed them, along with the lunch boxes we'd each taken to work that day. From above I heard my husband open bedroom drawers and rattle coat hangers.

Then he stood by the front door with a suitcase. Now really did mean now.

'What about this?' I waved the opaque Tupperware at him. 'You'll need it for your sandwiches tomorrow.'

He took it. 'I'll be in touch about money, the house . . . and stuff.' He made a vague gesture around the hall and I thought I detected a lump in his throat.

Even after he left, the tears didn't come. There was a steak pie in the fridge for our tea. It would be wasted on one. I cooked an omelette but it stuck round my mouth. I made more tea and let it go cold. I ran a hot bath. A hot bath, my cure-all for insecurity and anxiety. Confused emotions wouldn't allow me to use the luxury sandalwood bath oil Dave gave me for

Christmas, so I was liberal with the "Feel Pampered" Radox which had been 'buy one get one free' in the supermarket. Half an hour later, as the water cooled and the bubbles thinned, I realised I'd not told Dave my news. My news was also important and life-changing. It had been good news but now I no longer had a husband to support me, it was bad.

I'd been asked to take early retirement. The school was being forced to make cuts. We had a falling roll, and fewer pupils meant less money. Less money meant fewer teachers and I wasn't to be one of them — Latin not being a priority. I'd only lasted as long as I did because the head teacher studied Classics at Oxford and had a soft spot for the subject. Now he and a couple of others were going as well. I'd been pleased because I thought I was married with a husband and home to look after and one steady wage still coming in. But now I was in a post-lightning bolt universe. What would I do all day without a job? Liam lived in Canada so there was no family to fill my time. If grandchildren came along, I wouldn't be chief babysitter.

Liam! He needed to know that Dave and I had split. Dave wouldn't think to contact our son. Should I Skype him? No, an email would be easier and gentler — I'd be able to choose my words. Liam would be upset if he saw me sobbing on the webcam. There was no need to worry him yet. Best to wait until my head was calm before telling him. I'd email when things were clearer.

The next day I went into school as usual. I hadn't cried and I hadn't slept. I'd drowned in the darkness of my future. At lunchtime, the head was in the staffroom telling us how he was going to use his enforced early retirement to indulge his passion for family history. He had some grand scheme for writing a book but the details didn't register in my chaotic mind.

'What about you, Vanessa?' he asked. 'What's your passion?'

I jumped at the mention of my name and tried to think of a coherent answer. Until then, my passion had been my pupils. I thought about eleven-year-old Josh, who, on learning that Latin was a "dead" language, had asked me if I could help him contact his recently buried grandfather and ask where he'd hidden his stash of butter mints. I'd been passionate about making ancient Rome more interesting than mobile phones or computer games and was full of fun facts — did you know the Romans washed their clothes in urine for its bleaching properties? Or that they ate dormice and flamingos?

I didn't have another passion. Now Dave had left, I had nothing. With husband, son and job all gone, who was I? That's when the sobs finally came. I mumbled an incoherent excuse and fled the room. There was a sudden, humiliating buzz of conversation behind me before the staffroom door swung shut.

CHAPTER TWO

The following year

After thirty years of marriage, the divorce was like unravelling cold spaghetti. The strands of our individual lives had matted together and become indistinguishable. Through necessity, much of our joint existence was left soldered this way, even after the decree absolute. Dave's new partner had money. The housing and stock markets were in the doldrums. Selling didn't make sense until the recession cleared, so I stayed in the marital home. But after ten months of living alone I still wasn't used to the emptiness of the house. The piece of paper arriving, officially ending my marriage, didn't help. I didn't expect it to be formalised so quickly but Dave's girlfriend knew good solicitors and neither of us had put up a financial fight.

Now I had become a lady of leisure as well as a single woman. But the solidified spaghetti of our marriage still propped me up financially.

'Time for a new start, Vanessa,' my divorce solicitor had said, as she dotted the i's and crossed the t's. 'You've got a nice lump sum with your pension and your ex-husband is amenable to you continuing to live in the marital home for the time being. Go and do whatever you've always wanted to do.'

When she said that, my mind went blank. What had I always wanted to do, apart from grow old with Dave, captivate youngsters with stories about mock naval battles held in a purposefully-flooded Colosseum and indulge the grandchildren I'd thought Liam would provide? The future was a long, dark tunnel and I was without a torch, there wasn't even a pinprick of light to move towards. I broke down and wept. I cried my heart out in front of this immaculately dressed lady solicitor. She looked at her watch and sounded irritated as she asked her secretary for more tea and biscuits.

I blew my nose, put too much sugar in my tea and tried to explain that I felt my future had been snatched from me. Without my job or my husband there was no purpose to life. Dave had abandoned me and I'd grow old and bitter, alone. My son was thousands of miles away. The solicitor nodded like she understood but I knew she just wanted me out of her office as soon as possible so she could move on to her next appointment.

'The worst of it is,' I said, as I gathered up my things, 'he told me last week that he left me for a mature student — someone only a couple of years younger than me, not some young blonde floozy! How do you think that makes me feel?'

The expression of sympathy on the solicitor's face was fake. I wondered if that was how my marriage had been for the last thirty years; genuine love on my part and fake on Dave's?

The solicitor's remarks about doing what I'd always wanted to do made me think seriously about how to fill the years ahead. Eventually I settled on something I'd always fancied — running a tea shop. It might be a cliché but I wanted one of those quaint, homely places they have in Cornish villages, serving tea in mismatched floral china and huge homemade scones with great dollops of cream and strawberry jam. Places like that had me thinking of happy holidays when Liam was young and how we loved the treat of being served hunks of cake by a waitress. Cake that looked, as well as tasted, properly home-made instead of the cratered offerings that emerged from my own oven or the synthetic supermarket sponges I sometimes bought.

Over the summer I made several visits to Cornwall to trawl estate agents for successful businesses. But the cafés that were turning a profit were too expensive and the others lost money in the winter — something I couldn't afford with Dave's salary no longer in the background. As the school holidays drew to a close, I turned my thoughts to my home town of Birmingham. With the growing popularity of indulgent afternoon teas and many people preferring individuality rather than a coffee shop chain, a traditional teashop in Birmingham could be profitable all year round, especially if it was quintessentially English and attracted the many foreign tourists who now visited the city.

I finally found affordable premises but they were at the top end of my budget. The building was down a back street in the city's jewellery quarter, slightly off the main tourist route but if I found a unique selling point (I'd started attending a college business class and the lecturer was big on USPs) that shouldn't matter.

The property was much bigger than I needed. It was originally one of the smaller factories involved in pen nib manufacturing but had been through many guises since those days, including a beauty parlour and offices. The building had two floors, was old with character but in good condition. The downstairs would become my café — I planned on using pen nib memorabilia and old factory images to add atmosphere. The first floor could be let out to a craftsperson or artist as a studio-cum-gallery — thus bringing in extra money towards the loan I'd need and also generating increased footfall to the café.

My voice shook when I phoned the estate agent and put in an offer just below the asking price. Never before had I taken such a big decision on my own. I couldn't remember ever deciding anything bigger than what to have for tea without consulting Dave first. Now I had only myself to please; it was both frightening and exciting. And also lonely. Late at night my mind was engulfed with self-doubt, fear of failure and terror.

Jim, my lecturer at college, had helped me create a business plan that included a projection of the number of customers I might expect and how much they might each spend. Based on that, we worked out how big a loan I could afford to service, on top of investing my pension lump sum and a large chunk of my savings into the café. The old pen nib factory was more than I could sensibly afford but after viewing it twice I'd fallen in love with the place.

'Rent out the other floor and you'll be quids in,' the estate agent enthused. 'You'll have money to spare. We can handle the letting side of it for you, so it won't mean any extra work.'

I didn't take much persuading. I needed this place to plug the massive hole Dave had left. My roles of wife, mother and teacher had disintegrated and I was desperate for a new sense of purpose. Owning the teashop might even give me the impetus to perfect my own baking but until then I'd use top-notch bakeries to supply the fare I remembered from those Cornish holidays.

After I'd said yes to the purchase, everything happened quickly and within eight weeks the property was mine. The decorators began work straight away and I was able to open the tea shop in the middle of November. The estate agency sent me only a couple of prospective tenants to view the first floor. The first was a woman who sold her own hand-knitted garments and she felt the place was too big for her to fill with stock. The second was a man who wanted to set up a hands-on model railway experience and my first floor was too small for his needs. I started worrying. The teashop revenue wasn't reaching the theoretical projections. The empty first floor was an albatross around my neck, draining my cash reserves. Unsurprisingly, I was a failure, not only in marriage, but in business too.

I was beginning to wonder how much I would lose if I put the property back on the market and cut my losses, when my college lecturer, Jim, brought his wife along for a cream tea and to see how business was going.

'Bad.' I warmed a large teapot for the three of us to share and filled a tray with floral crockery.

'Can I see the accounts?' Jim asked after they'd both finished their first cup of tea and praised the scones. I didn't admit I'd had to buy the scones in as my own baking couldn't yet be inflicted on paying customers.

The accounts were homework I hadn't done. 'After I've worked singlehandedly all day in here, I drop into bed with exhaustion. Accounts are the last thing on my mind!' It was an excuse; the accounts weren't up-to-date because spreadsheets addled my brain. 'But it's obvious, even to me, that the takings are less than what I have to pay out. I'm subsidising the café from what's left of my savings but I can't maintain that long-term.' Suddenly I felt the need to cry. I put my head in my hands, sniffed and swallowed. Deep breaths. I would not let the tears out. The whole venture had been a stupid idea. Dave had scorned me and I'd acted impulsively, desperate to show him and the world that I could do something on my own. But I couldn't. I couldn't make things work on my own. I could only function as the weaker half of a couple. That was my role in life. And it was gone.

'It's early days, Vanessa.' Jim patted my arm. 'You need to experiment with another USP. This pen nib stuff' — he waved his arm at the sepia pictures and display boards on the walls — 'is no good because people can get the real thing at The Pen Room museum around the corner. Think outside the box. A bright intelligent girl like you will come up with something.'

'According to my calculations,' I said, 'I have twelve to fourteen months to start turning a profit. After that my savings will be gone. I need something that will grab the public by the throat and drag them in. And I need it quickly and cheaply.'

'Talking of which — this might be worth a read.' Jim's wife handed me a Sunday supplement magazine from her shopping bag. 'I was taking it for my mum; she likes the recipes. But there's an article about a museum in Zagreb. It would really suit this touristy area. The Museum of Broken Relationships.'

Great. My husband had left me and now I was being labelled as an expert in broken marriages. I wanted to move on in life, not wallow in the murk of what might have been. 'Thank you.' I tried to look grateful but my smile might not have reached my eyes.

The magazine had to wait. As Jim and his wife left, an elderly couple came through the door. The lady looked tired and was using a walking stick. The man, who I took to be her husband, was holding her hand in the manner of a child. Their clothes had seen better days and I wondered if a café visit was a rare treat for them. The lady ordered tea and scones for two.

'Would you like jam with the scones?' I asked. 'We've got strawberry, raspberry and apricot.'

She seemed about to say yes, but then glanced at the menu and changed her mind. 'Better not.' She'd seen the extra charge.

'It's complimentary today.' Making this old couple smile was more important than my balance sheet.

'Strawberry. Thank you.' The pleasure on the elderly lady's face was so good to see.

After I'd served them, I should've opened the laptop and made a start on those accounts but it was easier to flick through the glossy pages of the magazine supplement left by Jim's wife. I'd intended to skip the museum article but the bold headline sucked me in: *A MODERN MUSEUM ABOUT EVERYONE.*

The Museum of Broken Relationships is a place in which to treasure and share experiences of heartbreak and to leave behind those sentimental objects that draw us back to the past rather than letting us move onto the future . . .

11

I thought about my wedding ring sitting on the dressing table at home. I glanced at it several times a day and each time was like reopening a nasty, bloody wound. The only way to stop picking painfully at the scar was to get rid of the ring. But selling it might taint someone else's marriage and putting it in the bin felt like destroying all that had been good about our relationship and family life with Liam. The Zagreb museum would certainly be the perfect final resting place for it. And there must be other people in Birmingham like me . . . People with a life event that had soured both their present day and their memories. People for whom moving forward was like being fastened to a piece of elastic, tugging them sharply back whenever they reached a certain point. For me that certain point came when I looked at my wedding ring.

Perhaps Jim's wife was right. People might benefit from browsing the life stories of others, realising sadness is universal and leaving their own donation. "*Breaking the loneliness of suffering is healing in its own right*" said the article.

Zagreb was too far to travel for most of us. But Birmingham was one of England's leading cities, millions of people lived within easy travelling distance of my café and empty first floor. Thousands of them must have suffered a heartbreak which they'd like to put behind them so they could move on and find future happiness.

My thoughts raced, excitement tingled through my body. People could really empathise with a museum like this. It could be an establishment providing a genuine, caring service for people. The act of donating the symbol of their misery to the museum would give people freedom from the past and, if the act of giving made them feel emotional, there would be coffee and comfort food available at *The Mended Heart Café*. The new name for the café sprang fully formed from nowhere and I gave myself a pat on the back. After a moment's thought I also had *the Little Museum of Hope*. I wanted my museum donors to leave with hope for the future.

From the corner of my eye I saw the old lady give a little wave. I abandoned the magazine and took the bill over. She looked unsteady while she buttoned up her husband's coat before putting on her own. Age wasn't treating her well. I held first the interior café and then the main door open for them.

'Thank you.' The lady smiled at me but her husband didn't make eye contact; he was focused on twisting a glove around and around in his hands.

'Hope to see you again?'

'Yes, when we're having a good day.' She inclined her head towards her husband. 'Thank you.'

If there was a next time, I promised myself I'd engage the lady in conversation; she looked in need of a listening ear.

CHAPTER THREE

December
Tim

Rereading the magazine article made my enthusiasm for the museum idea soar. I had the energy and optimism of a new purpose. I needed to start the ball rolling: display cases. They don't tend to come cheap but fortunately for me, a large department store in the city centre was being closed and their fittings sold off at a bargain price. At first sight the second-hand glass cabinets didn't look attractive with all the sticky finger marks of shoppers pointing at silk scarves, feathered fascinators and chunky jewellery, but a good rub with a wet cloth and cleaning solution made them look just like new.

The biggest hurdle was going to be getting enough exhibits in place to open the doors of the museum and justify charging a reasonable entrance fee. No-one was going to come to see rows of empty cabinets. And I was still trying to keep the café open singlehandedly as well as launch the museum.

The first exhibit was obvious — my wedding ring. Expunge Dave from my life. I was an independent business woman now with no need for the baggage of a failed marriage and an ex-husband. Or, at least, that's what I was working towards. I put the gold band on a black velvet cushion in one of the glass cases on the first floor, in what I now thought of as the museum hall. I had to attach a story too. The true tale of just another middle-aged woman, gone to seed, whose husband decided that, having taken the best years of her life, he now deserved a different model, happened too frequently to interest the paying public. Poetic license made the back story more interesting. The laminated card I placed in the display case described a wealthy man who'd hidden his financial assets from the lawyers and flaunted a series of women on his arm. His wife ended up with nothing but bitterness and the memories of wasted years. Inventing someone who ended up in a worse position than me was cathartic. Even if I wasn't yet a fully independent woman, I had a fledgling business, a half-share of a house and the luxury of living there alone. When I tried, I could think positive.

Publicity was the next essential. I phoned the local free newspaper every day for a week before they agreed to run an article about the museum and print an appeal for objects with an emotional past. Tim, the reporter they sent, seemed to 'get' what I wanted to achieve with the museum and presented me with his own exhibit — a jam jar half-full of rancid-looking soil.

'It's mud from Glastonbury, fifteen years ago,' he said. 'Even then I was a bit old for camping knee-deep in festival mud but I met this wonderful girl there. We spent every moment of the festival together and I was sure it was going to be a forever relationship. We both took some mud home as a souvenir. She came from Newcastle and I live here so we arranged to meet in the middle a fortnight later. It was a disaster; without the atmosphere, the alcohol and the music, we had nothing in common. Neither of us admitted the failure but neither of us contacted the other after that weekend. I treasure the memory of that Glastonbury but it's time to get rid of the mud. I'm with someone else now. She's called Karen and this time we both think it's for forever.'

Now it was the reporter's turn to watch while I made the notes, only I couldn't match the speed of his coded shorthand squiggles.

'Can I use your real name?'

'Not surname. Just "Tim".'

'Thank you, Tim.' I finished writing. 'You don't know anyone else who might want to donate, do you?'

He hesitated. 'Karen has a story and an object. It's a mobile phone. Every time she looks at the thing, she's overwhelmed by guilt but she won't throw it away. I'll try to persuade her but I can't promise.'

'I appreciate that.'

No-one responded to the newspaper article but I was sure that once people came to the museum and saw what it did, they'd want to donate objects of their own. However, one glass case containing a wedding ring and a jar of mud wasn't enough to open and start charging entrance.

'I'm going to a jumble sale,' I told Jim and his wife when they made a pre-Christmas visit to see how I was getting on. 'I'm going to find some pre-loved items and make up some stories.'

I spent £20 at the sale and took two cardboard boxes of stuff back to the café to sort out and append fictitious back stories to. I kept the boxes hidden behind the counter so any customers wouldn't see what I was doing. An old naval cap inspired me to scribble a few sentences about a sailor lost at sea. An empty jewellery box became the symbol of a divorce where the husband had taken the wife's rings, bracelets and pendants before disappearing with another woman. A scratched garden gnome became symbolic of the gardener who'd lost his job and ended up living on the streets after a privately-owned manor house put its gardening needs out to tender and took the cheapest deal. There was also a large paperback book entitled *RPG IV — Get Started!* Inside was a message of love to Walter from Dawn. The printed pages were covered in examples of computer code.

'Walter and Dawn worked together in a computer department,' I muttered to myself. 'She bought him this book and it helped him win promotion. That brought higher status and more money. He became more attractive to women and went off with the boss's daughter.'

'I beg your pardon?' A well-groomed lady stood in front of me holding one of the café's menus. 'I wasn't sure whether it was table service or we had to order here?'

'Table service.' I was flustered now. How would I manage when I had visitors in the museum hall as well as down here in the café? 'I'll be right over to take your order.'

I jotted notes quickly while the idea was still in my head. Dawn took an awful revenge on Walter by splashing yellow paint on his new girlfriend's pride and joy — her brand new red mini. I smiled wickedly at the thought of it. A cautionary tale. Never date a work colleague.

The lady and her companion ordered and as the coffee machine hissed over their lattes, I warmed two mince pies and entered the order into the till. Doing many things simultaneously and under pressure stopped me brooding about Dave and worrying about the finances of the business. Until, that is, I was alone and exhausted while disinfecting, sweeping up and wiping down at the end of the day. Sometimes I felt like Cinderella without even the company of the ugly sisters and the wicked stepmother. That's when a longing for the comfortable, familiar presence of Dave would pop into my head. I wanted to return to those nights in front of the TV, me with a pile of Latin exercise books to mark and Dave with assignments to grade.

I carried the tray laden with mince pies and coffee over to the ladies' table and started to explain the concept of the new museum to them. The way they nodded and agreed with what I was saying showed that even the most well-heeled and well-dressed among us have secrets and heartbreak.

CHAPTER FOUR

January
Maxine

As per the newspaper advert, there was a small signboard outside the Little Museum of Hope indicating it was the "Grand Opening Day" and there were special offers in The Mended Heart Café.

Cheap coffee and half-price cake weren't the attraction for Maxine and nor was looking round the museum; she'd come to donate.

After reading about the museum in the paper it was her new year's resolution: she was going to make a gift to the museum and then move on with her life. The beginning of a new year demanded a new start. At least that had been the plan, now her courage was wavering.

A plump, middle-aged woman stood on the pavement next to the signboard and attempted to hand out glossy leaflets. People hurried past, heads down, without meeting her eye. Maxine walked up and down the opposite pavement. She'd forgotten her gloves and her hands felt frozen inside her pockets. It would be easy to go home and abandon the whole idea. The woman gave up trying to interest people and went through the museum's large black, wooden front door. A little further down the street in both directions, dropped museum leaflets formed piles of litter.

It was now or never. Maxine crossed the road and pushed open the black door. Arrows, printed on sheets of A4, in the deserted lobby indicated the museum was upstairs and the café to her left. A shot of caffeine suddenly seemed a good idea. Maxine placed a cold hand on her belly. It was too early for her pregnancy to show but the baby was going through a vitally important developmental stage; one coffee a day was her ration at the moment.

The café was empty. Maxine dithered over the choice of tables and then headed to the back corner of the room. She needed solitude to think and prepare herself for what she was about to do.

'Are you ready to order?'

'Eh . . .'

The waitress was on her before she'd had time to orientate herself. It was the same lady who'd been stood outside. She handed Maxine a laminated menu card.

'Sorry, I'm rushing you, love.' The woman put her hand kindly on Maxine's shoulder. 'I'll give you a minute. Don't forget the cake's half price.'

The menu was headed "The Mended Heart Café" and indicated, unless requested otherwise, tea was always served strong and sweetened, the coffee was milky and the hot chocolate came piled with squirty cream and comforting marshmallows. A message at the bottom of the menu said:

At the Little Museum of Hope we want to feed your soul. The aim of our menu is to offer the closest thing possible to an edible hug.

Maxine looked at the list of doughnuts, bread pudding and scones. She hadn't eaten breakfast and still didn't feel hungry. It was nerves and guilt at what she was about to do. She thought about the baby as she read the list of cakes; bypassing the calories yet again wouldn't be wise.

The waitress was hovering and must think she was a nutcase. How long did it take to choose? Her mind had gone to goo. All she could think about was parting with Daniel's bear. It was a betrayal of her first baby son. But he was an infant inside her head only — a newborn in a lemon babygro nestling in her mother's arms and suckling on a bottle. In real life he'd be almost a teenager, but Maxine still wasn't sure she wanted to relinquish his bear.

'I'll have coffee . . . and a doughnut, please.'

The woman disappeared and Maxine realised the hand clutching her handbag ached with tension. She took a breath and slowly released her fingers. To donate Daniel's bear, she had to learn to let go. She took another breath and put the bag on the floor between her feet.

'Enjoy.' The woman placed a large mug and a plate of sticky, sugary sponge in front of her. Instead of leaving, the waitress hovered.

Maxine shifted on her chair and tightened her feet around the handbag. Then the woman sat down on the chair opposite. Maxine wanted to tell her to go away but that wouldn't be good manners.

'I'm Vanessa. What's your name, love?' The woman's voice was gentle rather than demanding.

Maxine looked at her over the rim of her coffee mug. She was motherly in a way her own mother had never been. Mum had changed lately but when Maxine really needed her, she'd acted against her. Maxine was working on forgiveness but it was tough. If she started talking to this rounded matron in her white apron and cap the whole story would come out, including the part that made her so ashamed. No-one else knew everything from start to finish. Adrian had needed to know the bare bones but Maxine had left out certain details. Telling a stranger absolutely everything would be a relief.

'Maxine.'

'Have you brought something for the museum, Maxine?'

'Yes.'

'Would you like to tell me about it?'

Maxine took a deep breath and studied the tabletop.

'When you're back home, it might reassure you to know someone else has the full story behind your object. I can visit it for you when it's on display. You'll know someone here is caring for it in the same way you would.'

Maxine blinked, feeling the tears start.

'Only if that's what you want,' the waitress added.

Maxine opened her mouth and then shut it again. She didn't know where to start.

'How old are you, Maxine?'

'Thirty.' She took a bite of doughnut and a mouthful of coffee.

'Can you tell me about your object?'

The sugar rush and caffeine fix comforted her and Maxine started to talk. Her mind jumped back to her childhood and the events leading up to the total implosion of her life. Kaspar lived next door. His family had been there as long as she could remember. They bruised their knees in the same infant-school playground and he pulled her hair when they moved up to juniors. They both passed their eleven-plus exams, went off to single sex grammar schools and stopped hanging out together. Maxine still saw him coming and going from his house but as he entered his teens, he became scrawny and spotty. He let his hair grow shaggy. She ignored him and gave her attention to Robbie Williams.

While she was immersing herself in unattainable pop stars, Kaspar underwent a metamorphosis. One day, when Maxine was sixteen, a Greek god walked out of next door's house. It was summer and Kaspar's grey T-shirt outlined the muscles in his torso. Black jeans fitted snugly around his neat, firm bum. His blond hair was cropped close and he strode like a man.

Maxine watched him from her bedroom window. He turned, gazed up and his eyes locked on hers. While her stomach looped the loop and her heart did crazy things, she managed to raise her hand in what she hoped was a nonchalant greeting. He waved back.

After he'd disappeared down the street she lay on her bed with a confusion of thoughts. Kaspar had suddenly become attractive. He was up there on a par with Robbie.

Maxine noticed Kaspar's regular comings and goings. Sometimes she watched him, unseen, from behind the net curtain in the lounge. Other times, she stood, visible, in her bedroom. He always looked her way before heading down the street and when he saw her, they waved and exchanged a grin.

Soon she wanted more than this silent communication. He left for school before her, so one evening Maxine set her alarm earlier, hardly sleeping as she anticipated the next morning.

Make-up wasn't allowed at school but she brushed on a smidgen of mascara and applied a sheen of lip gloss. Ignoring her mother's protestations, she skipped breakfast to style her hair. Then she left the house early, at the same time as Kaspar went for his bus.

'Hi,' she said. She'd been practising to make it sound like a complete coincidence they'd bumped into each other.

'Hi.' His voice was deeper than she remembered.

Up close she could see his face no longer had the downy look of boyhood. He must have started shaving. They walked to the bus stop side by side. She wanted him to take her hand but there was no reason why he should. For all Maxine knew he had a girlfriend.

'I need to get to school early to go through some homework.' She'd planned what to say so he didn't think she'd engineered their meeting.

'OK.'

It was obvious things weren't going to happen between them on one walk to the bus stop. Maxine thought on her feet. 'In fact, I'll be going early most days. We're getting towards exams, there's more stuff to get done.'

'Don't I know it! See you tomorrow?'

He said it like a question, like he was asking her on a date. Maxine's heart thudded.

'Yes.' She tried not to grin too much and had to stop herself jumping up and down and waving her arms in the air. It was the first time she'd been asked on a date. All that day there was no room in her mind for anything else. It was filled with the bright orange anticipation of ten minutes with Kaspar the following morning.

The next day she coaxed on a little more mascara, smeared a tinge of Ruby Red across her lips before applying the clear gloss and then pinched her cheeks like she'd seen the heroines do in Sunday night TV period dramas before they set off to meet their suitors. Maxine would never have admitted it to anyone, not even her best friend, but she saw Kaspar as future husband material and the father of her children.

Then disaster struck. She was all dolled up for their second walk to the bus stop together but got the timing wrong. As she walked down the drive, Kaspar was nowhere to be seen.

Panic stampeded through Maxine. She looked at the blank windows of his house, sure he hadn't already left. She concentrated on his front door — willing him to open it with a wave and a grin. She gazed up and down the street. It seemed like everything was happening in slow motion. Old Mr Mallinson was walking his dog, a moth-eaten thing that looked as old and decrepit as him. The tortoise-like milk float, emblazoned with "Camberwell Dairies" lumbered past, travelling at walking speed even though it was naked of bottles. Maxine's dad came out with his lunchbox — cheese and tomato on white bread, the same as every day. He had no sense of adventure.

'Do you want a lift?' he asked. 'You don't want to be late for this homework club.'

She coloured at the mention of her white lie. Yes, would be the easy answer but she'd be too early for school and if she hung around here a little longer Kaspar might . . . In the nick of time, Kaspar came out of his front door.

'No thanks. I'll walk.'

'Looks like you won't be alone.' Her dad threw her a huge wink that Kaspar must have seen.

'Hi.' His voice was like melted Mars bar — heavenly. Kaspar was the hero in Maxine's own personal love story — a story guaranteed to have a happy ending.

'Hi,' she replied.

'Did you get your homework done?'

'What?'

'Why you're going to school early? Something to do with homework.'

'Oh, yes.' She patted her bag as if to indicate everything was in order.

Last night that orange feeling of anticipation had blocked her concentration — she hadn't written her French essay and, even worse, she hadn't practised any possible conversation with Kaspar for this morning. The only words running through her head the previous evening had been those she wanted to hear Kaspar utter right now — 'Will you go out with me tonight?'

Instead he said, 'My parents are going away for the night. It's Dad's fiftieth birthday. They won't let me have my mates round — they reckon they're a bad influence and will wreck the place.'

'Oh.' She watched his lips move as he spoke and wondered what it might feel like to kiss him.

Maxine had only been kissed by a boy once. It was at a party when she got off with a friend's brother who seemed to have even less idea of what to do than her. He had as much skill as a slug escaping from a muddy hole on a wet day. She knew there had to be something better and she wanted Kaspar to prove it to her.

'My parents like you, Maxine. They think you're a respectable girl from a good family.'

She didn't know whether this was a compliment or a quiet insinuation that she was as boring as her father.

'I don't fancy sitting on my own all evening,' Kaspar continued. 'So, do you want to come round?'

It took Maxine a few seconds to realise what he'd said. Kaspar was inviting *her* to spend the evening with *him* at his house. Alone. She nearly walked into a lamppost.

'We could play some music or watch TV,' he added.

Or kiss, she thought.

'Yes.' She hoped the joy pulsing through her body didn't show on her face.

When she left him at the bus stop she was gliding on cloud nine instead of walking on concrete towards double Maths. The news of her date exploded out of Maxine as soon as she saw her best friend, Emma. Emma heard nothing but Kaspar, Kaspar and more Kaspar. Wisely and with the experience of someone who'd been on three consecutive dates with the same boy, Emma pointed out that Maxine shouldn't rush around to his house that evening.

'Go at 8:23,' she said. 'Play it cool. If you go at 8:00 or 8:30 it looks like you pre-planned it. Go at 8:23 and it will look like you sauntered round when you had nothing better to do.'

It was the same with the outfit — Emma said Maxine had to look good but not as though she'd made any special effort. It had to be jeans and a T-shirt — but a newish one that hadn't yet been distorted or discoloured by the washing machine. Emma seemed as excited as Maxine. She'd seen Kaspar once, out of the window at Maxine's house. When they parted for the day she gave Maxine a hug and held up crossed fingers.

That evening, Maxine spent an hour in the bathroom. For most of that time her father was banging impatiently on the door. Maxine shouted back they should get an en-suite like everyone else. It took her ages to do her face so it looked like she hadn't done it at all, and to tong her hair so the waves looked natural — even though they hadn't been there that morning.

At 8:22 she told her mum she was popping next door. Her mum frowned and looked like she was expecting further clarification. Maxine didn't elaborate.

'You look nice?' her mum said, lifting the tone of her voice at the end of the phrase to add the question. After a pause, in which Maxine didn't speak, she added, 'Be back by 11:00.'

Maxine shrugged. She didn't want to commit herself to anything; Emma hadn't mentioned any rules about when she should leave. At 8:24 she was ringing Kaspar's doorbell. She could hear the television. For a minute she was terrified his mother might open the door and she'd, embarrassingly, discover she'd got this date business all wrong. There were footsteps in the hall and then Kaspar was ushering her inside a house with exactly the same layout as theirs. Two bags of crisps and an open can of lager were on a coffee table in the lounge.

'I'll get you some wine,' he said.

She stood awkwardly by the TV as he raced to the kitchen and came back with a glass and a bottle. He poured the clear liquid and handed it to her. She took a sip and tried not to pull a face. She rarely had the chance to drink alcohol and the only way she could usually drink wine was to mix it with lemonade. She wasn't going to tell Kaspar that.

'My parents won't miss the odd bottle,' Kaspar explained. 'Dad got given a load for his birthday anyway.'

She took another mouthful. Was he expecting her to drink the whole bottle? Perhaps the crisps would help it go down. They sat side by side on the settee and watched a repeat of *Absolutely Fabulous*.

'Salt and Vinegar or Prawn Cocktail?' he asked.

'Prawn Cocktail.'

The more wine Maxine drank, the easier it went down. When her glass was empty, Kaspar poured her another. She felt more relaxed than she'd ever felt before. The blood in her veins became warm and her limbs, heavy. There was a ten centimetre gap between Kaspar and her on the settee. Maxine looked at that space and thought how she didn't want to tell Emma about a missed opportunity. Making use of the Dutch courage coursing around her body, she wriggled closer to

Kaspar until their thighs touched. He put his arm around her and she knew her time had come. This was going to be better than the saliva covered slug at the party.

Kaspar bent his head and Maxine raised hers. He definitely knew what he was doing. He tasted of lager and salt and vinegar crisps. His tongue played with the tip of hers. Teasingly, he stayed only just inside her mouth. Maxine felt proper physical desire for the first time in her life. She could do nothing but respond and press herself closer to him. Her tongue caressed his and they both started to probe deeper.

Eventually they broke apart and neither spoke. Kasper stared into her eyes and caressed her face. At that point, in her teenage mind, Maxine knew he loved her as much as she loved him. His hand drifted downwards and found her breasts. Her nipples were plainly visible under the close-fitting fabric of her T-shirt. As he stroked, a delicious fire started between her legs. He placed her hand on his crotch.

Maxine was barely aware of Joanna Lumley and Jennifer Saunders on the television. For a long time they explored each other's bodies through the safety barrier of clothes. Then Kaspar refilled her glass. The bottle was half-empty and the mantelpiece clock said 9:45. There was plenty of time. Kaspar's hand slipped underneath Maxine's T-shirt and his fingers found their way inside her bra.

Maxine stopped dead in her narrative. 'What are you doing?' Vanessa was scribbling in a notebook and Maxine wasn't sure she wanted that; her story had always been private — there were certain things she was ashamed of.

'Writing down your story so visitors can make sense of your exhibit.'

Maxine frowned; she hadn't anticipated this. For some stupid reason she'd thought the museum would be like the inside of a charity shop — shelves of second-hand stuff and nothing to identify the original owners. She needed to rethink.

Looking down, Maxine noticed a skin had formed on the surface of her coffee. She pushed the beige membrane to one side with a spoon and then chased it around the inner circumference of the mug. It reminded her of the thick layer that used to form on the top of her grandma's home-made rice pudding. Maxine smiled; that skin had been luscious and caused innumerable playful arguments between her and her dad about who should have the honour of eating it. The mini quarrels usually ended with her squealing as she was tickled to death and Grandma decreeing Maxine the winner.

She stared at the coffee again and her smile turned to a broad grin as she remembered her one and only attempt at that old rice pudding recipe. Ignoring the handwritten, underlined instruction about the size of dish required, she'd tipped rice and milk into the first ovenproof dish that came to hand — oblivious to the fact that the rice and milk would both expand. She and Adrian had witnessed a rice pudding have a volcanic eruption that day.

Then Adrian had shown his true love for her: they'd cleaned the oven together. The satisfaction in their teamwork was a happy surprise to both of them.

Adrian never flinched from supporting her. Now she would do the same for him by carrying out her promise to move on from the past.

'Can you change the names? I don't want my baby . . .' She touched her belly again and glanced down.

'Are you expecting?'

'Only just. I've done a home test but it hasn't been confirmed by the doctor yet.' Maxine was surprised to find herself explaining this to a complete stranger.

'Congratulations! And don't forget baby needs energy too.' Vanessa pushed the half-eaten doughnut nearer to Maxine. 'What happened next with Kaspar?'

Maxine took a bite of doughnut and used her tongue to capture the sugar clinging to her lips. If the names were changed it would be all right to tell everything.

Kaspar wanted to go all the way that night, Maxine was sure. Intuition told her so. Despite the wine and her own physical longing, Maxine wasn't ready and he didn't suggest it. Perhaps he guessed how she felt. Maxine took it as a sign he loved and respected her and was prepared to wait.

She went home at 11:00, any later would've invited too much questioning from her parents. She ran upstairs. If she'd spoken to her mother on her way to bed she'd have guessed immediately what Maxine had been doing and would have seen how drunk she was.

After that evening, she and Kaspar started going out 'properly' — to the cinema, the pubs that would serve them and to the spate of teenage house parties going on amongst their friends. They kissed and groped but never had the privacy to go further.

Until Kaspar's parents went away again.

'Back by 11:00!' her dad called as Maxine scooted out the door before he or her mum could moan about how short her skirt was or tell her off for the tiny bit of cleavage her new, clingy top revealed.

This time they both drank cider. They drank too much, too quickly. Without discussing it they both knew this was going to be the night they consummated their relationship. Maxine had planned a little speech to Kaspar about condoms but the cider bubbles must have blocked her brain because she didn't utter a word of it.

By now they were practiced at turning each other on with kisses and caresses. When Kaspar led her from the settee to his bedroom she burnt with desire. Upstairs he pulled his clothes off and threw himself onto an unmade bed. Maxine did the same, pausing only to fold her new top.

The name of a football club was emblazoned on the quilt cover and a matching scarf was pinned along the wall over the bed. Looking back now, she couldn't remember the team or the colours but Kaspar's face would stay in her mind forever. His eyes had narrowed with the alcohol and there was no mistaking his lust. It was scary and exciting at the same time.

Maxine pushed herself against him on the single bed, their heads sharing one pillow. His lips were parted and he kept licking them as though, despite the alcohol, he was as nervous as her. He didn't speak but his body language was screaming urgency. He swung himself on top of her, resting on his elbows. For a moment they stared at each other. Maxine's whole body tensed and it was like she hadn't drunk a drop of cider. She wanted to ask if it was Kaspar's first time too. She wanted them to lose their virginity together. She wanted to ask him to be gentle and that little speech about condoms tried to make itself heard in her head. But she said absolutely nothing. Maxine lay there, rigid, wanting it and not wanting it.

He was quick, too quick.

'That was good,' he grunted as he rolled off her.

Maxine wanted to tell him it had hurt. She wanted him to cradle her in his arms and say that he loved her. Instead he muttered something about getting another drink. He pulled on his underpants and T-shirt and went downstairs.

It's not nice to be deserted in a strange male bed when you're feeling shaky and unsure. Suddenly home seemed a nice place to be. Maxine grabbed her clothes and went into the bathroom. She wiped herself with toilet paper and wondered if she dared have a shower. She felt sordid and wanted to get clean. But Kaspar was stomping back upstairs so she pulled on her clothes and went to meet him.

'I have to go,' she said.

'I got you another cider.' He looked forlorn and tried to hand her the can. There were goose pimples on the tops of his thighs.

Maxine shook her head. She wanted to cry. She had to go.

At home she locked herself in the bathroom and stood under a steaming shower for a long time. Her mother banged on the door.

'You spent hours in there before you went and hours in there as soon as you come back. What's going on?' she demanded when Maxine emerged wrapped in a towel.

Maxine didn't trust herself to speak. She went straight to her bedroom and closed the door. Her mother sighed and muttered on the landing.

Her mobile buzzed. A new message from Kaspar. *Soz.*
My first time too.

A few words but they meant a lot. She guessed he'd
done what he thought a man had to do. Neither of them
had known any better. At least now he realised he'd been
thoughtless and was making amends.

It's OK she texted back. Despite the disappointing experience she still loved him, especially now he was showing a
softer side.

The next day Maxine and Kaspar went into town
together and sat in Macdonald's, drinking coke and holding
hands. She felt closer to him than ever before. He explained
how he'd supposed he had to take the lead in the bedroom.
He was sorry he hadn't stopped to think or ask how she was
feeling. He said he'd been ashamed of his inexperience and
didn't want her to know he was a virgin. He hadn't realised
she wanted it to be his first time too so they could help each
other. Over the fizzy drink, Maxine felt their relationship
become deeper.

'I'm saving up,' Kaspar told her, 'to take you to a luxury
hotel. I want you to have the very best next time.'

They sat kissing in an upstairs corner of the fast food
outlet until the manager tapped Kaspar on the shoulder and
asked them to leave. He said their behaviour was 'inappropriate' in a place full of young children.

A couple of months later Maxine realised she hadn't
had a period since her one and only coupling with Kaspar.
Pregnancy crossed her mind briefly but they'd only done it
that once and it had been so quick. In her naivety she didn't
think it possible for sperm and egg to have met and do whatever they had to do to make a baby. But she'd been an ostrich
with her head in the sand.

Now, beneath the harsh café lights, Maxine rescued her
handbag from between her feet on the floor and retrieved
Daniel's bear. She kissed the top of its head before placing it
on the Formica surface of the table. The soft toy was worn.
She rubbed the bear against her face. It was like a sponge,

absorbing the tears trickling down her cheeks. She reached for a serviette and blew her nose.

'Go on with the story, love.' Vanessa gently pulled the hand with the teddy from Maxine's face.

Maxine did nothing about the missed period until it was too late. Her belly was well-rounded and the baby, kicking. Kaspar guessed before then. He tried to tell her that her breasts were heavier and her stomach bigger. Maxine muttered something about A level stress making her comfort eat. He pooh-poohed that and swore he'd stand by her. He wanted them to see the doctor together. The money he'd saved towards the hotel could be used for baby things, he said.

She ignored him. But this wasn't something that would go away. When Maxine's mum noticed, all hell broke loose. She took over and there was no chance of Maxine and Kaspar handling things their own way. She wouldn't even let him go to any of the antenatal appointments that followed.

'I think he's already done enough damage, don't you?' she said.

Maxine was glad when the doctor said she was seven months gone and it was too late to do anything but have the baby. If it had been early enough in the pregnancy, her mum would have made her kill it. How could Maxine have done that?

At the scan they said it was a perfect little boy. She called him Daniel. Maxine loved Daniel's kicks and wriggles. Kaspar loved them too. He'd sit with his hand on her stomach sharing each sharp movement with her. But that was only when Maxine could sneak round to his house. Maxine's mum didn't want her to have anything to do with Kaspar.

'This whole sorry state of affairs is his fault,' she said. 'He shouldn't have taken advantage of you like that.'

Maxine tried to tell her she'd been a willing participant but her mum wouldn't listen. She even blamed Kaspar's parents for going away and leaving him with an empty house in which to perform his wicked acts. Maxine's dad faded to a shadow of his usual self. He took no action and said nothing to Maxine, other than to pass the time of day. Sometimes she caught him looking at her with sadness in his eyes. She couldn't guess whether he shared her mum's anger or whether he was leaving things up to his wife because babies were 'women's business'.

Kaspar's mum and dad were supportive — maybe because they accepted some of the guilt being heaped upon them. They said they'd help Maxine and the baby financially as much as they could until Kaspar had done his degree and could get a job to keep the three of them himself.

Maxine bought a few things for Daniel with birthday money she'd stashed in the building society. She and Kaspar chose the teddy for him together. They checked it had the right safety labels so he couldn't hurt himself or choke to death. Maxine packed it in her overnight bag ready for when she'd need to go into hospital for the birth. It would make a nice first toy for their son.

'I don't know why you're bothering,' her mum said when Maxine showed her the bear. 'Keep that baby and your future is ruined. As it is, you'll be giving birth when you should be sitting your A levels. You'll never get to university now. At best you'll end up in some dead-end office job. More than likely you'll end up unemployable.'

'It's too late to do anything but keep Daniel,' Maxine said smugly.

'You can have him adopted.' It felt like a knife slicing into Maxine's heart. Her mother's voice was cold and her eyes hard.

'Never!' Maxine stomped from the room.

Day after day her mother gave the same talk. She gradually ate away at Maxine's confidence by telling her what a dreadful mother she would be and how Daniel didn't stand a chance of being happy if he stayed with her. She talked about what a fine life he would have if he was adopted. He would have two parents in a stable relationship with good money coming in — he would want for nothing, emotionally or financially. Maxine was totally confused about the best way forward.

She should've told Kaspar what her mum was saying but he was struggling with A level revision and she didn't want to give him any more hassle. Besides, she was ashamed of admitting her own mother thought she was unfit to look after a child. Maxine decided she would give birth to Daniel quietly at home — after all, young girls who don't even know they're pregnant do it all the time on the bathroom floor. At least Maxine would be prepared and know roughly when it should happen. Then she'd go away for a bit with baby Daniel and decide what to do; she still had money in the building society. Maybe she could get a flat near Kaspar's university and they could be a family from the start. She had no idea whether her savings were enough to rent a flat or to bring up a baby — but she had to try.

Maxine bought nail scissors for cutting the umbilical cord, a pack of nappies and a couple of lemon babygros with a blue duck motif on the chest. There was no need for feeding bottles because, like all good mums, she would breastfeed to build up Daniel's immune system.

In soap operas, babies are born within a single, thirty-minute episode and Maxine thought she could put up with any amount of labour pains for that long and manage it herself — it was a natural process after all. She repacked her hospital birth bag as a running away bag, for immediately after Daniel was born. She even slipped in her passport, just in case. Did new babies need passports? She had no idea.

When the contractions started Maxine was terrified. A vicious force took hold of her body. It felt like she was being squeezed in a vice. She locked herself in the bathroom. After each few minutes of respite, the pain would come again, stronger and more long-lasting than before. She stuffed the corner of a towel into her mouth and bit hard to stop the screams. Suddenly warm liquid poured down her legs. Her waters had broken. Overcome with fear for Daniel and herself, she howled.

Her parents came running and had to break the lock on the bathroom door to get to her. Her dad drove them to the hospital and her mum stayed in the delivery room. Somewhere in the back of her mind Maxine wanted to object to her mother's presence — Daniel's first breaths shouldn't be with a woman who wanted to give him away. Fear and agony chased away any coherent thought that Maxine could act upon. She breathed deeply on the gas and air. It didn't take the pain away so a white-coated man gave her an injection. Daniel finally emerged eighteen hours later. Maxine was too exhausted, sore and woozy to care. Her body felt as though it had been run over by a steamroller — a baby to look after was the last thing she needed. She wanted to curl into a cocoon and die. They took Daniel to the hospital nursery.

Maxine was given a side room on the ward and her mum stayed with her, dozing in a chair. Every time the midwife brought Daniel for feeding, Mum waved her away or gave Daniel a bottle herself, explaining that her daughter didn't want to breastfeed. Maxine acquiesced, too weak to argue and too young to know any better. The long labour had left her deflated and without the strength to put her own point of view. When Maxine's milk came in and her breasts were heavy and uncomfortable, still her mum sat there with a bottle. But the tingling of her nipples when Daniel cried was nature's wake-up call. Maxine tried to say that she should feed her son.

'Give it a bit longer. You've had a tough time.' Her mother's concern sounded genuine. 'Go back to sleep — you need the rest.'

Maxine gave in; the whole birth and baby business was much worse than she'd expected. Her lack of contact with the baby meant they didn't bond, which, in hindsight, was probably her mum's plan. Maxine's father came to the hospital just once, kissed her and Daniel and sat in silence, shaking his head every now and again.

Kaspar and his parents visited only once too. Kaspar brought a bouquet of red roses. Daniel was having a rare sleep and Maxine's mum refused to let them hold him in case he woke up. Kaspar sat silently by the bed holding Maxine's hand. In the years to come Maxine blamed him for not intervening to ensure Daniel came home and they became a family. But, coupled with revision, it was too much for an eighteen-year-old boy to cope with.

At the end of that single visit he kissed her and whispered, 'I'm working my socks off for these exams. Eventually I'm going to have a brilliant job and take care of you and Daniel.' The intention was there but it never came to pass.

A parade of social workers visited. Such was Maxine's utter confusion, terror, exhaustion and apparent inability to bond with her new son, she bowed to her mother's pressure and let Daniel go to what her mother called 'a better life'. Kaspar went mental when he found out but by then Maxine had sunk into a depressive lethargy. They tried to keep their relationship going through the summer months but there was a great wedge between them. Maxine couldn't bear Kaspar to touch or even kiss her. She was petrified of things going too far and getting pregnant again.

Then Kaspar went away to university and Maxine enrolled at the local college to redo the second year of her A levels. At first, Kaspar came home at weekends and they tried to make things work but the glue had dissolved and they drifted apart.

CHAPTER FIVE

'Do you feel better now, love?' Vanessa asked. 'For having talked about it to someone?'

Maxine was holding the bear close against her chest. 'I haven't finished.' If she was finally going to tell her full story, she was going to do it properly. 'You'll hate me for what comes next. This is the bit no-one else knows.'

Vanessa raised her eyebrows.

Maxine took a deep breath and ploughed on. 'Let's jump forward three years . . .'

Maxine told how after his graduation, Kaspar got married — to Emma, Maxine's best friend from school. They'd ended up at the same university but didn't get together as a couple until their final year. Emma was worried Maxine would be upset but she gave them her blessing. After Daniel had gone, her feelings for Kaspar had dissolved too.

Maxine's agony restarted when Emma got pregnant. She could do nothing but compare the situation to when she was expecting Daniel. Emma bloomed during her pregnancy. Everyone was pleased for her and Kaspar — especially Maxine's mother. Maybe she felt this baby would right the wrong she'd inflicted on Kaspar by letting Daniel be adopted or maybe she just wanted to emphasise to her daughter how bad she'd been a few years earlier by not conceiving within the security of marriage. Maxine's mum talked about Emma like some prize, pedigree breeding cow, whereas pregnant Maxine had been something to hide away and be ashamed of.

Emma had a little boy. They called him Joseph. He'd have been Daniel's half-brother but Maxine's mum gave him a welcome one hundred times better than that of her own grandson. She bought a massive bouquet and insisted Maxine sign her name on a greetings card decorated with blue ribbon. Maxine tried to refuse, not out of spite for Emma, but as a protest at how her mother was behaving with this baby compared to her own flesh and blood. Maxine's mum accused her daughter of making an innocent new baby suffer for her own whorish actions with Kaspar.

'If you'd waited until you had a ring on your finger, things would have been so different,' she said. '*You* could've lived the "happy ever after" instead of Emma.'

Maxine wrote her name but didn't give her congratulations in person, even though Kaspar and Emma were staying next door for a while so Kaspar's mum could help with baby Joseph.

Early one morning, as Maxine was trying to decide what to wear for another boring day behind a desk in the bank, an ambulance screamed into the cul de sac. She pulled the bedroom curtain slightly open. Kaspar was outside. For a split-second Maxine had a vision of herself as a teenager watching and lusting after him. But, unlike all those years earlier, he didn't turn around with a grin and a wave. Instead he almost dragged the paramedics from their vehicle.

Something had to be wrong with Emma or Joseph. When Maxine went downstairs, her mum was pacing the kitchen, wondering aloud if she should go next door to see if there was anything she could do.

'What can you do that the paramedics can't?' Maxine's voice was too sharp but her mother had never shown any anxiety over Daniel and her, yet here she was, worried sick about people she hardly knew.

It was Joseph they carried out to the ambulance. Emma climbed in too. She looked like she'd just got out of bed and pulled on the first thing that came to hand — jeans and a gruesome turquoise hoody. Kaspar and his parents got in the car and followed the ambulance.

Later, they announced it was a cot death. Maxine's mum cried. But Maxine felt her own suffering with Daniel had been much greater and was still ongoing. Somewhere in the world, her baby would be starting school and she knew nothing about it. At least Emma had been able to enjoy Joseph for a few weeks and she still had Kaspar — they could have another baby.

Maxine's mum organised a collection amongst the neighbours for a wreath. Maxine refused to accompany her mother to the funeral. She didn't want to watch her caring about someone else's dead baby in a way that she'd never cared for her own live grandchild. Then her mum did the unforgiveable.

'They're burying the little mite,' she said. 'He'll be alone in the cold and dark. I'm taking this to leave on the grave. You've got no need for it.' She picked up Daniel's teddy from its home on Maxine's pillow and popped it in her handbag.

'No!' Maxine tried to snatch the bag from her.

It was too late. Her mum slammed the bedroom door, putting a wall of wood between them. Maxine tried to follow but her mum was in the car before she reached her. Afterwards, Maxine rang in sick to work. Then she lay in bed sobbing. She pretended a stomach upset when her mother came home. The fabricated physical discomfort became real when Maxine had to listen to how Daniel's teddy had been gratefully received.

'With all the wreaths, the plot looked too grown-up,' her mother said. 'That cute little bear reminded everyone a baby had passed on.'

Maxine was devastated. That teddy was all she had left of Daniel. She feigned illness again the next day and, when her mum had gone to work, got the bus to the cemetery. It was a damp day and a fine mist of rain hung in the air.

She walked up and down the geometrically arranged plots, looking along the rows for freshly dug earth indicating a new grave. Then she saw Emma and Kaspar. They were kneeling beside a mound of flowers. Maxine stopped and turned back but they'd already seen her.

'Maxine!' Kaspar called her over.

Reluctantly she walked towards them. His face was pale. There were dark circles under his eyes and the wetness in the air was making his hair cling to his skull.

'I never got a chance to thank your mum for the teddy.'

Maxine stared at him. How could he have forgotten? Didn't he recognise the bear they'd chosen for their son? Why thank her mother when she'd caused nothing but trouble between them?

Daniel's bear was propped against a makeshift wooden cross at the head of the grave.

'No headstone?' Maxine said. They obviously didn't love that baby if they'd left him in a virtually unmarked grave.

'You can't get them straight away and Emma's too upset at the moment to decide on the wording.'

Emma hadn't even looked at Maxine. Her shoulders were heaving with grief. She was Maxine's friend and Maxine should've comforted her, but she could only think of retrieving poor Daniel's sodden teddy.

'Sorry to disturb you,' Maxine muttered and walked away.

From a café across the road, she waited until Kaspar's car pulled out of the cemetery. She finished her tea without tasting it and went back out into the wet. The cemetery was deserted now. The rain was heavier and she didn't have an umbrella. In moments she was soaked through. A few more days like that and her beloved bear would've been nothing more than a sodden, mouldy lump. She found Joseph's grave again. Daniel's teddy was still sitting in pride of place. She grabbed him and gave a gentle squeeze. A trickle of brownish liquid oozed out. She put him in her pocket, cradled in her hand.

The heating was off at home and she had to fiddle with the controller until it flicked into life. Then she turned up the radiator in her bedroom and balanced Teddy on top of it. At intervals she turned him over so he dried out evenly.

A few days later her mother muttered something about vandals having stolen the bear from the grave. Maxine ignored her. From that point Daniel's teddy stayed with her constantly, in her pocket, her handbag or underneath her pillow.

In the museum café Maxine realised her voice had dropped to a whisper and Vanessa was leaning across the table in order to hear. She stopped talking, clutched the bear to her cheek and put her hand on her stomach. Would giving up Daniel's bear to this museum really ease the pain of his absence and help her move forward with his new half-sibling?

'Don't you want to keep the bear for your new baby?' It was as though Vanessa had read her mind.

'No.' She had promised Adrian she would do this. 'I'm trying to make things work with someone else now. Adrian knows about Kaspar, Daniel and Teddy. He says I must let go and move on. He says that's the only way the two of us and our new baby can have any kind of future together. He's right.'

Maxine placed the worn brown bear on the table between them. After a deep breath she continued her story.

She left home as soon as she could afford a place of her own and met Adrian when he was transferred to her branch as a supervisor. Maxine refused his invitations to have a drink together several times before finally trusting him enough to say yes. He was her first boyfriend since Kaspar. As they got serious, she had to explain her past and also her non-existent relationship with her mother. Adrian was the perfect gentle-man — sympathetic and supportive. He encouraged Maxine to patch things up with her mum.

'That must have been difficult for you.' Vanessa put her hand on top of Maxine's. Maxine swallowed the emotion building in her chest; if only her mother had had a tiny bit of Vanessa's empathy when Daniel was born, life might have been so different.

'At that first meeting, Mum and I were both wary, like two circling wild animals waiting for the opportunity to pounce. In the end I just came out with it and asked her why my baby had to go. She talked in clichés about wanting to give both me and her grandson a better life. I screamed at her. Tried to tell her she gave neither of us a better life!'

The tension and frustration from that meeting knotted tightly across Maxine's shoulders, making her free fist clench and reopen. Vanessa's thumb gently rubbed the back of her other hand on the table. Maxine focused on that pressure and the knots started to relax.

'Don't be too hard on her,' Vanessa said, slowly. 'Your mum's sentiments were natural. I have a child. Liam's grown up and a long way away but that protective lioness feeling never goes away. If I could make his life better in any way, I'd be there like a shot. If there were grandchildren, I'd bend over backwards for them as well. As mothers we only go wrong because we can't always be sure exactly what the best thing is for our children.'

'That's the whole point!' Maxine didn't want anyone taking her mother's side. 'What she did wasn't in our best interests.'

'She probably had reasons she thought you wouldn't understand.'

'She did! And maybe if she'd told me at the time, I could've made her see that she and I were different people at the age of eighteen. I didn't want the same things she wanted when she was young. But she didn't tell me when it could have made a difference.'

Vanessa didn't respond and, robbed of a sparring partner, Maxine calmed down. She explained that her mother had shown her a photograph. It was Daniel in his plastic crib at the hospital. Maxine hadn't known the photo existed and she remembered the dumbstruck feeling it produced in her.

'I look at this picture every night,' her mum said, 'and say a little prayer for him.'

Maxine had wanted to dismiss those words as trite and a poor excuse for despicable behaviour but when she noticed how well-thumbed the picture was, she was forced to give some credence to them.

'Your dad told me I was being too hard and cruel on you. I'm sorry if it seemed that way but if my emotions got involved, I couldn't have let Daniel go.' Then her mum had cried like Maxine had never seen her cry before. 'Now I realise I was wrong but at the time it seemed the right thing to do — because I loved you and I wanted you to have the future that I didn't.' Her mother paused, as though realising she'd said too much.

'What future didn't you have?'

Her mum took a deep breath. 'I was about to join a cruise ship as a hairdresser when I fell pregnant with you. I didn't hesitate to marry your dad and keep you, but it was hard watching my friends enjoy their freedom while I endured sleepless nights and a life with very little money. I wanted you to have something better. The opportunity to be young only comes once.'

Maxine didn't know what to say. She couldn't imagine her mother as a young woman experiencing feelings of lust, love and longing. She'd always been a middle-aged killjoy. Had her mum resented her all these years for being conceived as an accident and spoiling her life? Or did her sacrifice show she truly loved Maxine?

Slowly, as if expecting rejection, her mother took Maxine's hand and squeezed it. After a moment Maxine squeezed back — she was beginning to realise her mother was a real person with a real past. The first tentative planks had been laid in bridging the gulf between them.

'When Daniel's eighteen will you help me trace him, Mum?'

'Yes,' she whispered and pulled her daughter close. Then she explained she'd put Daniel's teddy on Joseph's grave to ease her conscience — Daniel, her own grandson, was out of reach but at least she could do something for little Joseph.

Now Maxine pushed the worn teddy bear across the Formica to Vanessa. 'After that conversation I understood her motives and her life as a young woman. I'm trying to forgive her.' Maxine blew her nose and dabbed her eyes. 'But I can't forget the times I shared with Kaspar and I don't want to forget Daniel. Adrian says Daniel and Kaspar are like a barrier between us. We got engaged last week and I owe it to Adrian to remove that barrier — otherwise I'll spend my whole life dreaming about what might have been.'

'The decision to donate Daniel's teddy to the museum is yours,' Vanessa said. 'It's not Adrian's, nor anyone else's.'

'Please look after him.' Maxine clumsily wiped her tears. 'Please look after Teddy for Daniel. I hope my first-born son is having a better life than I could've provided as a silly, naïve teenager. When I trace him, I'll bring him here to see Teddy and find out the whole story.' She put her hands protectively on her flat stomach. 'I should have said sorry to Kaspar, Emma and Joseph for stealing Teddy. But it was Daniel's bear and I wouldn't have got through the last few years without him. So, if I'm honest, I'm not sorry.'

'Will you go back to work after the baby's born?'

Maxine looked down at the table. Vanessa's question had struck a raw nerve and another well of potential guilt. 'I've no choice. Adrian doesn't earn enough to pay the mortgage on his own and the bank is being awkward about my request for part-time work.' She tried to smile. 'So, yes, I'll go back. The nurseries where we live are very good and Mum has offered to childmind a couple of days a week to save us money. But I'm not sure about that. Wouldn't she get to enjoy my baby more than I would? Maybe she doesn't deserve that just yet.'

Maxine stood to put her jacket on. She hadn't finished her coffee and a third of the doughnut was uneaten — emotion having robbed her of what little appetite she had. She watched Vanessa examine the small brown bear. He'd been well loved but not in that overzealous, rough and tumble way of a child. The older woman wrote a final sentence in her notebook and then appeared to be thinking. Maxine waited for her to look up so she could say goodbye.

'Would you like to work here, Maxine? Instead of the bank. Now the museum's open I can't be in two places, selling tickets upstairs and serving drinks down here. I need someone part time to cover our busy periods. Maternity leave won't be a problem and if you're breastfeeding feel free to bring the baby with you. They sleep most of the time at that age.'

'Oh!' Maxine was taken aback. She'd hoped, at best, to walk out of here with a positive outlook on the future. The offer of a new job was more than she'd expected. Did she want to work here? Yes! She hated the bank's atmosphere of targets, pointless emails and petty regulations. Vanessa gave this place a feeling of acceptance, calm and being cared for. Maxine wanted to pass that on to others like herself, who'd suffered in life. But she had to push that altruism to one side and think about why she had to work at all. 'The pay would be less, I guess?'

Vanessa nodded. 'I can only afford minimum wage. But because you're in with me at the beginning, if we make this place a success then your status and salary would grow. Some of your hours would be weekends when Adrian could child-mind, if that helps.'

Maxine tried to switch off her emotional longing to be in the museum and to look at the job offer logically. Weekend working or bringing the baby in with her would save a significant amount of money, meaning a lower wage was doable. By the time he or she was older and needed to be in nursery this place might have taken off. Her enthusiasm was bubbling now; there was so much scope in a place like this.

'I could do social media for you. Photos of the objects would be great for Instagram and Twitter.' Maxine's imagination was bounding forward. 'You could franchise this concept and reach out to more people!' She might end up with a profitable financial interest in the place. It was worth a gamble. Adrian would understand.

'Don't make me run before I'm barely walking!'

'I'd love to work here.' Maxine was excited. This job was going to have much more purpose than staring at a computer and looking busy even though nothing was being achieved. 'I'm supposed to give a month's notice but I've got some holiday owing so I'll ask to leave in a couple of weeks.'

'Thank you. I'm so pleased, love!' Vanessa gave her a hug and Maxine smiled. No-one gave her a hug and made her feel so wanted at the bank.

CHAPTER SIX

February

Dave had always complained that I was a collector of lost souls. Strangers on buses told me their life stories. At Christmas I invited people home who would otherwise go turkey-less. Dave tired of me striking up conversations in cafés, queues or wherever we happened to be.

'Stop taking everyone under your wing,' he'd say. 'Let them stand on their own two feet.'

He'd have said that about employing Maxine too. 'What! You've employed her without an interview, references or even a trial to see if she can make a decent pot of tea?'

But I was steering my own ship now, albeit nervously, and none of that formal admin stuff bothered me. It was easy to tell the genuine people. However, I did worry that Maxine had given up a secure job with a pension in order to work in the museum. My attempts at the museum accounts weren't entirely precise but it was obvious that after five weeks fully open, takings were up only slightly on the café-only, pre-museum days. The increase wasn't enough to sustain me, never mind an employee as well. Maxine was a gamble. Before Maxine I'd calculated a twelve-month financial cushion but now, with wages to pay, that was looking precarious. Unless my new employee brought enough added value with her, the museum might not see the end of the year. A dark thought — with Dave gone, my son in Canada *and* no business, it would be a desolate empty stretch to the final curtain.

Maxine was a quick learner in the café and was as happy defrosting the fridge and cleaning the toilets as chatting to visitors. Plus she bubbled with business ideas of her own.

'I've created a Twitter account,' she said one day, above the hiss and gurgle of the big silver coffee machine, as she concocted a tray full of lattes and cappuccinos for a party of ladies.

'You've what?' Social media wasn't my strong point.

'It's a way of getting free publicity and it can't do any harm.' Maxine started to gabble and I realised she'd misinterpreted my frown of incomprehension for disapproval.

I curved my mouth the other way up. 'I'm sure it'll be fine but you need to explain what and why.'

With such an enthusiastic teacher, the importance of hashtags, handles and attention-grabbing photos soon became clear.

'What about a Valentine's Day event?' she suggested next. 'Lots of our objects have romantic connotations. We could have heart-shaped pink biscuits in the café and a quiz sheet about the items on display, with prizes. The fourteenth is next week but we can move fast.'

'Heart-shaped biscuits?' The cost of quality cakes from the bakery was already more than I'd anticipated and there wasn't the budget for much more. 'Are they something you could make, Maxine?'

'Me?' Her eyes were wide with disbelief. 'I can't cook to save my life. Can't you do that if you own a café?'

'At school my cookery teacher wrote on my report: "Vanessa's written work is far better than her practical work".'

Maxine sniggered. 'My one and only rice pudding erupted.'

'In class my pastry always ended up in crumbs on the floor and my Yule log refused to be rolled — I took home a mountain of crumbs stuck together with buttercream. My dad asked me if there was a yeti living in there somewhere.'

Maxine laughed out loud. 'And you chose to open a teashop!'

It was a couple of minutes before we were solemn enough to continue the conversation.

'We definitely don't bake the biscuits,' I said.

* * *

With only a seven-day lead time and even with the help of Twitter, we pulled in very few extra visitors on Valentine's Day and I was left trying to sell off the expensive bakery-bought biscuits for the rest of the week. On the plus side, organising the event meant there was barely time to register the most romantic day of the year go by for a second time without Dave's customary box of dark chocolate mints. While the mints were his favourite, the card-shop propaganda had at least always propelled him to buy me something.

'Our next event will be better,' Maxine asserted. 'At the moment we don't have enough followers to make social media effective. I'm on the case.'

She was empathetic too and donors were happy to open up to her.

'Look!' she said one day and waved a naked Barbie doll with matted hair under my nose. 'There are twin five-year-old girls on a barge holiday. Only one remembers to take her doll. They fight over it and one of the girls falls into the water and drowns. I've got photos of the boat and of the twins on their first day at school just before the tragedy. This has to be the centrepiece to the museum.'

'No!' Making money out of an awful tragedy like this wasn't part of the ethos of the museum. It surely couldn't help the parents or surviving twin move on. 'This is one story we have to diplomatically decline.'

Maxine held up a finger indicating there was more to come. 'Afterwards,' she continued, 'there was always animosity between the surviving twin and her mother. Then the mother saw that newspaper article about the museum and it made her think. She dug the Barbie out of the loft. It had to go up there because she couldn't bear to look at it. She took the doll to her surviving daughter's and they had a long and honest chat. Afterwards they came here together and made the donation. Hearing about the museum reconciled those two people — it lessened their hurt and that has to be good, doesn't it? It's a message of hope; the doll has to go into the museum.'

Maxine was right; the story fitted. I gave her a hug. She was becoming indispensable and her optimistic enthusiasm was infectious. But she hadn't seen the accounts and the precarious nature of her position at the museum. It felt wrong to hide that from her. There was no point worrying her for the sake of it, so I asked Jim if he'd go over the books with me and calculate how long the museum could realistically survive at current visitor levels and with Maxine's wages factored in. It felt akin to asking whether I'd die prematurely from a terrible disease. Did I want to officially acknowledge that I was a failing business woman as well as a failed wife? For Maxine's sake I pulled my head out of the sand.

'I'll assume the worst-case scenario,' he said as he set up his laptop at a table at the back of the café and I brought him his first coffee. 'That is, visitor levels and takings remain as per the last six weeks.'

'Couldn't you work on slightly higher figures — a small increase in numbers would be realistic, wouldn't it?' I was frightened that Maxine would have to go straightaway.

'It never does to be over-optimistic but I'll assume five per cent growth each month.'

An hour later Jim waved me over and tried to explain the spreadsheet. 'October,' he pronounced, 'will be make or break month. With five per cent growth per month you've got around eight months' head space which takes you to October. Every month that you grow more than five per cent then you buy yourself extra time. If you don't achieve five per cent growth then you lose time.'

'So, what do I tell Maxine?'

'That's your decision but in a standard business it wouldn't be wise to start scaring the horses until absolutely necessary.'

'Thanks,' I said, glancing over to where Maxine was holding the door open for an elderly couple to come into the café. I recognised them as customers from my café-only days. Maxine hurried to pull out chairs and help the lady get seated with her stick. I wasn't sure I had the guts to tell my assistant that by the time her baby was born, the family-friendly job I'd promised might no longer exist.

'I'll be off then.' Jim packed his laptop away. 'It should be straightforward for you to keep that spreadsheet up-to-date and check whether you're on track for October, beyond, or, hopefully not, sooner.'

I showed him out and we shook hands. I wished I'd remained ignorant; eight months wasn't long and then the dark abyss of my future would open and take me again. And Maxine as well this time. I caught up with my assistant behind the café counter. The old lady had ordered tea and scones again. I added complimentary apricot jam to the tray Maxine had prepared.

'I'll take it over,' I said. 'Please could you keep an eye on the reception desk upstairs?'

'No problem. I'll get those historic Birmingham post-cards into the display rack and point them out to people as they're leaving.'

It would be cruel to quash Maxine's consistent, youthful optimism and initiative with Jim's harsh reality. Selling a few postcards wasn't going to make a great deal of difference to anything.

'Special offer on the jam again,' I said to the old lady and, after unloading the crockery, I sat down.

She was alone, her husband wandering between the tables.

'It's always nice to have a sit down and cup of tea, isn't it?' October loomed like a great stone wall in my mind. I needed some chat to distract me.

'Even better when you don't have to make it yourself or do the washing-up.' The old lady looked across to where her husband was moving his hand from one empty chair to the next as he walked. 'I'm sorry about my husband. It's difficult for him to sit still.'

'No problem. I'm Vanessa. Shall I pour?'

'Polly. Yes, please.'

We made small talk for a few minutes and she commented favourably on the introduction of the museum above the café but seemed reluctant to talk about herself. Then her husband spotted the scones and came back. He ate clumsily, like a child, and Polly seemed embarrassed. To save her feelings I left them to it.

October. I had to smash that wall down. I'd promised Maxine a flexible job to fit around the baby. The museum was becoming a necessity for me too. What else was there in my life? The odd email from Liam, who still hadn't been told about the divorce, and the many uninvited thoughts of Dave and what I'd done wrong to lose the man I loved.

That evening I stepped out of the shower, towelled the condensation from the full-length mirror and stared at myself. Had I let myself go in a way that repulsed him? There were curves and cellulite. Should I have become a gym bunny and reclaimed the figure from my twenties? There were laughter lines and plain, short nails. Would facials and manicures have done the trick? Was my appearance much worse than any other woman my age? What did his new girlfriend look like? She was only a couple of years younger; didn't we all carry an extra pound or two along with the wrinkles and salt and pepper hair? Or had she gone in for expensive artificial help?

'You are a loser!' I leaned towards the mirror and growled at my reflection. 'You let yourself and your marriage get stuck in a rut. Dave was bored with you!' I stamped my bare foot on the bathroom lino and then kicked angrily at my failure and at my ex-husband who'd given no warning that he was unhappy. Shouldn't he have had the decency to do that?

'Ow! Ow!' My toes collided with the bottom of the mirror at speed. I managed two hops on my good foot before crumpling to the floor in agony.

I sat there for several minutes, sobbing and massaging my reddened digits. The tears weren't just for my physical pain. Dave should have told me what was wrong and given me chance to fix it. He never said anything. Never. Never rocked the boat and then all of a sudden — bam! He was off in a cloud of dust. I banged my fist on the floor and tried to recall if there'd been warning signs that I'd ignored. No. There'd been nothing, I was sure.

'Our whole marriage was probably a sham,' I said to the ever-patient Maxine the next day. 'For three decades I thought he loved me but all the time he may have been lusting after other women. There might have been hundreds of affairs for all I know.'

'Unlikely.' Maxine's expression was wiser than that of most thirty-year-olds. 'He couldn't hide it for all that time. You'd have sensed or seen something.'

She was probably right. Dave was a non-descript, ordinary sort of man; someone you wouldn't look twice at. It was hard to imagine women throwing themselves at him or him chasing after them. But I'd fallen head over heels for him when we met and his new girlfriend must have found an attraction. So why not others?

'What was going on inside his head?' I persisted. 'I wasn't woman enough for him. And he's in love with her, so it's emotional as well as physical betrayal. That feels much worse.'

Maxine squeezed my hand. 'We don't know what's behind his behaviour. Stop poisoning today because of what happened yesterday. Remember the good times and move on. That's what we tell our museum donors.'

Move on. Easier said than done.

A week or so later, we'd just opened up when Polly and her husband came into the café again. Polly in front as usual, using her right hand to lean on her gnarled, old walking stick. A Mrs Thatcher style handbag hung in the crook of that elbow. Her left arm was stretched behind her, clutching her husband like a mother might hold on to a toddler who was likely to make a run for it at any moment. Malcolm was staring around the café in wonderment, as if he'd found himself in some magical place instead of somewhere he'd been several times before. His jacket was a serviceable speckled grey tweed that had obviously been worn a lot. Polly's tights were thick, wrinkled and mud brown. She probably didn't know about the ladder running up the back of her right calf. As before, they both looked like they lived off a pension which didn't stretch far enough.

'Sit down, Polly.' I pulled out two chairs.

It was a slow process. She leaned the stick against the table. It immediately clattered to the floor. I picked it up and wedged it securely upright. She put the bag on the table and eased herself down onto the chair. Malcolm had wandered off. He was steadier on his feet than his wife and was walking around the perimeter of the café, trailing his fingers along the surface of the wall.

'Malcolm!' Polly turned to me with watery eyes. 'I'm sorry. His dementia is getting worse.'

I'd already guessed but it was the first time Polly had volunteered her husband's illness. I squeezed her shoulder. With Polly's permission I upgraded them from scones to Victoria sandwich cake.

While I brewed the tea and cut the cake, I watched Malcolm make his umpteenth circuit of the café, his hand still running over the sparkling new white paintwork. Selfishly, I hoped his hands were clean but immediately flung the thought from my mind. A damp cloth could put right any damage he did but nothing could put right his health.

'I'm sorry,' Polly said again when I carried the tray over to her table.

'Don't worry. Here let me be Mum.' I poured myself a cup too and sat down.

'You two must have been married a long time?'

'Yes.' Her eyes kept flitting anxiously towards her husband. 'He's been my rock over the years. Now he's ill, I'm trying to be there for him. He would never want to go in a home. But it's not easy.'

She turned towards me with sad eyes.

'Would it help to talk about it?'

She nodded and took a deep breath.

CHAPTER SEVEN

Polly

Malcolm had been Polly's first boyfriend and she'd never looked at another man since the night he first asked her to dance. It was the youth club Christmas social in 1952. They were both sixteen and as soon as he held her for the waltz, the electricity between them sparked. Her skin beneath his fingers on her waist and shoulder was burning, even through the fabric of her dress. She'd never experienced anything like it before. Every fibre in her body tingled and when she woke the next morning her heart was still singing with joy. Malcolm hadn't kissed her goodnight, it was too soon, but she knew it would happen, eventually.

The kiss was longer coming than she expected because their free time never coincided. Malcolm was working as a clerk and studying accountancy in the evenings. His free time was at the weekends but, on Sundays, Polly had to care for her grandmother in order to give her mother a break. Saturdays too if her aunty was busy. They saw each other at youth club on Saturday evenings but Polly's dad always arrived promptly to walk her home. Malcolm and she could do nothing more than smile and wave at each other. There was no chance of a few minutes alone.

Things had got no further by February and, when nothing arrived in the post on Valentine's Day, Polly thought she'd imagined the strength of feeling between them. It had just been wishful thinking on her part and she should start paying more attention to some of the lads at church or even the errand boy in the office where she was a junior filing clerk.

They'd just finished tea at home on that Valentine's Day and Polly was doing the dishes when there was a loud rap on the door. Her dad always insisted on answering the door himself, something to do with being the man of the house. She remembered him putting down his newspaper with a sigh, as though whoever was calling was a nuisance.

'I'm not expecting anyone,' he muttered. 'It's not the right day for the insurance man or the pools.'

'Good evening, Mr Hinchcliffe. My name's Malcolm Stroud and I've come to see Polly.'

At the sound of the familiar voice, Polly's heart zinged like a Catherine wheel. She stopped scrubbing at the frying pan in the sink and stood absolutely still so she could catch every word.

'Oh!' Her father sounded as surprised as Polly felt. She'd never had a male visitor before.

There was a long pause and she was terrified her dad would send Malcolm packing. She crept to the kitchen door and tried to peer into the hall without being seen. Malcolm looked nervous and her dad was inspecting him from head to toe like he was a soldier on parade.

'You best come in, lad.' Polly let out her breath when she heard those words. 'Polly! A young man to see you.'

She dried her hands on the tea towel hanging by the oven and went into the hallway. Her mum emerged from the living room. Her dad had closed the front door and was standing next to Malcolm like a guard with a prisoner. Malcolm had one hand behind his back. As Polly walked into the hall, he brought it forward and offered her a single red rose.

'Ooh!' Polly's mum said. 'How lovely.'

Her dad gave a grunt — whether it was of approval or disapproval, Polly couldn't tell.

'Thank you.' She accepted the flower with a shaky hand. The stem was tightly wrapped in a piece of damp newspaper.

'To protect you from the thorns and to keep it moist.' Malcolm caught her eye as she looked up from the newspaper.

Polly wished for her parents to disappear. But instead they fussed as they always did when they had a visitor who wasn't family and therefore needed impressing.

'I'll get that tall glass vase we had for a wedding present. It will make the rose look grand,' said her mum.

'Come and sit down, lad.' Her dad directed Malcolm into the living room.

Polly was left in the hall bereft of both rose and suitor.

'I was hoping to take your daughter for a walk.'

Polly remained in the hall and crossed her fingers.

'In the dark, lad?'

'We won't go far and only where there's street lights. And we won't be long. I need to get home to finish some work for the accountancy course I'm doing at night school. I work at Fishers and they're paying for me to study.'

'I see.' Her dad's voice told Polly he was impressed. 'I'm sure Polly'd love to go for a walk. But have her back here in an hour, mind.'

'Thank you very much, Mr Hinchcliffe.'

Heart thudding with anticipation, Polly put her shoes on and was adjusting her jacket collar in the mirror as her dad and Malcolm came out of the lounge and her mum came out of the kitchen with a tray of tea things.

'You're not going out?' Her mum's smile turned to disappointment. 'I've got the tea and scones ready.'

Polly's dad made a strange head gesture at her mum. 'Malcom's training to be an accountant.'

'An accountant,' echoed her mother. 'That's nice.'

'They're going for a little walk.' Her dad made the head gesture again as though it was a secret code between him and her mum.

'Nice to meet you, Mrs Hinchcliffe,' Malcolm said. 'Perhaps we could have the tea and scones later.' Then he propelled Polly out of the door with his hand on the small of her back.

'Thank you for the rose,' Polly said once they were clear of listening ears, 'and sorry about my parents.'

He took her hand and squeezed it. A tingly warm current raced round her body. She squeezed back. They walked down the road hand in hand. She wished it was a light summer's evening so people could see them together.

Malcolm paused at the entrance to the park. 'We could sit on a bench if you don't mind the dark. There's no streetlights in there.'

'I don't mind.' Polly's heart was thumping so much she was sure it must be audible to Malcolm.

It should have been cold, damp and miserable sitting on a park bench in the dark on a February evening but Polly felt warmer than in the hottest heatwave. Malcolm put his arm around her shoulders. She leant against him. They didn't need conversation. They turned their heads towards each other at the same time and it seemed perfectly natural that their lips should meet. It was better than Polly had dared hope. Her insides fizzed uncontrollably. His strong arms enveloped her and she thought she'd died and gone to heaven. After their kiss they sat quietly for a while, just holding hands. She gazed at the dark shapes of bushes and trees around them. There wasn't any need to talk, it was enough being alone together. She said a silent thank you to her father for allowing Malcolm to take her out.

Malcolm broke the silence. 'When I'm qualified, will you marry me?'

Polly sat upright. His words had to be in her imagination. It was too soon for a marriage proposal. She said nothing, afraid she'd look stupid if the wrong words tumbled out.

'I'm sorry, Polly. You must think I'm far too forward but I didn't want to wait and then lose you to another man. Please tell me you'll at least give it some consideration?'

'What?' Was he really asking her to be his wife?

'Will you marry me? In a few years, I mean, after I'm qualified. I can't support a wife until I'm qualified.'

This was totally unexpected. A proposal the first time they'd properly walked out together. Unexpected but she didn't need to think about the answer. 'Yes.'

He kissed her again. Through all the years they shared together, Polly never had any doubt that she made the right decision that night. When their hour was nearly up, Malcolm walked her home and they arrived with one minute to spare. They didn't tell her parents about the proposal and her parents didn't ask about the great big grins on their faces. The four of them ate scones, drank tea and talked about the terrible storms that had claimed so many lives at the beginning of the month. But her parents must have sensed they were serious about each other because Malcolm was invited to tea twice a week. He came after work and before night school. Polly's dad would often take him into the shed for a chat and her mum always gave him extra cake to take home.

A couple of years later, with some exams passed and promotions obtained, Malcolm could afford an engagement ring. They went public about their betrothal and both sets of parents were over the moon. The ring was the most beautiful thing Polly had ever seen and was set with the tiniest diamond. They married when Polly was twenty-one and Malcolm twenty-three.

Polly spread the fingers of her left hand on the café tabletop and looked at the two worn bands of gold on her fourth finger. On the upper-most, a diamond, little bigger than a pinhead, sparkled beneath the ceiling strip-light. 'Next year will be our sixtieth wedding anniversary.'

'It's a gorgeous ring,' I said, 'and a beautiful love story.'

'Pol! Pol! Pol!' Malcolm had relinquished the wall and was now standing alongside them at the table.

'Sit down and have some cake.' Polly spoke in the kindly way that adults speak to children.

I stood up and pulled a chair out for him. 'I'll leave you to it. Give me a shout if you need any hot water to top up the teapot.'

When Polly asked for the bill, I didn't include the cake. She queried it but I explained it was today's special offer which wasn't yet chalked on the board. A few minutes later I watched Polly make her slow way out of the café, walking stick in one hand and the other gripping Malcolm securely. It was the perfect scene for showing what it meant to keep marriage vows for life. The familiar feeling of abandonment crawled over me. I had to keep busy or I'd drown in a mess of self-pity, anger and worthlessness.

The café was quiet for the rest of the morning and, with Maxine holding the fort upstairs, I opened Jim's spreadsheet on my laptop. I tried to enter the final February figures for takings and visitor numbers but the spreadsheet developed a life of its own and refused to produce the correct answers. Computers were just one more thing I had no aptitude for. I closed the laptop and fetched the mop and bucket.

The floor behind the counter and in the kitchen area needed regular washing to keep it clear of crumbs and splashes. It was a satisfying task with instant results and no brain work required. As I bent to manoeuvre the mop head into the corner behind the fridge I spotted dark grains of rice on the white vinyl, probably walked in on someone's shoe from the takeaway around the corner. I was about to swirl them into oblivion when I realised what they were.

I loosed the mop and raced upstairs.

'Maxine!' The museum hall was empty and I dragged my assistant down to the café, pausing to switch the sign on the door to "Closed".

I propelled Maxine towards my discovery and said it how I saw it, 'We've got rats!'

My legs were wobbly and my stomach heaved. How could this have happened? We were constantly cleaning. We had all the proper hygiene certificates. We never left food lying about. I glanced again at the droppings and then tucked my trousers into my socks and motioned to Maxine to do the same. She ignored me, took a knife from the drawer and started poking at the rodent poo.

'Not rats. A mouse.' She stood up, grinning. 'I had pet mice when I was a kid. They're lovely.'

'We have to get one of those traps.' I mimicked the action of a guillotine blade coming down hard and fast on a small head.

'No. We can catch it humanely and release it in the park.'

'I am not chasing a mouse into a cardboard box.' My legs prickled at the thought of it. I sat down on the nearest chair and pulled my knees up to my chest.

'There's a place on my way home that sells humane traps. We stick a bit of cheese or peanut butter inside and it's job done. I'll be mouse monitor.'

'Until it's caught, we need to do extra cleaning,' I cautioned and then forced myself away from the safety of the chair. 'We are now shut for the day. We need to get behind that fridge. And we need to be liberal with the disinfectant.'

The kitchen and café gleamed by the time we went home. I didn't remove my socks from my trousers until I was safely outside with the door locked behind me.

CHAPTER EIGHT

Stephen

The museum's door was locked but the notice said it was open all day. Stephen tried pushing, pulling and turning the door handle several times. Then he spotted the doorbell, small and rectangular with a push button like on a residential front door. He pressed and waited. The sound of a faint ring was just discernible. He pressed and waited again. Time wasn't on his side; it had been a long journey down from Yorkshire and there were only a few hours before his return train. He wasn't going home without leaving his donation. He leaned on the doorbell, making it ring continuously.

'Five more minutes,' he muttered. 'I'll give them five more minutes to answer the door and then I'm going to tweet something derogatory.' He got out his phone to take a photo of the list of opening hours.

'Can I help?'

'Oh!' Stephen jumped. He'd been busy with the picture and hadn't noticed the woman come up behind him on the pavement. 'I wanted the museum.'

'That's me.' The woman was flushed and a little out of breath as though she'd been hurrying. The strap of a shoulder bag went diagonally across her chest, from one shoulder to the crook of her waist on the opposite side, leaving both hands free for large supermarket carrier bags. 'I did put up a sign to say we're closed until two o'clock.' She looked round, presumably for the sign.

'There's no sign. Only this.' Stephen pointed to a poster, taped face outwards on the inside of a ground floor window. It listed the museum's regular opening hours. 'It says you stay open all day until 5.00 p.m. every day.'

'Drat. There it is.' The woman moved away, indicating a puddle ten feet further down the road. She put down the bags and fetched the mud-smeared piece of laminated card. 'We set this and pop it up when we need to close for an hour or so.'

A clock face with moveable hands had been fashioned on the card using split pins. Two holes were punched at the top and threaded with black ribbon.

'It should have been hanging on the door handles but kids must have pulled it off.' The woman wiped the dirty puddle water from the plastic surface with a tissue from her pocket. 'My colleague's gone to antenatal clinic and the milkman didn't turn up this morning so I had to go out. A café's no good without milk.'

'Can I come in? I want to donate something. I've only got a couple of hours until my train back to Yorkshire.'

'Absolutely. Follow me.'

'Let me take your bags.'

'Thank you.' She smiled at him gratefully. Her warm, open expression made him want to smile back. And, unusually, Stephen wanted to keep that smile on his face. The flush on the woman's skin and the sparkle in her eyes expressed a cheerfulness that was contagious. He followed her through the front door and off to the left.

'You can leave the bags there,' she said, pointing to a spot just behind the café counter. 'Thank you very much. Have a sit down and I'll be with you in a minute.'

The café was spotlessly clean. Stephen chose a table near the counter. Two daffodils nestled in a thin glass vase in the centre of the table; a reminder spring was on its way, despite the chill outside. He placed his carrier-bag wrapped object on the table. There was a lot in Stephen's past that he wanted to relinquish. This book embodied the man he'd become: secretive and unable to trust or share with other human beings. Unless that changed, he faced a very lonely future. He hoped that leaving the book here would help him kick-start the process of change.

When the woman came over to take his order, she'd swapped her coat for a white apron and her silver-speckled auburn hair was now hidden under a little cap. He chose a pot of tea and bread pudding from the menu. The woman joined him at the table, bringing two pieces of a moist bread, raisin and peel concoction plus spoons. It was served with clotted cream and tasted like nectar. Suddenly breakfast seemed a long time ago. Lunch had been a takeaway coffee in New Street station and Stephen realised he was hungry.

'Did you miss lunch too?' the woman asked as she tried to manoeuvre both pudding and cream onto her spoon simultaneously. 'A salad sandwich would have been better for me but right now I need an energy boost. When Maxine's not here I'm up and down those stairs like an Olympic sprint medallist.'

This woman was easy to be with. He wanted to be like that. Open with people and kind. He felt an attraction to her too. It was something he couldn't quite put his finger on but he liked the way her smile made her eyes dance, the way her voice was easy to listen to and the way she demanded nothing from him.

They cleared their plates without speaking further, each chasing the final sticky crumbs with the spoon and then using fingers to snare the last bits. When they'd both moved on to their hot drinks, the woman picked up a spiral bound notebook.

'I'm Vanessa. What's your name?' She had a pen at the ready.

'Stephen.' He'd looked at the museum website and knew they liked to get the full story behind the objects. He took a deep breath.

Vanessa made a note of his name. 'So, what have you brought to the museum, Stephen, and what's the story behind it?' She momentarily placed a hand on his. 'I know it won't be easy, so take your time.'

Stephen delved into the carrier bag and brought out a smallish, red, hardbacked book emblazoned with gold lettering: *DIAGRAMS*. He put it on the table between the two of them.

'May I?' Her large hazel eyes, framed with dark lashes, were expressive and engaging. He nodded.

Vanessa pulled the book towards her and opened it at a random page. 'No pictures?'

The comment threw Stephen for a second and then he realised Vanessa had taken the book title literally. The book didn't contain actual diagrams or illustrations, only columns of numbers with zig-zag red and blue lines running through them. There was a small heading at the top left-hand corner of the open page, "83 Oxford Treble Bob". At the bottom of the page in red lettering it said "Major".

Vanessa frowned. 'Are you a spy? A code-breaker? Did you work for GCHQ?'

Stephen laughed. 'No. I'm an accountant. These aren't codes. The important thing's at the beginning of the book.' He flicked the book back to the flyleaf. It was inscribed, "*To my darling, Stephen. Now all that hunting makes sense — it led me to you! Always and for ever, Naomi XXX.*"

'Naomi is your wife?' Vanessa was looking at the gold band on Stephen's left hand.

'No. My wife died.' Stephen touched the ring. 'I stopped wearing it for a while. I wanted to avoid questions about my wife. But things got out of hand. It's hard to escape the past.'

'We all have things in our past that didn't work out.' Vanessa's voice dropped and she fiddled with her pen. Then she perked up again. 'Can you start from the beginning? What you just said makes as much sense to me as the numbers in that book.'

Stephen nodded. For a moment there was silence as they both sat back, lifted their cups and drank. Then Stephen put his elbows on the table and leaned towards Vanessa.

He and Trish had both been thirty when they married. They'd met at work a couple of years previously and, despite the cliché, they really were soulmates. She understood his passion for tinkering with old cars and never complained if he wanted to spend Sunday with his head underneath a bonnet. Similarly, he understood that her ultimate ambition was to make it big as a novelist and didn't mind helping around the house to give her time to write. They both loved to travel and planned their leave from work meticulously to get the most out of their annual quota. Stephen couldn't remember them ever arguing during their first five years of marriage.

Everything changed when the twins came along. Trish got pregnant within two months of dispensing with contraception. When the sonographer pointed out two babies on the first scan it was a shock — but in the nicest possible way. There were raised eyebrows and knowing looks when it was announced Trish was expecting twins, but only one friend was brave enough to ask to their faces what everyone else was thinking.

'Was it IVF? With it being twins?'

When they said no, the friend coloured and muttered something about it being a stupid assumption to have made but because of their age and the fact they'd waited five years before starting a family . . .

Trish was too nice to let anyone suffer for long.

'Don't worry.' She hugged her friend. 'That would have been my first thought as well.'

Nicholas and Robert were like a bomb exploding into their lives. Cars and novel writing went out of the window. Everything focused on feeding and changing two tiny babies on a continuous loop, day and night. Trish was amazing. She survived on virtually no sleep for the first three months in order to breastfeed both boys. They were weaned on to bottles by six months so she could go back to work part-time.

But even though Trish was working only three days a week, life was hellishly complicated. The boys picked up a succession of coughs and colds. Neither Stephen's nor Trish's families lived nearby, so they both took turns using valuable holiday entitlement to care for the twins when they were too ill for nursery. And the infants were never poorly at the same time. Stephen tried very hard to not complain and to do his share but inevitably, because he was higher up the career ladder and the major breadwinner, his job came first.

'It's not working is it?' Trish said one day when Robert had a temperature and needed quiet time at home with his mum rather than being despatched to be sociable with a bunch of other babies. 'This career woman lark? Having it all, even on a part-time basis, doesn't work. Something has to suffer.'

'It'll get easier as the boys get older.' Stephen couldn't admit out loud that things weren't great with both of them working. Whatever his wife was feeling about it now, he didn't want to be labelled in the future as the one who made Trish abandon her career.

'I'm going to resign.' Her voice was firm. She'd obviously thought about this. 'I'll do it today. It's not fair to leave Robert at nursery when he's off-colour like this and my leave is almost gone. I'll take him with me to the office, hand in my notice and then come home for good.'

Stephen made sure it didn't show on his face but at that moment his heart was singing. Financially Trish's resignation would make little difference because most of her salary went on childcare but having his wife at home would make both their lives much easier.

Trish never went back to work, even when the boys started school. She used her organisational abilities to great effect at the playgroup and then the PTA. When the boys moved to secondary school she talked about starting her own business as a virtual assistant.

'Entrepreneurship is on the up,' she explained. 'But these inventive, ideas-led people who want to go it alone aren't necessarily good at the basic admin involved in running a business. That's where I come in. Their phone calls and emails can be redirected to me. I can look after their social media and publicity. I can do anything the business owner finds tedious. And I can do it all from home and fit around the boys' activities. I might even find time to resurrect that novel.'

Trish excelled at everything she put her mind to. It wasn't long before she was a profitable business woman as well as a great mother and the best wife any man could want.

Stephen picked up his cup, saw it was empty and put it down again. Vanessa caught his cue, lifted the lid off the floral china teapot, peered inside and stirred.

'Only lukewarm now. I'll make us another and give the museum hall a quick check, if you'll excuse me.' Vanessa took the pot over to the counter.

While she was gone, Stephen tried to read what she'd written. He didn't want to be spotted turning the notebook round so tried to decipher the upside-down scrawl from a distance. It was impossible to make out more than his own name and the odd word.

After racing up and down the stairs and making the tea, Vanessa was flushed again. It suited her. She wasn't a fashion magazine beauty but had a sort of inside-out attractiveness that Stephen liked. And those hazel eyes kept drawing him back to her face.

'So, this Naomi who signed the book.' Vanessa put a fresh milk jug and the teapot on the table. 'Who was she?'

Stephen frowned. Without thinking, he played Mum and stirred the pot. 'She comes later.' So far most of what he'd said was irrelevant to the red book but it was essential to set the scene for what came next and this preamble would, hopefully, explain his motivation. He didn't want to be rushed. He wanted to be understood.

'Sorry, please carry on.'

For a while everything was great. Trish talked excitedly about the clients she was acquiring, mostly through word of mouth. The boys were doing well at school — Robert captained their year group football team and Nicholas, the rugby team. But like most things that seem too good to be true — it was. Very soon Stephen's whole world came crashing down. And he felt it was his fault.

Stephen's sister was getting married for the second time. It was a small do with mainly family. Trish offered to drive but Stephen wanted her to relax and let her hair down after all the work she'd put into getting her business started. Knowing he was going to drive, Stephen limited himself to one glass of red wine with the meal and a couple of mouthfuls of the sparkling wine toast — both a good few hours before they headed home. The boys had to be up early the next morning for sports matches so Trish suggested they leave at 9.30 p.m. for the sixty-mile drive home. Everyone dozed in the car, except Stephen.

The last set of traffic lights before home was a right-turn. Stephen positioned the car in the middle of the junction and waited for a gap in the stream of oncoming traffic. For late on a Saturday night, the road was uncharacteristically busy. The lights changed from green to amber and then to red before the gap came. Stephen pressed on the accelerator to get across the junction before the traffic started flowing across from right to left. A massive jolt winded him. The car filled with airbags. Stephen was aware of yelps and groans from Trish and the boys but no-one screamed. It took him a second to realise what had happened. The passenger side of the car had been rammed by a vehicle coming across the junction. It must have been travelling at speed, otherwise the driver would have seen their car, trapped trying to turn right, and stopped.

'Trish? Are you OK? We should get the boys out of the car. It might go up in flames.'

The groans stopped. No-one spoke.

'Rob! Nick!'

No response.

That's when Stephen knew. That's when he started screaming.

Someone pulled open the driver's door and Stephen half fell and half stumbled onto the road. He struggled to walk, not because of any injuries but because of what he feared had happened to his family. Someone helped him onto the grass verge. He pushed against them, trying to get back to the car to rescue his family. The memory was hazy but from the reactions of onlookers and the emergency services he guessed he must have been incoherent and raving. The police breathalysed him. He was well under the limit. The first ambulance to leave the scene on a blue light carried the driver of the car that had smashed into them.

Stephen shouted at the policeman who was trying to guide him to a patrol car. 'Why him? What happened to women and children first?'

'The ambulance crews have to prioritise.' The statement was supposed to calm him but it enraged Stephen further.

'He caused the accident. My family should come first!'

From the backseat of the police car he watched hi-vis personnel swarm around his car. It seemed like hours but was probably only minutes before the people most precious to him were stretchered from the wreckage and taken away at speed under more blue lights.

'They will be all right, won't they?' He repeated the same phrase over and over again to the police and then tried to explain what happened. 'I couldn't turn right because of the traffic coming the other way. I couldn't get us safely off the junction. It was my fault, wasn't it?'

Nobody said his family would be all right. Nobody said he hadn't been at fault. At the hospital a policewoman gave him sweet tea in a paper cup. Stephen's hand shook as he held it, his brain unable to tell the muscles to stop juddering. He was frightened of spilling and drank the sugary liquid quickly while it was still scalding hot. Afterwards he felt marginally calmer. They took him into a small room. There was a doctor behind a desk. He made Stephen sit down and then broke the news that Trish was dead. Stephen yowled like an animal. Someone had pulled the rug from beneath him. He was tumbling, falling. A voice was asking if there was someone they could call but Stephen couldn't marshal his thoughts.

'My boys?' he managed finally. 'Do they know she's dead? I want to tell them myself.'

He had no idea what words he would use but the twins shouldn't hear about their mother's death from a stranger. The people in the room exchanged uncomfortable glances.

'What is it?' A fresh wave of panic engulfed him. Not his boys as well. Please, not his boys as well.

'It's not looking good, Stephen.' The only woman in the room had pulled a chair up and was holding his hand. She might have been a doctor, a policewoman or a nurse. He didn't know and didn't care. If she had a uniform, he didn't see it. 'You can see each of them now if you'd like.'

Someone took his arm and they walked down an endless corridor. Vaguely Stephen registered the entrance to the intensive care unit and the command to use the hand-sanitising gel at the door. Both Rob and Nick were wired up to tubes and monitors. They could all be the stars in a TV episode of *Casualty*. The camera had focused on the happy family dancing the Conga at a wedding and then, in a split second, all of that happiness was blown to smithereens and lost forever. For his sons, life had become a thin strand of cotton, about to snap at any minute.

The hospital asked again if they could call someone. Around dawn Stephen gave them his brother's number. He lived a distance away and had been at the wedding too but he came straight over. Stephen insisted he wanted to stay with the boys but the people in charge thought he needed a break and some sustenance. With the blessing of the nursing staff, Stephen was taken by his brother to the hospital cafeteria. His brother tried to insist on a proper breakfast.

'You've got to keep your strength up.'

'You sound like Mum.' Stephen managed a feeble smile at his own remark but all he could eat was one slice of buttered toast.

He'd just swallowed the last difficult mouthful when the nurse appeared. She sat down. Stephen was the last to realise what she was about to say. His brother had already dragged his chair closer to Stephen and put his arm around him in an awkward hug. Their last physical contact had been as fighting youngsters.

'I'm sorry,' the nurse said. 'We thought your sons were stable but it seems their hearts couldn't cope. They went within seconds of each other.'

Stephen hadn't been there. It was the last thing he could've done as their father and he hadn't been there. It was some comfort the twins had gone together. They'd entered this world together, fourteen years ago, and left it together and, just as at their birth, Trish, their devoted mother would be waiting for them. Stephen was the only one missing. Stephen was the one left behind. Stephen was the one who had to find some way of continuing his life without everyone he held dear. He didn't know if he could. He didn't want to even try.

Stephen was relieved that Vanessa had turned to one side to write in the spiral bound notebook. It was embarrassing for a man to cry in public. He fiddled with his handkerchief, keeping it close to his face for longer than necessary. Vanessa's pen was still moving. Several pages must now be covered with Stephen's story and he hadn't got to Naomi yet.

'More tea?'

Stephen nodded.

* * *

Standing at the counter, with my back to Stephen, I swallowed hard a couple of times. When that didn't quash my urge to cry, I reached for a serviette and blew my nose. It was impossible to imagine the trauma of losing your family in one fell swoop like that. Deep breaths, deep breaths. Don't break down in front of the customers. I had just about regained control when Maxine walked into the café carrying a shopping bag.

'I bought cake ingredients on my way from antenatal,' she explained. 'When we close tonight, we bake!' She unpacked the bag onto the counter with excitement as I slowly shook my head. 'Hazelnuts, chocolate, double cream, four cake tins to cook it all in — there's no point in just making one cake at a time . . .'

'This all looks very' — I didn't want to burst her bubble of enthusiasm but — '*ambitious* for two people who profess to not being able to bake?'

'The fancier the cake, the more we can charge. Isn't that what it's all about? And if we bake our own cakes we won't need to buy-in and will save ourselves shedloads.'

I was aware of Stephen turning around in his seat to stare at us and lowered my voice. 'Isn't there a saying about not running before you can walk?'

'Relax. We're simply obeying the ethos of the museum. We're leaving behind our "failures"' — she made her hands into quotation marks — 'and moving forwards positively.'

I still didn't feel comfortable but this wasn't the moment for arguing. 'Could you man the museum hall, please? We can catch up later.'

'Aye, aye, sir!' My assistant gave a mock salute and left as I returned to Stephen with the fresh tea.

CHAPTER NINE

For Stephen, the months after the accident went past in a tear-stained blur. Somehow, with the help of medication, he survived the triple funeral. His brother and sister-in-law helped go through the boys' clothes and Trish's belongings. Stephen didn't want stuff to go to the local charity shops — imagine the pain if one day he walked past and saw his wife's favourite dress on display? They drove a hundred miles away and distributed them to hospice shops. The accountancy firm he worked for were generous with open-ended compassionate leave. In hindsight that was a mistake. He wallowed at home with photographs and self-pity. After three months his brother delivered a long lecture and a kick up the backside. Stephen went back to work. It was a relief to have some structure to the day again. He started sleeping better and eating proper food at proper meal times rather than staying up late and having cereal for dinner. But nothing could ever be normal again.

At work he was given a new client. The client's employees didn't know Stephen's personal history and treated him normally, without any mawkish words of condolence or awkward embarrassment when they forgot his bereavement and accidentally mentioned their own wife and kids.

Occasionally, for whole two-minute blocks of time Stephen would forget he was a widower and enjoy a conversation about football or the weather.

The colleagues he'd known before the accident were uncomfortable around him. They no longer talked about their home life. The regular office night out to the local Indian was suddenly branded staff only, no partners. No-one said anything but it was obviously supposed to make Stephen feel better in some weird way. He went on these outings but instead of having his usual beef madras he chose chicken korma — it was what Trish always had and eating that made her feel closer.

It was much easier to feel comfortable with people who'd never known him during his life with Trish and the boys. He began to actively seek new people out. He dipped his toe into the world of Rotary but the average age at the local branch was too old for Stephen. Racket sports had been his passion as a teenager but neither the squash club nor the tennis club were a good fit — they felt cliquey and unwelcoming to someone turning up on their own and wanting a game.

Walking the streets in the evening became a compulsion. It was better than staying at home with reality TV and memories. One evening he passed the local church. The bells were ringing. Stephen stood at the bottom of the tower where the noise was loudest and let the rhythmic peal replace the dismal thoughts that constantly surfaced in his brain. It was strangely soothing to have nothing in his mind but bells.

A young woman, ten years his junior, paused alongside him and smiled. 'There's nothing as English as the sound of church bells,' she said. 'Are you a ringer?'

Stephen shook his head.

'Come on up.' She pointed to a small wooden door set into the stone wall at the bottom of the tower. 'Come and see how it's done. If you've got time?'

He nodded. He had all the time in the world. No-one was expecting him home. Ever again.

'I'm Naomi.' She offered her hand.

'Stephen.' He shook her hand.

The stone spiral staircase felt like the stairway to the top of a helter-skelter and Stephen remembered Enid Blyton's Faraway Tree books. The twins had loved those stories featuring the Slippery-Slip, a giant helter-skelter built inside a tree. With their imaginations sparked, Nick and Rob had become masters at searching out the tall, corkscrew slides at any seaside town.

Naomi paused at the top of the staircase. Beyond her Stephen could see a brightly lit room, about ten feet square. Eight people stood around the edges pulling on ropes. The doorway was partly blocked by one of these ringers.

'Stand!' The order was shouted by one of the male ringers.

The noise of the bells stopped and the ringer in the doorway stepped aside so that Naomi and Stephen could enter the room.

'Stephen's come to have a look at what we do.' Naomi ushered him into the centre of the room.

Ten pairs of eyes acknowledged him and there was a murmur of greetings. Stephen gave them a nod and smile before feeling awkward and gazing at his feet. He was stood on what looked like someone's old 1970s lounge carpet, all orange and brown swirls and slightly worn.

'Welcome, Stephen. I'm Bill, the tower captain.' Stephen shook hands with the older man. 'Sit down there and we'll ring some more. Keep your feet flat on the floor and don't talk while we ring.'

Stephen sat as he was told. The ropes went up and down. Some of the ringers' lips moved silently — Stephen later learnt they were counting their bell's position in the pattern of the other bells. Other ringers appeared to be communicating with each other using only eyes and a gesture of the head. Apparently, they were acknowledging that their bells were 'dodging' — which was some special change in the ringing pattern. Occasionally there was a sharp, shouted command from Bill. Some of the ringers stretched up to reach their ropes. Some seemed to be using a degree of physical strength each time they pulled on the furry part of the rope. Others appeared to put no effort in at all.

'Stand!'

As the ringing stopped again Stephen realised he hadn't thought about Trish and the boys for almost ten minutes. Guiltily, he acknowledged he'd enjoyed the liberation.

'Come and have a go.' Bill beckoned him over to one of the bell ropes. 'You'll do the handstroke and I'll do the backstroke.'

Bill demonstrated how he wanted Stephen to pull on the furry bit of the rope, known as the sally, and he would take care of the end of the rope, known as the tail end, as it snaked up towards the ceiling. Stephen gripped the soft, red and blue sally and pulled with all his strength.

'Too hard! Much too hard. Bell ringing is technique not strength,' Bill said.

After a few pulls Stephen got the idea of how much strength was needed. He watched some more ringing by the team and then Bill let him hold the tail end of the rope while he controlled the sally. The concentration needed to coordinate his movements and follow Bill's commands left no room in Stephen's head for stray thoughts about Trish, Nick and Rob. From then on, Stephen was hooked by bell ringing and the mental as well as physical skill required to ring as part of a team. Bell ringing was something his family had never been part of and it carried no associated memories. And best of all, it cleared his mind of all things past.

After the weekly bell ringing practice there was a trip to the pub with the rest of the band to look forward to and Naomi always seemed to grab a chair next to Stephen. She was chatty, pleasant and had an alluring elegance, even in jeans. Stephen had stopped wearing his wedding ring because he didn't want anyone to make conversation by asking about his wife. Instead he kept the ring by the bed and, through it, every night he wished Trish goodnight before he put his head on the pillow. Every night he felt the loneliness of a double bed half-empty.

'You're not married?' Naomi asked quietly one evening when the others were discussing the intricacies of a bell ringing method far beyond Stephen's comprehension.

'No.' It wasn't a lie but Stephen should have offered some further explanation. He didn't. He wanted bell ringing to be something not tainted by the sadness of loss.

Naomi looked awkward when she spoke again. 'It should probably be the man doing the asking, but nothing ventured, nothing gained. I'd like to cook you a meal one night. Will you come?'

Stephen opened his mouth to speak but no words came out. Trish had been dead almost two years. He was being asked on a date. Was this a betrayal of his wife? He hadn't been on a first date for over two decades.

'If you don't want to, that's OK.' The words tumbled from Naomi's mouth and she looked awkward.

'I'd like to come.' Stephen wanted to reassure her after the gamble she'd just taken and the words were out before he'd properly weighed up the implications.

She grinned. 'Great. Next Saturday? Any special dietary requirements?'

'I don't eat fish.'

'No fish — that's fine.'

Before leaving for dinner at Naomi's house, Stephen placed his wedding ring in the palm of his hand and had a long chat with Trish. He explained she would always be the love of his life and the only woman to ever bear his children. But the prospect of spending the next three or four decades alone scared him. What he'd loved most about their relationship was the sharing and he needed that again, otherwise life would be too dark to bear. Stephen hoped that, hovering somewhere out in the ether, Trish understood and gave him her blessing.

Naomi's dining room was candle-lit. There were flowers and crystal wine glasses and gentle music playing. She had romantic expectations. Stephen was nervous he might not be able to live up to them. He wasn't yet sure he could ever kiss another woman.

The food was good. The wine mellowed him. Naomi had a fund of funny stories from her student backpacking days. Stephen said little about his past other than describing his love of vintage car restoration.

'It's a hobby that's gone on the back burner for a while,' he said. 'Work pressures and stuff, you know?'

She nodded.

'But I'm thinking of looking around for a new project now. Things are a bit quieter and I've got more time.' It was a thought that just popped into his head. A new car project would give him focus and a reason to get up at the weekends.

After the meal they talked about their common ground — bell ringing.

'You're reasonably competent at bell handling now,' she said. 'The next step is to learn plain hunting. It's a way of changing the order in which the bells are rung. Let me show you on paper how it works.'

Naomi extinguished the candle and opened the dimmer switch to give them more light. She started writing out a column of numbers and drawing lines through the numbers that represented a particular bell. Stephen sat next to her on the settee, their shoulders touching as they both studied the same piece of paper. She turned her head towards him to make a particular point and their lips were level. There was a momentary pause when anything might happen. Stephen was aware of her subtle perfume, the coffee on her breath and the light touch of her hand on his arm to draw his attention to the paper. Naomi was the one who moved her head to bring their mouths together. Maybe it was the wine, the relaxed atmosphere, loneliness or simple lust, but kissing Naomi was extremely enjoyable. Afterwards she made more coffee, poured brandy and selected music to fit the new mood between them. It was midnight before Stephen made his excuses. Their goodbye kiss at Naomi's door was accompanied by comments they almost whispered about how enjoyable the evening had been.

On the walk home, in the cool air, his mind was a cauldron of emotions. He felt guilty, like a betraying Judas, but he also wanted more of Naomi. He wasn't in love with her but he wanted more of the human closeness that she could offer. Before he went to sleep he apologised to Trish but, unusually, he couldn't feel her presence through the wedding ring.

The following week, as a return gesture, he took Naomi out for a meal and the next weekend she went with him to look at a potential car restoration project. He'd seen it advertised online but, in the flesh, it needed a lot more work than the internet post indicated. With Naomi at his side, Stephen bartered the price down and arranged for it to be delivered. Suddenly there were things to look forward to again.

* * *

Soon Naomi and Stephen were seeing each other nearly every day. Sometimes he stayed over at her house. The first time after Trish hadn't been nearly as bad as he'd expected, slightly awkward initially but then it happened naturally. Thankfully Naomi didn't question why she wasn't invited to his house. Bringing her into Trish's territory would have been a step too far.

They'd been together a few months when Naomi gave Stephen the copy of *Diagrams*. Now he pushed it over the table to Vanessa and explained it was a book of bell ringing methods. They could be called tunes in layman's language but were more like mathematical combinations. The basic technique of changing the order in which the bells ring is called 'hunting' — which was why Naomi's inscription was so clever. Stephen leaned towards Vanessa and opened the front cover again. "*To my darling, Stephen. Now all that hunting makes sense — it led me to you! Always and forever, Naomi XXX*".

'There's a bell ringing school here in the Jewellery Quarter,' Vanessa offered. 'We hear them every Saturday morning.'

'I've read about it. But I've given up the bell ringing.'

'Oh?'

Stephen was like a teenager with his first girlfriend when Naomi gave him the copy of *Diagrams*. The paper was slightly worn where he continually ran his finger over her signature. Being with Naomi liberated him from what had gone before. She led him out of the darkness. With Naomi he barely had a minute to himself. She took him to other churches' practice nights so he could progress more quickly at ringing, she suggested films and took him walking in the countryside on Sunday afternoons.

All of this made Stephen more positive. The directors at work noticed — he got promoted and given charge of a big new client up in Scotland. This meant flying to Glasgow every Monday morning and returning Friday evening. Naomi wasn't happy.

'How long is this going to last?' she said.

'There's no end date but once the initial audit is over I won't be needed on site as much.'

They spoke every day. She carried on ringing at various towers and Stephen found a church near to where he was working that was happy to have him ring on practice nights. At weekends he and Naomi made up for the time they'd been apart during the week. After a couple of months, Stephen came home one weekend and at the supermarket bumped into Phil, a ringer from a neighbouring tower. Phil looked embarrassed, as though he didn't want to talk. But he did.

'I don't know whether it's my place to say this' — he looked over his shoulder as though frightened someone might be listening — 'but Naomi has started seeing Oliver Brown. I saw them outside the Red Lion, heads close together and looking like . . . well, you know . . . and his car's been seen outside her house . . . at night.'

'What?'

'As I said, with you being away and her being an attractive woman. She's hardly going to become a nun, is she? I thought it only right to give you a heads-up.'

It took a second for the meaning of Phil's words to sink in. Then Stephen abandoned his trolley mid-aisle and drove straight to Naomi's. There were tears pricking at his eyes but he wouldn't give her the satisfaction of seeing him cry.

He searched his memory for signs of infidelity. Naomi had picked him up from the airport the previous evening and they'd spent the night at her house. Everything had been normal. Stephen had left her warm bed reluctantly that morning, but his cupboards were bare and the post would be building up. He'd even decided now was the right time for inviting Naomi back to his house, but first there was tidying and hiding to do — Naomi still didn't know about Trish, Nick and Rob. She thought he'd never been married. It was better that way. She couldn't come round until he'd hidden the photos and other evidence.

Stephen had to ring her doorbell for almost five minutes before she eventually answered in her dressing gown with a towel wrapped round her head. Her smile of pleasure looked genuine but Stephen's anger and hurt had multiplied with the wait.

'I must give you a key,' she said and then added unnecessarily, 'I was in the shower.'

She closed the door and moved down the hall to the kitchen. Stephen followed, his heart thumping. He didn't know if he had the words to say what was needed. To his knowledge, he'd never been two-timed before and the last time he'd ended a relationship was in his teens.

'Coffee?' She filled the kettle, flicked the switch and reached for the cafetière.

'No.' Stephen had to raise his voice to compete with the boiling kettle, which sounded as though it was about to take-off.

'You don't mind if I do? I'm gasping.'

Stephen shook his head, trying to formulate the right words.

She warmed the glass jug. 'Sit down. You look all awkward. What's the matter? I thought you were going to the supermarket?'

The kettle reached a crescendo and then cut to silence. Stephen spoke to Naomi's back as she dug a spoon into the reflective silver coffee bag.

'You've been seeing Oliver Brown.' Saying it out loud made it real and the end of the sentence got caught in the back of his throat.

Her face coloured. 'Well sort of . . . yes.'

The admission was like a kick in the stomach.

'We're finished.' Stephen turned and walked back down the hall, trying to hold his head up and shoulders back. He would not cry. He would not cry.

'Stephen, wait!'

He couldn't wait. He didn't want her fabricated explanation. He held the tears back until his own front door shut behind him. Then he banged his fists on the wall and sobbed. He'd been stupid. He should never have got involved with Naomi. It was too soon after Trish. He was vulnerable and looking for comfort. He'd jumped in with both feet when he barely knew her. The landline rang, his mobile rang. Stephen ignored them both. Eventually, even though it was the middle of the day, he slept.

When he woke the landline was ringing again, his eyes were puffy and he had a headache. He lifted the receiver by the bed and mumbled.

'Stephen! It's not what you think.'

He put the phone down. He ignored the dozen text messages from her and deleted the voicemails without listening. He had a shower and a cup of tea. A new determination was creeping in. The worst thing that could ever happen already had. Anything else was water off a duck's back. Stephen made beans on toast topped with melted cheese and ate it at the kitchen table at the back of the house, making it easy to ignore the arrival of her car and the banging on the door. She'd never been here before and it had been a mistake giving her his address.

He went back up to Glasgow on the Monday. He had to put his phone on silent and scan it occasionally to spot any business calls in-between the unwanted messages from Naomi. Every day he stayed at the office as long as possible and then blasted the hotel treadmill, shocked the exercise bike and ripped the rowing machine. He spent the rest of each evening working on his laptop in the hotel. Never had he been so physically fit or on top of the job. He could only sleep if absolutely exhausted. He stopped bell ringing, both in Glasgow and back home in Yorkshire. A clean break from everything Naomi-related was the only way Stephen could stay sane.

'And you're donating *Diagrams* to the museum so that you can move on with your life?' Vanessa touched his hand again.

Stephen looked up and caught her eye. Something passed between them and he wasn't sure how to decipher it. 'Yes,' he said. 'But that's not quite the end of the story. Do you want the rest? There's time before my train.'

'Yes. Please.'

A couple of months later, the Glasgow job finished and Stephen was back home trying to avoid anyone and anything connected to Naomi. Most of the time he had his head under the bonnet or was working on the chassis of the vintage wreck that now inhabited his garage. But in a market town it's not possible to hide for ever. He bumped into Oliver Brown. These things always seemed to happen in the supermarket. Stephen could see him further down the aisle by the tinned fruit. Stephen was about to do a U-turn when Oliver spotted him and came powering down the aisle, driving the trolley one-handed and waving with his free hand. Stephen took a breath and composed his face into an 'all's fair in love and war expression'.

'So glad I've seen you mate,' Oliver said.

Stephen nodded and let his lips turn up slightly in acknowledgement of the other man but he said nothing. They weren't mates. Oliver had stolen his woman.

'No-one's seen you for ages. What's up?'

'Working away, in Glasgow.' Surely the moron could guess the real reason why he'd been keeping a low profile?

'But Sundays? We'd really appreciate an extra ringer over at Greater Beaton and Hailton is wondering what they've done to lose one of their best learners. It's more than working away, isn't? Besides, Gary Jones saw you in the gym last Wednesday — only from a distance, mind.'

Stephen wanted to punch Oliver Brown in the face. He wanted to flatten and bloody his nose. He wanted to see him sprawled on the floor, as vulnerable as Stephen had been the day he cried after discovering Oliver and Naomi were carrying on behind his back. He took a step towards him, his fists clenched in his jacket pocket.

'Naomi's rung her first peal. Did she tell you?' Oliver seemed oblivious to Stephen's tense, unwelcoming attitude. 'She thought she'd never be able to concentrate for three hours solid ringing. But she did wonderful and not even a blister to show for it at the end.'

There was nothing Stephen could say. To the other shoppers they must have looked like two old mates who'd bumped into each other and were now inconsiderate enough to block part of the aisle while they had a good chinwag.

'I gave her some extra help beforehand. We discussed the bobs and singles in Stedman Triples time and again at the pub and I went round to her house a couple of times too.'

'Just a couple of times was it?' Stephen couldn't help the dose of sarcasm that dropped out with his words.

Oliver frowned and his face rested in a puzzled expression.

'From what I've heard it was more than a couple of times and discussing Stedman was only the tip of the iceberg of what you got up to.'

'Whoa, mate. You're barking up the wrong tree. But now I understand why you two split up.' Oliver took a step back, shook his head and gave a look that said he doubted Stephen's sanity. 'Everyone thought you and Naomi were the perfect couple but no wonder it didn't work out if you didn't trust her. That peal was going to be a surprise for you — she was going to have it dedicated to your birthday. But when she said you two were finished, we sent it to *The Ringing World* as rung for the thirtieth wedding anniversary of the vicar and his wife. They were pleased but Naomi's been on a downer ever since you split.'

Oliver was treating Stephen, as though *he* was the one in the wrong. Stephen had to put him right. 'The break up was not my fault. Phil told me what you and Naomi were getting up to in my absence.'

An elderly lady was hovering close by taking a long time to choose between two different brands of tinned pears.

'Phil's an old woman. He likes to gossip.'

The lady cast them a dark look, put one tin of each brand in her trolley and walked off.

'So, you and Naomi weren't having an affair?'

'No way. I swear to God.' Oliver crossed himself. 'Look at me — I'm at least twenty years older than her, podgy round the middle and I hate the theatre and culture. I have nothing to offer a lovely woman like Naomi — except my knowledge of Stedman.'

Stephen's fists unclenched and he breathed, trying to exchange anger for logical thought. Was Oliver telling the truth? But beauty's in the eye of the beholder and . . . Stephen needed to see Naomi.

For the second time he abandoned his trolley mid-aisle and drove round to Naomi's. But this time he was filled with hope for the future, a shared future. Again, he leant on the doorbell until she answered. This time she was fully dressed in jeans and a long red and blue checked shirt that almost covered her denim-clad bottom.

'Oh!' Her face looked different. It may have been the shock of Stephen turning up on her doorstep but, on closer inspection, it was more than that. The cheek bones were more prominent, her eyes were warier and lips narrower. Something of her carefree attitude seemed to have evaporated.

Naomi gestured him inside. This time he accepted the offer of coffee. This time he planned to be here for a while — making up. The ritual of brewing the coffee afforded the opportunity for small talk before Stephen stated his purpose.

'I'm sorry, I don't have any biscuits.'

She looked like she'd lost weight.

'I've just seen Oliver Brown.'

A frown crossed her forehead.

'He said you rang a peal. That he coached you in Stedman. That was why he came round here and was with you outside the pub.'

She nodded with an I-told-you-so expression.

'I'm sorry,' Stephen said. Her hand was on the table, he put his on top and took a deep breath. 'Can we try again?'

'You didn't trust me.' She removed her hand.

He looked into his mug. He had no answer, no excuse. 'I'm sorry.' It was all he could say.

'You jumped to conclusions. You wouldn't let me explain. And you kept a massive secret from me.'

Stephen's eyes flicked up to meet hers.

'You never told me about your wife and sons. For all those months I thought I was seeing someone who'd never been married. Someone who'd never had children. But you misled me. It hurts that you didn't tell me the truth. It makes me feel our relationship was some dirty little secret just like their existence appears to have been.'

'Trish and the boys aren't a dirty little secret!'

'But I am?'

'No. You've misread everything I've said and done.'

'I'm not the one who's kept secrets. I didn't deny you the right to explain your actions. I'm the victim in all of this.'

Silence.

'How did you find out about Trish?'

'The weekend after we split, I went round to your house to wait for you coming home. It was to be my last attempt at explaining things. You never showed up.'

'I stayed in Glasgow. It would have been too painful to come home.'

'I looked through your windows and saw a wedding photo. One of your neighbours struck up a conversation and told me.'

Stephen felt ashamed. Keeping Trish, Rob and Nick under wraps was the only way of moving forward after his life had been ripped apart. Naomi was right; he'd made his family look like a dirty secret to be hidden away. He hung his head, desperate for a way to make things right again.

'I'm sorry. Really sorry. Can we try and make it work between us?' Only now could he admit to himself how much he'd missed Naomi. He'd loved her without realising it. He wanted physical contact with a woman again. He wanted not to be alone for the next four decades.

'You have to tell me everything,' she said. 'Everything. Relationships with secrets don't work.'

Stephen nodded. Naomi felt duped and he had to put that right. 'Maybe tomorrow.' He put his arms around her. Being close physically was much easier than talking. Caressing Naomi was easier than sharing Trish and the twins with an outsider. He didn't want anyone invading that precious world.

Naomi pulled away. 'Now. Or we're finished . . . for ever.'

They sat on the settee and he gripped her hand. He apologised silently to Trish and then ploughed in. He told Naomi everything, hesitantly at first and then the words cascaded without control, sometimes drowned in tears and sometimes caught in the emotion at the back of his throat. Naomi held him close when he cried. She had the decency not to promise that everything would be all right. She let him take his time. It was mid-afternoon when she knew everything. Stephen was exhausted but felt as though a great weight had been lifted from his shoulders.

'Now I want to go to your house,' Naomi said. 'I want to see their photos and to know how you lived. And how you live now.'

He trembled. It was this, or face decades alone.

As soon as they arrived he thundered upstairs past Naomi. 'You don't want to see yesterday's underpants on the bedroom floor.' Like the rest of the house, this room was pristine but there were nooks in the past where he refused to take Naomi. He pushed Trish's wedding ring, which he'd taken to talking to again at night, and the photo of her with their newborns, Rob and Nick, into a bedside drawer.

Then he guided Naomi around the house and, following some pressured persuasion, talked her through two decades of photographs. Pictures he hadn't had the courage to look at since the accident. He cried a lot more. It felt as though Naomi was torturing him for his secretive ways. They took a break at eight o'clock to order a takeaway but Stephen struggled to swallow the spring rolls and lemon chicken. Instead he drank wine; it made the sharp beheading of the scabs easier to bear.

Later Naomi held him close and then she slept on Trish's side of the bed. He couldn't make love. He was disorientated when she woke him in the morning with coffee and toast.

'It's the best I could do for breakfast,' she said. 'You're almost out of milk and there's no eggs.'

Stephen grappled for the events of the previous day. 'I abandoned the shopping to see you. My trolley's probably still sitting in the tinned-fruit aisle.'

Later he watched her go through the meagre contents of his cupboards and fridge and make the longest shopping list he'd ever seen. They went to the supermarket together and then she helped him put it away, fussing around and wiping dust out of his cupboards like a mother hen.

'Sit down.' He pulled at her hand. She'd promised they could go back to how they were, if he told her everything. But this wasn't how they'd been. 'I want a girlfriend not a housekeeper.'

She gave him a weird look and sat down next to him. 'You shouldn't be here alone when you're feeling emotional. Or do you want to come to mine and have a break from all the reminders?' Then she gently held both his hands, as though he'd only just lost Trish. Suddenly he felt smothered.

'What I'd really like is some time alone, if you don't mind. Nothing personal but I've got used to my own space.'

For a moment she looked insulted and then swiped her face into neutral. 'OK. I'll be back in a couple of hours. Call if you want me sooner.' She kissed him briefly before leaving.

Stephen stretched out on the sofa and closed his eyes. Trish and the boys were there waiting for him.

Naomi was back with a suitcase within two hours. He didn't have the bad manners to tell her he wanted to spend the night alone. The night turned into several claustrophobic days and then she suggested they sell one house and live together.

'After all you've been through.' She traced his cheek-bones and then his eyebrows with her index finger. 'It's not right that you brood alone on the past.'

'No!'

Her eyes widened.

'Sorry.' He placed his hands on her shoulders. 'I need space, Naomi. Maybe one day I'll be ready for a new live-in relationship. But not quite yet.'

Naomi didn't push him and Stephen did his best to engineer the relationship back to how he'd enjoyed it before the split. He started bell ringing again, they stayed over with each other two or three nights a week and they resumed theatre and concert trips. But knowing about his past had changed Naomi. She refused to just let him be so that the wounds of grief could heal in their own time. Instead she tried to persuade him to see a counsellor.

'Nobody loses their whole nuclear family without gathering scars. All those bottled-up emotions have got to come out at some point. Better now than in a nervous breakdown later.'

She wanted him to buy the house next to hers when it came up for sale. 'I accept your need for space but I want to cook for you more often and chase away those black thoughts when you feel overwhelmed.'

She made a point of planning an activity for every significant date in Stephen's family history: the day he and Trish got married, the twins' birthday and the day of the accident. 'It will stop you brooding but still mark the occasion with respect,' she said as she produced tickets for the London Eye on the day the twins would've turned seventeen.

None of this helped him. She made him want to bury his past deeper, not celebrate it. He knew she'd told the other ringers when they patted him on the back, refused to let him get a round in and stopped making stupid jokes at his expense. Stephen stopped trying and admitted it wasn't the right time for him and Naomi. He ended their relationship as gently as he could.

She took it on the chin. 'I guess you can only properly love one woman in a lifetime and, for you, that was Trish.'

He nodded but part of him hoped that in time it would be possible to love again.

Stephen never went back to bell ringing. Instead he threw himself into the vintage car scene in an attempt to push everything but the present day from his mind. For a few years, he kept himself to himself, not daring to risk another doomed relationship.

'It still hurts when I think about Trish and the boys,' he explained to Vanessa. 'But I feel strong enough now to leave what was our family home. I want a new start where people accept my past but won't judge my current needs by what happened.'

Vanessa nodded as though she knew exactly what he meant. During the whole telling of his story she hadn't once offered sympathy, given reassurance that time is a great healer or tried to advise him on how to move forward. She was just *there*, listening. He liked that. The museum café was the most comfortable place he'd been since losing Trish.

It was time to leave for his train. He didn't want to go. The place made him feel peaceful and Vanessa had a magnetism about her. Stephen suddenly realised it was significant that she was the only woman he'd confided in, totally and willingly, since Trish died.

Vanessa saw him all the way to the museum door and they shook hands.

'See you again soon.' He meant it.

'I'll look forward to it. By the way, how did you hear about the museum?'

'Twitter. I was torturing myself looking at #ValentinesDay and came across one of your tweets. Started following you and here I am.'

CHAPTER TEN

'He looked nice,' Maxine said later as they locked the front door, 'in a mature sort of way. Too old for me but now you're on the market again . . .'

'Thank you for the reminder that I'm old and decrepit.' But Maxine was right, Vanessa had liked the look of Stephen. Most women over the age of fifty would fancy him but she wasn't likely to attract his attention. She pushed him from her mind. 'Baking, you said.'

'Yes, it's the obvious way to cut our costs. No more high prices from the bakery; we simply buy our ingredients from the cash and carry and hey presto.'

'It will need more than hey presto on my part. When Liam was little he used to chunter on about my "swimming pool" cakes. I finally realised what he meant; they always had a sunken hole in the middle which I let him fill with jam or cream.'

'Sounds yummy.'

'Possibly, but not something we can serve here. I can only hope you have more talent than me. And I need a guarantee — no volcanic rice puddings.'

Maxine chuckled at my smile. 'The recipe doesn't involve rice. If we take it slowly, it will all be perfect.'

Was it my imagination or did Maxine sound like she was trying to convince herself as much as me? I patted her on the arm; she really was putting her all into the museum.

Maxine passed me a couple of sheets of paper printed from an internet recipe site: "Hazelnut Tiramisu Cake". The picture showed two deep round sponges sandwiched together with cream and covered in a chocolate topping and finished with grated chocolate. My mouth watered. Then I saw the number of instructions and steps.

'Don't look so nervous. If you can run a business, you can make a cake — especially with me to help you.'

She gave me an overly wide smile as she pointed at the four brand new cake tins, the roll of greaseproof paper and the tub of margarine. 'Get greasing and lining. We are making two cakes. One to serve tomorrow because the Victoria is all gone and one to put in the freezer.'

Never skimp on the greasing. It was my mother's voice — if a cake won't come out of the tin, it's ruined.

Maxine put the hazelnuts in the oven to roast and then unearthed our brand-new electric whisk that I'd bought in my first flush of ambition and optimism. She held it steady and grinned as it smoothly combined the butter and sugar.

Wow, we were actually doing this. Very soon the museum would be serving cakes "a la extraordinaire" — made by us!

But then I saw it.

'Mouse!'

My cry was more shriek than scream, but whatever, it ended up in a bit of a choked yelp. The creature was sat brazenly alongside Maxine's humane trap washing its whiskers. I moved very, very slowly so as not to attract its attention and, notwithstanding my greasy hands, bent over and pushed my trouser legs into my socks. Only then did I realise cake mixture was raining down from the whisk held aloft by Maxine. 'Maxine!'

'You made me jump and now I can't turn it off! Will you *stop* backing away and help!'

I made a leap for the socket and pulled the plug from the wall.

There was a sudden silence and we both looked at the mouse and the mouse looked at us too — as if we were mad.

'You overreacted. Again.' Maxine was pinning the blame firmly on me.

'You told me the mouse had gone of its own accord.'

'It didn't take the bait so I thought it had. And there were no more droppings. And talk normally instead of hissing! It's why he's looking at us like that!'

We both returned our gaze to the mouse — only he was gone. And not into the trap.

'Look . . .' Maxine seemed to be attempting a casual shrug of her shoulder. 'It's clearly just come in from somewhere as there's been no droppings and has clearly gone right back out again. Panic over.'

I took a long deep breath. 'Fine.' I'd happily believe that. 'But we are scrubbing this place all over again and . . .'

And then I smelt it. Something was burning and we hadn't even got the mixture in the pans yet.

'Maxine, can you smell that?'

'Nuts!' She shot forward and rescued the tray from the oven. 'They're not quite black so I think they'll be OK. Right, you get the flour and milk ready.'

* * *

By the time the cakes came out of the oven, we'd scrubbed the kitchen with industrial amounts of disinfectant and Maxine had re-primed her useless trap that she swore would be full in the morning.

The cakes . . . ?

When we went home there was a single chocolate-hazelnut four layer swimming pool cake sitting in the fridge — with lashings of extra whipped cream and a tub of Nutella filling its pools — and it all made me realise how much I missed Liam.

'We won't get distracted next time,' Maxine asserted.

Next time?

CHAPTER ELEVEN

April

'See you again soon.' Stephen hadn't meant he would actually *see* me again soon. It was one of those things people say, like, 'You must come round' or 'We'll have a drink sometime'. They were empty comments and 'sometime' never came. Why would Stephen want to see *me* again? A rejected, slightly overweight, middle-aged woman with a failing business had nothing to offer a broad-shouldered silver fox, who wore his jeans well and had a high-flying career. And he lived in Yorkshire — miles away from Birmingham. It was the museum he wanted to see again, not me. He probably wanted to check the story displayed against the *Diagrams* book was correct. He didn't trust me to get it right. He thought I wasn't as efficient as his entrepreneur late wife, Trish. But even now, a month after his visit, Stephen kept popping into my mind. I pushed him out.

He wouldn't return and I had more than enough to think about.

Liam for a start. He needed to know about the divorce. I'd continually put off breaking the bad news. Dave left all the keeping in touch with our son to me. When Liam mentioned saving his annual leave for a long visit home, the time had come to tell him. He Skyped me a few hours after I sent the email.

'You OK, Mum?' His native Brummie accent had developed a Canadian twang. He quite bizarrely didn't sound like my son any more.

'Fine. The café and museum keep me busy. Lots going on. Nothing stays the same for ever.' Bright and breezy, that's how I needed to sound. No point Liam worrying over milk already spilt. Sound positive and you almost believe it yourself. I was getting over Dave. I was getting over Dave. If I said it enough times, I could almost believe it. Except in the middle of the night when, tired and befuddled with sleep, I reached for him, touched the empty reality on his side of the bed and sobbed.

'You take care, won't you, Mum? I reckon Dad will soon be back with his tail between his legs.' Liam had gone too far away and for too long to be upset by the split or understand the reality of our everyday life. 'If you need a break from everything come and see me instead of me coming over there.'

Hearing his voice stirred that longing in my heart. I wanted to see my son. And hold him. I wanted to feel I wasn't alone in this world. Liam misinterpreted the pause. 'If you're nervous about travelling on your own, get Dad to come with you. I've two spare bedrooms. We could all be together. It might even mend things between you two — I could be like a cupid's arrow. I'll drop him an email and suggest it.'

Had Liam grasped the meaning of divorce? It would be nice to all be together but could we really sweep Dave's unfaithfulness under the carpet for the sake of our son? And would Dave's new woman allow him to go away with his ex-wife?

Liam sent flowers — a mass of pink and red chrysanthemums and carnations. A brownie point for effort but I'd have preferred a real-life hug. Half of me had hoped he would jump on a plane and rush home for Easter. The flowers needed the tall crystal vase Dave's parents had given for our engagement but it was in the charity shop with all the other tainted memories; mostly dispersed before the museum came into being. Tears pricked as I split the blooms between a glass water jug and an inferior emerald green plastic vase.

That crystal vase hadn't had much use. Dave wasn't one for rash romantic gestures, unless you counted the Valentine chocolate mints. The one time he excelled himself was when we brought newborn Liam home from hospital. A huge bouquet decorated with a blue ribbon waited on the kitchen table.

'You were fantastic,' Dave said. There was the shine of tears in the corners of his eyes. 'You seemed in such pain, I . . . I was frightened you might die.'

At that point I truly believed he loved me. And it was a delicious sensation to feel so wanted as a vulnerable new mum.

Now I had to cope alone and was on a mission to wipe away Dave's existence and betrayal. Selling the house would be the biggest and best step forward. Moving somewhere new would stop the memories crowding in on me. But selling up came with its own difficulties. Our individual half shares of the proceeds would be barely enough for a studio flat each. Not that Dave needed a flat; he had his woman. I could be awkward and force a sale but the thought of living somewhere little bigger than a bedsit depressed me. So, I did nothing, even though knowing he still owned half my home made moving on difficult.

Instead I removed all trace of him from what I now saw as *my* four walls. I boxed up his books, CDs and other paraphernalia and asked him to collect them while I was out. But he came when I was in. At least he had the grace to knock rather than use his key. Our doorstep greetings were awkward. We didn't invade each other's personal space with fake hugs and air kissing. I watched to see if he showed any signs of regretting his decision. There was nothing. He didn't squeeze my hand or give me a peck on the cheek. He gave no indication at all that he might have made a mistake in leaving me.

I hadn't anticipated him dragging out the loft ladder and pushing the boxes into the eaves. Apparently, his girlfriend's place was too small to house it all so I wasn't going to be completely rid of him yet.

'One day Gillian and I will get married and buy a bigger place together, then I'll take all this out of your way,' he said.

I shuddered at his mention of marriage; the memories of my wedding day further tainted by the image of Dave making the same promises to someone else. Had he ever taken our vows seriously? Would he give her the same wink he'd given me when he lifted my veil at the altar? I was glad my wedding ring now sat in the museum with a false story. It was only a tiny defiant gesture but significant. If he could treat our relationship with a pinch of salt, so could I. The future might be a lonely place but with the museum to cling to, I could make it work. I had to.

Professional decorators gave my master bedroom a makeover. In the past, mindful that it was half Dave's room, I'd avoided anything overtly feminine but now I didn't hesitate to go with shades of pink and a large floral pattern on the feature wall. It was time to celebrate and enjoy my womanhood. My ex-husband was not going to destroy my confidence as well as our marriage. Not to say that my ability to face the world didn't feel destroyed on my weaker days but I was fighting it.

The charity shop did well from my clearout, receiving the watercolour landscapes Dave had chosen, the barbecue he always captained as though he was a Michelin-starred chef and the ugly, brown velour armchair that he swore was the most comfortable thing he'd ever sat in.

Being alone in the house was difficult. Before the café and museum, the evenings were long and mournful. The TV programmes, Dave and I had enjoyed together lost their shine. Drinking wine alone seemed a terrible sin and a loud silence hung in every room. Concentration was difficult and I spent my time channel-hopping, scanning magazine articles and wondering if I'd ever be brave enough to go out on my own. Or even to start dating again. Did women date at my age or did they just acquire a cat and a rocking chair? When I started the museum, things improved. Now I was on my feet most of the day and at home all I wanted was food and sleep. Sometimes I dreamed Stephen kept his word about seeing me again and that he arrived at the museum in shining armour to whisk me off my feet.

Five weeks after his first visit, that dream came, partly, true. I was trying to fathom why the income from ticket sales seemed to be dropping when it felt like visitor numbers were increasing. The arrival of April meant I was already more than one third of the way through the financial cushion as calculated by Jim. If things didn't improve soon, I'd no chance of breaking into the black by October.

'Hello, Vanessa.' He startled me at the museum reception desk.

'Stephen!' Without conscious thought my right hand went to my hair and my left covered my mouth. I felt my cheeks go warm.

'I said I'd be back. So here I am.'

'It's lovely to see you.' Act normally, Vanessa.

'Likewise.' He grinned at me for several seconds before swivelling his eyes and gesturing at the computer screen. 'And I'll be able to pop in regularly and boost your visitor numbers.'

Then his gaze moved back to me and I felt as though he was drinking me in. Or maybe that was wishful thinking. Whatever it was, I couldn't even string a full sentence together. 'How?'

'I'm relocating to Birmingham.' He grinned at me again. 'Oh!'

'A fresh start will do me good. I have cousins here who'll put me up until I get sorted. I've got a part-time contract as an internal auditor, which gives me a few months to consider my options. It shouldn't take too long to find a permanent job. But it must be right, maybe in the not-for-profit sector, a housing association or a charity. I want something I can feel passionate about, like you do this place.'

This new Stephen was fired up, enthusiastic and ready for anything, compared to the Stephen who'd brought his book to the museum and appeared to be carrying the weight of the world on his shoulders. This energy added to his attractiveness and forced me to turn my head back to the computer screen so he didn't think I was staring at him.

'That's great,' I said to the spreadsheet in front of me. 'Not many people can engineer themselves a new start. Make the most of it.'

He was silent for a moment and I looked up. A shadow of the old despondent Stephen had crossed his face. 'Not having dependents, other people to consider . . . well, I suppose it makes things easier.'

'It's called moving on,' I said in my best matter-of-fact voice. 'We all have to do it. Children fly the nest, jobs and partners rarely last for life. Sometimes the best things emerge from the worst things.' I gave him a little punch on the arm. 'Let's look to the future. Both of us.'

'I want to do voluntary work.' The spark was back in his eye. 'On the two days I'm not doing proper work. My next stop is the volunteer bureau in Digbeth. Perhaps I could help a small charity with its accounts or teach kids about money.'

'Great idea — whatever organisation gets you, will be very lucky.'

'What are you working on?' He moved closer to look over my shoulder. His odour was spicy and male. I held myself tense and still to avoid brushing against him and transmitting the fact that I found him attractive. As somebody else's reject, fancying Stephen was punching far above my weight.

'Visitor numbers and museum income,' I explained, 'but something's not right. Visitor numbers are up but our income isn't.'

'It's the formula that's wrong. May I?' He pointed at the mouse.

'Be my guest.' I stood and moved away so he could have my seat. 'I'll fetch us some tea from the café.'

On my way downstairs I couldn't help making a detour into the Ladies. Stephen's presence made me want to check my hair and make sure my clothes weren't rucked up. When I came back with the cups, he explained in easy words what the problem was and how he'd already put it right.

'I could do with you working here!'

'Really?'

I'd said it as a joke but Stephen was looking at me seriously, as though that was something he'd like.

'Yes, really. But I can't afford an accountant's salary.'

'You could be my two days' voluntary work. Well, for the next six months until my contract ends and I have to make decisions about the future.'

And I thought I'd hit lucky with Maxine . . .

Was he really offering to be my own private, free, *attractive* accountant? To take away one of my biggest headaches? But doing the accounts wouldn't take up two whole days a week. And . . . *really*?

I wasn't going to look a gift horse in the mouth. Except that I did want to look at Stephen's mouth, I wanted to look at every bit of him. 'Would you mind using some of that time to cover for Maxine? She's part-time and does a bit of everything.'

'I'll do whatever you want. It's so comfortable here, with you, in the museum.'

With you? Meaning *me*? A slip of the tongue. I knew he simply wanted an antidote to a standard office job — he'd admitted as much when he talked about working in the not-for-profit sector.

'I can't magically turn the business around,' he warned, 'but I'll do my very best.' Then he offered his hand and we shook on it.

If Stephen felt the same tingle as me run up his arm, he didn't show it.

* * *

Polly and Malcolm arrived after Stephen had gone but before I could wipe away the silly grin he'd put on my face.

'You look happy,' Polly said when I took their order.

'It's been a good morning.' I tried to tone down my expression but the thought of working with Stephen made the edges of my mouth turn up again.

'Tea and scones, please. And I've brought you something.' Polly was holding out a small, boxed Easter egg. 'To say thank you for looking after us. Finding a welcoming place to go with Malcolm is . . . difficult. You are a godsend.'

'Oh, Polly! Thank you.' Now the grin was gone and tears were pricking at my eyes. I bent over and hugged her. This was a much greater, more worthwhile reward than money. This was why I had to keep the museum open beyond October — for people like Polly and for my own sanity in a newly empty life.

I fetched her order and sat down opposite her. Malcolm was prowling again but the scarcity of customers meant it didn't matter. I told her about my good fortune in Stephen offering his services for free.

'Him taking the accounts and business stuff off my shoulders is a godsend but we have limited time before we have to make a profit or shut down. This place hasn't become as popular as I'd hoped.'

'Well, you'll never make any money if you don't charge for the jam or cake. Make sure it goes on my bill this time.'

Polly might be old but she was on the ball. I smiled and squeezed her hand. She looked at me with sad eyes and then started to cry.

'Oh, Polly, what is it?'

'I love him so much but it's really not easy.'

'Tell me about it,' I said gently.

She blinked hard and then told me about her daily struggle.

The worst times were when Malcolm got overtired or hungry. Then he would follow Polly around while she was trying to get the tea ready and pull and push at her to convey his discomfort and frustration. His speech was almost gone and he'd resorted to toddler tactics. When someone's tugging and shoving you, the first reaction is to push them in return and create some distance between you and them. It's an instinctive act not malicious. But Malcolm took it as an indication that you wanted to fight, so he retaliated with slaps and punches. He'd always been a strong man and there was power behind his blows. Polly had to cower in a corner, arms over her head until his anger was spent.

Melissa came to visit the day after it happened the first time.

'We'll have to put him in a home,' she said. Her voice was matter of fact, like she was talking about a dog that had turned out to be too boisterous and needed to be rehomed.

'No. You're talking about my husband.' Polly tried to explain why Melissa's dad couldn't go in a home. 'We've looked after each other for nearly sixty years. I can't get rid of him because he's ill. I promised "in sickness and in health".'

'Mum, nobody expects you to keep that promise in these circumstances.'

'Had it been the other way around, your dad would've kept the promise.'

'It would've been easier for him — you don't have the strength to hurt him physically like he can you.'

After that Polly didn't tell Melissa about the further violent outbursts. If Malcolm left a visible mark, Polly delayed Melissa's visit until it had faded enough for her to hide it with make-up.

Polly looked like she had more to tell but Malcolm arrived back at the table and she immediately slipped into carer mode, buttering his scone and helping him with his drink. Then Maxine appeared with the message that there was a salesman upstairs wanting us to stock books about the Jewellery Quarter. I went to talk to him and Maxine slipped behind the café counter. Later she told me that Malcolm had become cantankerous and Polly had had to take him home before finishing her pot of tea. I felt sad for the old lady who was beginning to feel as much a friend as Maxine had become.

CHAPTER TWELVE

I spent the evening eating the whole of Polly's Easter egg. I was regretting all that chocolate when the doorbell rang. It was 10.30 p.m. My first thought was for Liam — was it the police to break bad news? Dave had never got around to putting in a spyhole or affixing a chain to the door, so I leant one ear against the wood and heard footsteps receding down the path. Whoever it was had given up or changed their mind. Not bad news after all. My shoulders sank with relief and I turned to go upstairs.

As my foot touched the bottom stair there was the trundle of wheels over the path outside. I listened at the door again. The trundling came nearer, stopped and was replaced by prolonged ringing of the bell. The letterbox rattled and was held open. I stood to one side, out of the line of sight, my heart thudding. A draught swept into the hallway followed by laboured breathing. Then there were words, panted rather than spoken.

''nessa. It's me. Open up, please. I've lost my key.'

Dave. My heart didn't know whether to sink or soar. I opened the door a couple of inches and peered into the night to make sure it really was him. He stood on the doorstep between two suitcases, one sitting unevenly with a broken wheel.

He offered me a bunch of slightly wilted pink carnations and a box of chocolate mints. 'Can I come in?' His breathing was almost back to normal now. 'Sorry about the flowers. They were all the garage had left.'

I took the cellophane wrapped stalks and dark green box, opened the door wider and stood out of his way. He half dragged, half carried each of the suitcases over the threshold. Under the bright light of the hall I could see there were bags under his eyes and his hair was greyer. Neither of us spoke. Then we both opened our mouths together and our words collided in mid-air.

'I've left—'

'What do you—?'

'You go first.'

'No, you.'

Thirty years of marriage and we were complete strangers being polite to one another.

'I'll put the kettle on,' I said.

He spoke to my back as I headed down the hallway to the kitchen.

'Gillian was a mistake . . .'

I deliberately drowned the rest of his words with thundering water from the tap into the kettle. I needed time to think. He could not tear my marriage apart and then turn up again out of the blue because he'd realised the grass wasn't greener. More than eighteen months had passed since Dave announced his adultery and walked out. We couldn't, at the drop of a hat, pick up where we'd left off. Even though in my weaker moments, when I was tired, like now, I wanted to. I didn't like being lonely.

I played for time by putting biscuits on a plate, stirring the dark liquid in the teapot, warming mugs and decanting milk into a jug — things I usually did only for 'proper' visitors, not my husband. Ex-husband. I cut the cellophane flower wrapping, found the ugly green plastic vase that had been home to Liam's flowers only a couple of weeks' earlier, filled it with water, sprinkled in the contents of the flower-food sachet and added the carnations. Then we sat at the kitchen table and I poured the tea. His suitcases were still by the front door.

'I've left Gillian.'

At my lowest ebb I'd pictured this moment in glorious technicolour. We would fling ourselves into each other's arms, consumed by the relief of being back where we belonged. But now I didn't move. Neither of us moved.

'Why?'

'I'd rather be with you.'

My heart missed a beat, my mind filling with warnings to tread carefully. 'But for over a year and a half you preferred to be with someone else.'

'Call it a honeymoon period, a midlife crisis, chasing the greener grass. But now I realise that what I had in the first place was the best.'

'You wrecked what we had in the first place and that exact same thing can never be available again.'

'You're still the best, 'nessa. And I'd like us to try again. If you'll have me?'

A second beat missed. I was feeling tired and weak. My heart could not be allowed to make this decision now.

'It's too late at night for decisions like this. Let's meet on neutral ground somewhere another day.'

'But I need somewhere to stay tonight.'

'Not here.'

'I still own half the house.' He spoke slowly, as if reluctant to use this weapon. 'I can use the spare room. I'll do my own cooking and washing. Yours as well, if you want.'

'No. We're divorced. That means we don't live under the same roof.' I would call the shots, not him. Now I regretted being too cowardly to swap this comfortable three bedroomed house for a souped-up bedsit.

'So, I have to squander my salary renting a tiny flat while you have empty bedrooms?'

I didn't like his change in tone but could see his point.

'Sorry, that came out wrong,' he continued. 'How about we give it a few months as housemates and see how we get on?'

Or we could sell up. But I couldn't cope with selling up and moving home, as well as keeping the museum afloat. Dave's suggestion was a fair compromise. 'Purely platonic and with separate lives,' I stipulated.

He reached for my hand. 'But we can be friends.'

I pulled my hand away. 'I don't keep friends who use me for thirty years and then walk out.'

'I didn't set out to hurt you.'

'Bollocks!' Dave was visibly shocked by my language. 'As soon as you took an interest in her, you knew it would hurt me. You don't get the chance to stick the knife in twice. Find somewhere else to live.'

'Half of this house is still mine.' His voice stayed calm. 'Let's give ourselves time to get used to each other again. I'll take my things up to the spare room.' He went to fetch his suitcases.

What choice did I have? It was nearly midnight. It was only half my house. He had nowhere else to go. I was tired and it was a weak moment.

'This is temporary,' I warned. 'I work seven days a week so you'll have the place to yourself most of the time.'

'I heard you started some kind of museum. Good for you. There's money to be made when you're your own boss.'

I ignored his praise, rinsed my mug in the sink and went to bed. Dave thumped his suitcases up the stairs. Water ran in the bathroom then the door of the spare room closed. I hoped he'd brought his own toothbrush and had remembered to put the toilet seat down. Sleep was a long time coming. Tension knotted my back. My fists clenched and opened. A fairground waltzer of emotions raced in my head. I was furious that Dave had barged into my home but I also felt the pathetic reassurance of having a man in the house. Alone at night I heard noises and worried about a burst pipe or blown fuse. He had dealt with all that stuff for thirty years and it was hard not to want his practical help back. Having Dave in the house was going to be a complicated situation.

The next day I deliberately stayed later at the café, ostensibly to give the floor a thorough cleaning, making sure I got into all the hard to reach areas where crumbs, and possibly mice, gather, such as between the wall and the cake display cabinets and behind the fridge. I refused to look in the direction of the humane trap. There'd been no more sightings of our friendly mouse or his droppings but the last thing I wanted right now was a conversation with a rodent whose whiskers were covered in peanut butter.

'You should go home,' Maxine said when she pulled on her own coat. She had a small baby bump now and didn't bother with the buttons. 'You look dead on your feet. I'll help you first thing tomorrow to get that done.'

I shook my head and waved her away. Maxine didn't need to know that I couldn't face going home to spend time with my ex-husband. On the way I bought a ready-made lasagne for one — I wouldn't give Dave any reason to think I would step back into my old 'wife' role.

In the kitchen there was a restaurant-level smell of bolognaise, garlic and cheese.

'Great timing!' Dave called as if there was no big wall of animosity sitting between us. He'd just taken a bubbling, golden brown dish of home-made lasagne from the oven. The mass-produced version in my carrier bag turned to cardboard.

The kitchen table was set for two. The salad bowl was full of multi-coloured goodness, there were two glasses of red wine and a small bowl of roughly grated parmesan.

'You go ahead.' My stomach rumbled. I tried to ignore the assault on my senses of his culinary activities. I worked in a café all day but it was weeks since I'd had a proper home-cooked evening meal. I didn't have the energy or the inclination to go back in the kitchen after serving customers all day. 'I'll eat later — I grabbed something on the way home.'

Dave looked from the steaming dish in front of him to the cardboard-sleeved plastic tray that I was trying to push into the fridge without him seeing. He took it from me, jabbed his foot on the pedal bin and let the packet fall. 'Sit down.'

When was the last time someone had cooked for me? There was fresh fruit salad for dessert and wrapped chocolate mints with our coffee. It felt like a bistro without all the hassle of getting dressed up and travelling. And there was no bill to pay.

'Gillian was a bit of a foodie.' Dave poured us another glass of wine. 'It was catching and she taught me to cook.'

I flinched at the mention of the woman who'd usurped me. She'd obviously been superior to me in more than one department.

'But I'm well rid of her,' Dave continued. 'And I'm happy to cook for us every night — my way of paying you back for all you did when we were married. Now, are you making money at this museum?'

'It's early days,' I responded vaguely, wondering at the domestication of my husband. Then I smiled, remembering yesterday's surprise visitor. 'I've got myself a volunteer accountant to help with the business side of things. Stephen.'

'Stephen.' Dave looked suspicious. 'A man? And he's doing it as a favour?'

'Yes.' I realised Dave was jealous and that made me smile even more. I liked him thinking that another man found me attractive — even if, in reality, Stephen didn't.

Dave had cooked so it was only right I offered to wash up. He gave me the tea towel and took the sink for himself, like when we were married. Initially it felt awkward but old habits die hard and soon we were laughing about how we used to bath Liam in the kitchen sink when he was tiny.

Dave emptied the water away, dried his hands and put an arm around my waist. 'It's good to be back.'

For a moment I was where I belonged, close to the man I'd lived with and loved for thirty years. I looked up into his eyes, seeing the familiar flirting twinkle that he always used to get me into bed. He still found me attractive. Then a scarlet warning flag dropped. My husband had lied, cheated and walked out on me.

'Shall we?' He inclined his head towards the kitchen door and the bottom of the stairs.

Our bodies were close and his smell familiar and welcoming, but I couldn't shut out what he'd done.

'No.' I pulled away.

Dave frowned. 'Gillian was a stupid midlife crisis. I want to be with you — we're good for each other.'

'We *were* good for each other. We had a comfortable rut. But you jumped out without me and things are different now.'

'We can make it work again. I know we can.' He squeezed my hands.

'No. If you stay here it has to be platonic.'

Dave frowned and then nodded. 'But maybe in the future . . . ?'

I shrugged. He looked hurt. I felt guilty; I liked to please. But my heart would never mend if Dave broke it for a second time and, until he'd proved himself, I didn't trust him not to be careless with it.

CHAPTER THIRTEEN

Stephen started work at the museum on the last day of April. I showed him Jim's spreadsheet again and where I'd unsuccessfully tried to put in the figures for February and March.

'April's figures can go in now as well.' I handed him the notebook, open at "April", where I kept a tally of weekly takings and visitor numbers.

As he took the book, Stephen glanced at me with a smile that lit up his eyes. The lurch in my stomach was the same sensation I'd had as a teenager when I saw David Essex in concert and was convinced that, as his eyes rested on my section of audience, his look was just for me.

'At least you've kept manual records,' Stephen said. 'You wouldn't believe the mess some small businesses get into.'

He hardly moved from the laptop on the reception desk all day and, mid-afternoon, he said we needed to talk. I made us coffee and plated the last two bits of chocolate cake that would become dry if left until the next day.

'Jim was right. You can't afford Maxine.' Stephen was solemn and had lost his twinkle. 'Even that one employee on minimum wage is too much. The five percent growth figures were too optimistic. Over the last three months takings are only up by two percent per month.'

I went cold inside. I couldn't tell Maxine she'd given up a secure banking career to end up on the scrap heap. And I'd miss her. Doing everything on my own had been hard and lonely; I couldn't go back to that. 'There must be a way.'

'It's nearly always possible to turn a business around through innovation and elbow grease. But there's the risk that by staying open and continuing to employ Maxine, you're throwing good money after bad.'

'I'm in too deep. I can't give up now. What can we do?'

'You were on the right lines with the Valentine event. People need a particular reason to visit the museum. With the right event, a city the size of Birmingham should easily fill this venue.'

'We're a museum, not a social club.'

'But not a normal museum. A museum like this should be a social amenity as well as an exhibition space — it's all about improving lives. Like it did mine.' For a second the gravitas left his face; he grinned and I felt good. Then Stephen turned serious again. 'To give you until October to turn things around, I advise reducing Maxine's hours.'

'I can't. With a baby on the way she needs the money. She's already part-time.'

'Perhaps if we talk it through with her, she'll understand and possibly be able to manage financially.'

'No. I refuse to worry her before the baby is safely delivered.' It wasn't businesslike to be emotionally involved with staff but I couldn't help it. The thought of telling Maxine her job was finished or her hours reduced brought me close to tears. It was the end of the day, I was tired and the waltzer in my head was still circling on full speed about the rights and wrongs of having Dave back in the house. My face must have been a reflection of my distress. Stephen gave me a sudden hug. The physical contact lasted only a few seconds but the sensation of having him so close remained far longer. I composed my face before looking up at him. He seemed as surprised as I felt and then a sort of apologetic grin crossed his face but he never took his eyes away from mine.

One of us had to speak. 'Your coffee's going cold,' I said.

Stephen became professional again. 'I've painted the blackest picture but you've got me here to turn things around and I'll do my utmost. But I insist on one thing.'

He paused and I waited for the next bombshell.

'We tell Maxine.'

'Tell Maxine what?' My assistant walked into the café before I could silence Stephen.

There was no way out of it. 'Sit down,' I said and then looked at Stephen, indicating he could break the news.

'Things aren't good with the museum finances, Maxine. Notionally we only have until October to turn things around, possibly less. Even a part-time employee isn't sustainable if we are being realistic.'

'But I can't manage without you, Maxine.' I blundered into Stephen's explanation.

'With all three of us on board,' my new business manager continued, 'there's more chance of turning things around. Are you happy to risk there being no job after the baby is born? Or, would you prefer to see if the bank will take you back?'

No-one spoke while Maxine processed the information. She frowned. She placed her hands flat on the table and stared at them. She moved them to her belly and looked down. She pursed and straightened her lips.

'The money I earn is essential,' she said eventually. 'I can't pretend it's not. But none of my colleagues ever looked happy working at the bank. And I certainly wasn't.'

I willed her to say she'd stay.

'This is my chance at a worthwhile job and I'll stay as long as possible.'

'Yes!' I felt triumphant.

Maxine grinned, stood up and raised her right arm. She motioned for Stephen and me to do the same. We stood in a tight circle.

'One for all and all for one!' she declared.

'One for all and all for one!' Stephen and I repeated with feeling. His eye caught mine and we both grinned.

'There is something else we can do,' Maxine said. 'Revisit our baking.'

'Noooo!' I cried.

'It's an obvious thing to do,' said Stephen. 'And whoever heard of a tea shop owner who couldn't bake?'

I felt the flush rise in my cheeks and gave a reluctant nod Maxine's way.

She grinned. 'YouTube here I come!'

CHAPTER FOURTEEN

May
Joanne

Joanne ventured into the museum with her donation, not sure whether what she had to say or to give would be interesting enough. Since her mother died, she'd felt like a snake, shedding her past like a scaly, unwanted skin. For three decades life had been lived in a dark grey shadow but now light was shining in and pulling her forward.

Joanne chose a table in the middle of the café. She moved the stand-up laminated menu onto a chair, ran her fingers over the tabletop to check for sticky marks, and then took a large photo album from a carrier bag. She sat down and began to slowly turn the pages. The album had been in the family for years and had opaque inserts between the pages to protect the pictures.

'Can I get you anything?'

Joanne looked up. It said "Vanessa" on the waitress's name badge. She was in black, topped with a white apron and her likable, open face was make-up free.

'Tea, please.'

'What about something to eat? Lemon drizzle is our "Cake of the Day" — it's on special offer.' Vanessa indicated the menu that Joanne had moved onto the chair.

Joanne hesitated and glanced down at her soft, plump waistline. The elasticated waistband of her trousers wouldn't mind. 'Yes, I'll have a piece, please.'

She closed the album. Now she was here Joanne felt calm; there was no need for a last frenzied look at the pictures. The decision was made. She would go home and the album, along with all her resentment, would stay here. As long as the museum felt it worthy of their collection. She watched Vanessa go behind the counter, fill a teapot, slide a wedge of cake from the chilled display cabinet onto a china plate and gather a milk jug, sugar bowl and serviette.

'Are you donating the album to the museum?' Vanessa asked, transferring the tea things from the tray to the table. Joanne moved the book to one side to make more space. 'Or maybe just one picture?'

'I want to get rid of the whole thing.'

Vanessa sat down. 'So why didn't you just bin it? Why make the effort to bring it here?'

Joanne took breaths, the bitter feelings coming back as she thought about what she'd really like to do with the album. 'I nearly had a bonfire — imagine the pleasure of seeing a thing like that burn! I actually piled up fallen branches in the garden and put the album on top. Then I couldn't strike the match. It was too . . . final. I want to put everything behind me but this' — she gestured at the book, the tension tight across her shoulders again — 'this is too big a part of me to destroy but I need it out of the house before I go insane.'

'What's your name?'

'Joanne.'

'Would you tell me about it, Joanne? I saw you having a look around upstairs so you've seen how we work, when the album's on display, we like to tell its back story.'

'It will be anonymous?'

'I promise.'

'This is our family album.'

'Before we start, are these recent pictures? Will people be recognisable? That would destroy your anonymity. And we might need the permission of other people in the photos.'

'No, they're old, mostly me as a child and my parents, who are dead. No-one will recognise me now.'

'OK. Could you talk me through the pictures please, Joanne?' Vanessa rearranged the crockery to make space for the album to be opened again. She pulled out a spiral-bound notebook. 'You don't mind if I jot down your story?' Vanessa looked like she was expecting pearls of wisdom to drop from Joanne's lips.

Joanne shook her head. 'That's fine but I've not had the most exciting or fulfilling life.'

Trawling through the story of her wasted life, with a stranger, wasn't going to be easy, however kind Vanessa seemed, but perhaps it would be cathartic. Whenever Joanne thought about all those grey, frustrating years she got angry. Even after the counselling she still fumed but she'd accepted that clinging to negative emotions was ruining the remainder of her life. That's why the album had to go. But complete destruction was too final — it *was* her whole life after all.

Joanne turned to the first page in the album. A picture of her, aged one. She was gripping the handle of a push-along dog. It was the size of a toy poodle, well-worn, brown and cream and of no identifiable breed, with a blue collar around its neck. The animal was fixed to a red metal frame on small black wheels. Joanne thought she remembered using the dog to take her first few steps or maybe that was a false memory created by seeing the photo so often.

'Tell me about this?' Vanessa was pointing at the picture.

'It's a long story if we talk about all the pictures. Shall I just get to the point and tell you the crux of the matter?'

'No, please, I'd like to hear it all.'

'OK.' It was a good job she had nothing else planned for the rest of the day. 'This is the earliest photo there is of me.'

The toddler picture was taken in the mid-1960s. Auntie Sylvia was in the background clapping her hands. She was home from university for the summer holidays. Joanne's parents had bought the dog from a second-hand shop. Apparently, it was Joanne's pride and joy and she'd walk around and around the garden chuntering incoherently to the soft toy. Her mum had made the cute dress with hand-sewn smocking across the chest. The photo was black and white so the red and blue stitching against the pink fabric couldn't be appreciated but Joanne had had the colours described to her many times. After her mum died, she found the dress wrapped in tissue paper at the back of her mother's underwear drawer. Joanne found a lot of things after her mother's death.

In the next picture Joanne was a couple of years older and paddling on the beach in a baggy swimsuit. She was staring downwards into the water, clutching a small bucket in one hand and, with the other, holding her dad's hand. He grinned broadly for the camera but Joanne frowned in concentration.

'You were looking for fish,' Joanne's father used to tell her about this picture. 'You worried about standing on a fish and hurting it. We tried to explain that fish didn't live in the shallows but still you paddled everywhere on tiptoe, convinced you'd accidentally kill one.'

There were more summer holidays on the following pages but Joanne turned the pages quickly. There was nothing worth saying about those. She stopped at an image of her aged six, standing next to her mother. Joanne's mum was holding a baby dressed in a great long christening gown. It was one of those family heirlooms that got passed down the generations, worn by boys and girls alike. Joanne wore it when she was christened. Auntie Sylvia was her godmother but Joanne had never found any photos of her baptism; with hindsight it's possible her mother destroyed them. The baby in this picture was Joanne's cousin and Joanne was looking up at him in her mother's arms instead of grinning at the camera. There was only the ghost of a smile on her mum's lips.

Joanne had no true memory of the christening but she did remember Auntie Sylvia, Uncle Rodney and little Kevin coming to stay with them at Christmas and Easter. Joanne always wished they'd come more often because she liked taking Kevin by the hand and showing him her rabbits and then sitting him down on the floor with her dolls and giving him juice from her toy tea set. Sylvia was her mum's sister and Joanne was desperate for a sister of her own. Joanne's mother was never happy when they came to visit. Once Joanne overheard her parents talking after the visitors had left. She didn't understand at the time but it stuck in her head and finally made sense years later.

'It's as though she wants to rub my nose in it,' her mum had said. 'Twice she's done something I never have and she thinks that makes her superior to me. All she talks about is Kevin this and Kevin that.'

'I'm sure she doesn't mean it like that, Audrey, love.' Dad tried to placate her. 'Every parent's proud of their child, just as we are of Joanne. Sylvia's proud of Joanne too — she always makes a fuss of her.'

'It's not the same for us though. And she's got that wretched degree — she thinks that makes her cleverer than the rest of us.'

Joanne was pleased her dad was proud and the other remarks got filed away until she could understand them.

Kevin's sister Emma was born a couple of years later. When she heard she had a little girl cousin, Joanne was desperate to go and visit. But Mum made them wait a few weeks. Then on the appointed day her mother had a bad headache and said she'd have to stay in bed. Joanne and her father went alone. It was two hours in the car each way and on the way back they stopped in a café and had what Joanne's dad called a 'Full English' even though it was teatime not breakfast time. Joanne asked why they had to live so far away from Auntie Sylvia and from both her grandmas.

'I changed my job when you were little. Your mum saw a better one advertised in Birmingham and she thought it would be a good city for you to grow up in.'

The brains of grown-ups seemed to work in strange ways. The fields around Auntie Sylvia's house were a much more exciting place to play than the playground at the bottom of Joanne's street with its litter, chewing gum and graffiti.

Joanne caught Vanessa's eye as the waitress looked up from her notepad. 'Is this the sort of thing you want to know?'

'It's great. I'm jotting down a few sentences for each picture. The album will be in a glass case and we can have it open at a different page each day. It will be good for encouraging return visitors. They can learn your story bit by bit. We're considering an annual season ticket to cover unlimited visits.'

Joanne frowned; she hadn't expected her story to be exploited for its commercialism. Did she want this? Would a bonfire be better after all?

'I'm sorry.' Vanessa must have read the distaste on her face. 'We're not a tabloid newspaper or a celebrity magazine. Your photo album won't be sensationalised. You've seen that all exhibits are treated respectfully.'

Joanne nodded. It was going to be anonymous so it didn't really matter. She picked up the cake plate and ate a couple of forkfuls, being careful not to let the sticky citrus drizzle drop onto the album. Then she went back to the pictures.

'These next few pages chart various milestones in my life. There's me dressed for Brownies — I got to be a Sixer. And that's my school uniform.'

Joanne moved on to a party picture — she was dressed up as Alice in Wonderland for her tenth birthday. Her dad had declared that reaching double figures was 'an achievement' and deserved a special party. He hired the church hall and suggested it should be a fancy-dress do. Her mum was less keen.

'It'll be a lot of work,' she said. 'All that food to prepare and the hall to clear up afterwards.'

'I'm sure Sylvia will be happy to help,' Dad said. 'Rodney's got a company car now so he won't mind the drive.'

'There's no need to ask her. Joanne can butter bread and mix fairy cakes.'

Joanne was more than happy to help. Her party was the talk of the class at school and, because they'd hired a hall, she could invite absolutely everyone. She did a list and made sure that each person dressed up as someone different.

The party was a great success. Auntie Sylvia, Uncle Rodney, Kevin and Emma came — but only by the skin of their teeth. Joanne overheard the discussion between her parents about whether to invite them.

'It's a long journey for them to come just for an afternoon,' her mum said. 'Let's not bother.'

'They're family,' her dad said. 'Let's give them the option.'

'Really, there's no need. They won't know anyone and Kevin and Emma will be too young to join in properly. And Sylvia will *interfere*. Because of . . . she thinks she has the right to interfere in everything.'

For Joanne the party was going to be a great opportunity to show off her lovely little cousins to her schoolmates. And her friends would like Auntie Sylvia too with her being young and pretty — just how Joanne wanted to look when she was grown up. 'I want them to come,' Joanne declared, abandoning *Blue Peter* and walking into the argument in the kitchen. 'Please invite them.'

Her dad's lips wriggled as though he was trying to suppress a smile and he wrote out an invitation card. Joanne licked the stamp and ran to the post box.

It was lucky they were invited because at the party Joanne's mum had a headache and had to sit down most of the time, so her dad and Uncle Rodney took charge of the games and Auntie Sylvia was in charge of serving food. They played Musical Chairs, The Farmer's in his Den, Pass the Parcel and, especially for Kevin and Emma, Ring a Ring o' Roses. Everyone joined in with a great big: 'Atishoo! Atishoo! We all fall down!' Little Emma rolled around on the floor giggling for ages.

Afterwards Joanne helped Auntie Sylvia wash up. Dad and Uncle Rodney swept the hall and got rid of all the rubbish. Emma was laid on the backseat of the car for a nap and Kevin tried very hard to read *Five on a Treasure Island*, which Joanne's best friend had brought to the party as a present. Every two minutes he had to ask Joanne to read the difficult words for him. She felt very grown-up.

Joanne was still over-excited from the party when she went to bed and was lying awake when her parents came upstairs. Her mum sounded grumpy from her headache that hadn't gone away.

'Why did you let Sylvia and Rodney take over like that?' She was trying to whisper but her voice was cross and she spoke loud enough for Joanne to hear.

'Because they offered and I couldn't manage thirty children on my own.'

'You made Sylvia look superior to me. Sylvia is twenty years younger than me and not only has she given birth to "super kids" Kevin and Emma but she can also run a children's party at the drop of a hat.'

'You're twisting things, Audrey. Don't be jealous of what your sister has. Be proud of Joanne — she's our daughter and she's a lovely, kind young girl.'

This argument, which Joanne didn't understand, was spoiling her memories of the lovely party. She put the pillow over her head, hummed Ring a Ring o' Roses and remembered how everyone had laughed.

It was a year or so after the party that Joanne started to realise her mum and dad were older than everyone else's parents. The next photo in the album was from a nativity concert during her first year at grammar school. Joanne had cut the picture from the local paper. She was eleven and played the Angel Gabriel. Her mum used her sewing skills to turn an old sheet into a wonderful pure white, angelic gown and her dad made a headdress from an old wire coat hanger and some sparkly silver tinsel. It was even cleverer than the Advent crown they made on *Blue Peter* every year, except Joanne's headdress didn't have candles.

She was nervous about the performance but her dad practised the lines with her and she was word perfect on the night. At the end of the show her dad rushed up for a hug and her mum was just behind him. There was a photographer from the local paper there.

'Lovely,' he said. 'Let's have the grandparents congratulating one of the stars of the show.'

'They're not my grandparents,' Joanne said immediately and probably too loudly. 'They're my mum and dad.'

There must have been a lull in the general conversation in the hall at that point because her voice echoed around. Suddenly everyone was looking at Joanne, her mum and her dad. It felt like she'd said something wrong but she'd only said the truth. Her mum was always complaining about her wrinkles so Joanne knew she wouldn't want people to think she was a grandmother. Joanne had to put the photographer straight.

'I'm sorry.' The photographer was looking awkwardly at his feet. 'I didn't mean anything by it. It was just—'

'Forget it, lad,' Joanne's dad said. 'Let's get this picture taken. It's our Joanne who's important. It doesn't matter who we are.'

The photographer arranged the three of them in a group and pointed a huge camera. It was much bigger than the one they used for taking photos on holiday. In the picture Joanne's dad was as proud as punch with his arm around her shoulders but her mum was standing slightly to one side, glaring at the man behind the camera.

After that Joanne never looked at her parents in the same way again. She noticed the furrows around her mum's eyes were deeper than those of her friends' mothers and the clothes she wore suddenly appeared dowdy and old-fashioned. When her dad waited with the other girls' fathers to collect her after ballet or Guides, his hair was noticeably greyer and thinner. He wore braces over his work shirt — and braces definitely weren't trendy back then.

'How old are you?' Joanne asked her mother when they were drying the dishes.

'Old enough,' she said evasively. 'Don't you know it's rude to ask a lady her age?'

She wouldn't tell but Joanne's dad did. Joanne brought the subject up when they went to fetch fish and chips for tea one day.

'Fifty,' he said. 'We're both fifty.'

'So, when I was born you were thirty-nine?'

Her dad was a silent for a second and he had a funny look on his face. 'Yes,' he said eventually, 'when you were born, we were thirty-nine.'

When Joanne was thirteen her dad got ill. At first she wasn't told but it was obvious that something was wrong. Conversations stopped when she walked into the room. Her dad started taking time off work, something he'd never done before. Both her parents looked even older and greyer and they were worried all the time. One day, Joanne's dad sat her down when she came home from school.

'I've got to go into hospital, Joanne.' His voice was shaky.

'What for?' She gripped the kitchen chair. She could tell from his expression that it was something serious.

'I've got lung cancer.'

If they were a touchy-feely family that would have been the time to do the tears and cuddles. Instead her dad gave her a quick hug and then she stared at the floor and he patted her shoulder. Then her mum appeared in the doorway.

'You've told her, then?'

Dad and Joanne nodded in unison.

The weeks that followed were a blur. Mum visited Dad every afternoon. Joanne went to school as though everything was normal. At teatime they both pushed their food round and round their plates. Then her mum scraped most of their meal into the bin and they did evening visiting at the hospital together.

Homework slipped down Joanne's list of priorities. The teachers started noticing and had words with her. It made no difference; her head was far away in a hospital ward with her dying dad. So they sent a letter home.

Joanne's mum cried when she read it. 'Your father will be so upset. How could you do this? He'll blame me.'

'He doesn't need to know, does he?' Joanne couldn't bear the prospect of his disappointment. 'I promise I'll do better. Please don't tell him!'

Joanne did do better. Each day, for two hours after school, she forced the image of her dad's newly bald head and diminishing frame from her mind and replaced it with French verbs, Maths equations and Shakespearean quotes from Julius Caesar. A few weeks later she was able to announce that she'd been commended by the head teacher for her mid-term test results. Joanne's father gave a now rare smile and clapped his hands together slowly.

That was the last time she saw him smile. He died two weeks later.

Joanne halted in her tale. She steepled her fingers and rested her elbows on the Formica table. She chewed on one of her thumbs.

'Take your time,' Vanessa said. 'There's no hurry.'

* * *

After a short break to visit the Ladies and regain her composure, Joanne turned the page. There was a jump of a few years to the next picture. Joanne was still recognisable but now she looked about sixteen and was wearing the navy blue skirt and V-necked jumper of a senior school uniform. There was a blue and white striped tie at her neck. The huge knot hung loosely a couple of centimetres below the open top button of her white blouse. She was in a group with three other girls. They had their arms around each other's shoulders and were kicking their legs out as though dancing the cancan. Their faces were full of exuberant laughter.

Joanne took a sip of tea from the cup in front of her and pulled a face. She added more sugar to the cup and stirred. After taking another sip she carried on.

'That's our last official day in the fifth form. The following week O level exams started and then lots of my classmates left school and got jobs but some of us stayed on into the sixth form.'

Joanne blamed the dearth of future photos on her father's death — nothing happened that was worth capturing on film. Joanne went to school and her mum carried on being a housewife. Then, like most of her sixth form schoolmates, Joanne got a Saturday job in a shop. She and her mum did nothing else. The life insurance money had paid off the mortgage and there was enough left in the form of a pension to keep Joanne and her mum. Joanne started looking forward to university and being independent in the big wide world. Eventually she wanted to be a teacher.

As time went on Joanne's mum went out less and less. She stopped meeting friends for coffee and gave up the WI. When Joanne started in the upper sixth her mum even stopped going out to do the food shopping. Instead she gave Joanne lists of things to buy on her way home from school. Joanne thought it odd but didn't worry. Looking back down the years she tried to work out why she'd buried her head in the sand for so long. Perhaps she'd been a typical teenager — wrapped up in her own world with little brain space left to take much notice of her mother. Or maybe she just wanted to be like everyone else, and nobody else at school worried about their mother. So Joanne pretended that everything was all right at home.

Either way, her mother's increasing reclusiveness didn't impact Joanne directly until she got her A level results and a place at Durham University to read English. She expected her mum to be over the moon. If her dad had been alive, he would've cracked open the champagne.

'You can't go,' her mum said, when Joanne burst into the house with a shout after collecting her results envelope from school.

'What? Why not? I'll get a full grant. Money won't be an issue.'

'Who'll do the food shopping or go to the bank to pay the bills?'

'You will.'

Her mum looked at the floor, shook her head and then said in a small voice, 'I can't.'

'What do you mean, you can't?' This was news to Joanne. She thought her mum asked her to do the shopping because she passed the shops on her way home from school. She thought her mum was getting lazy and it would do her good to do her own errands for a change.

Joanne's mum was quiet for a while, as though working out what to say. Then she spoke quickly without making eye contact. 'Just after your dad died, I went to the supermarket and was trying to choose some fish for tea when I came over all funny. I started shaking and thought I was going to collapse. An assistant found me a chair and they called a taxi to take me home. After that I was scared of the supermarket and I only went to the smaller shops closer to home. Then I had the same frightening experience at a WI meeting in the church hall so I had to stop going there. The final straw came in the newsagents around the corner. I was in the queue when my heart started to pound and my hand was shaking so much, I couldn't get the coins out of my purse. Now I can't even get outside the front door without my heart behaving like a racehorse and feeling like the world's going to end.'

'Why didn't you tell me?' Joanne was shocked that all this had gone on without her noticing.

'You're young. You don't want to be worrying about me.'

'Can't the doctor help? Antidepressants or something?'

Her mum shook her head. 'I don't want drugs. They turn you into a zombie. Sylvia would never be dependent on antidepressants and I don't want her to have reason to think I'm not coping with life. She feels superior to me as it is, what with me having you. And with your dad being gone.'

'What do you mean? What's wrong with having me?'

Her mum was crying now and refused to answer questions. Joanne was confused, worried and very angry. Angry because unless her mother made a miraculous recovery, Joanne would not be going to university. She wished her mum was younger, like her friends' mothers then maybe this wouldn't have happened. Then she blamed her dad for dying. He died when she was young because her parents were already old when she was born. This was all their fault for being old parents.

Joanne thought about calling Auntie Sylvia for advice. But it was obvious, for reasons she wouldn't share, that her mum felt inferior to her younger sister and wouldn't thank Joanne for broadcasting her problems. Joanne was angry with her mother but she couldn't betray her.

Sylvia sent a huge glittery congratulations card when she heard about Joanne's exam results. Sylvia had been the first in the family to go to university and was pleased Joanne was following in her footsteps. Joanne had to write and tell her she wouldn't be going to Durham after all. Out of loyalty to her mum she made it sound like she'd got cold feet and wanted to postpone leaving home for a year or so. Sylvia said she understood but the tone of her letter showed she was disappointed.

Joanne got a job in a bank, living at home to look after her mum. Joanne's friends and teachers were aghast she'd turned down a place at Durham but shame stopped her giving them the real reason why.

At first Joanne resented the job but that changed when she fell in love with Christopher. He was tall and handsome with wavy fair hair and green eyes. His lazy smile made her toes curl up and he had a way of making her feel special. They'd chatted when their coffee breaks in the bank's rest room coincided and once he dealt with an awkward customer at Joanne's till but it was the branch barbeque at the manager's house when they got together properly. A burger covered in fried onions and ketchup escaped from its bun and slithered down Joanne's T-shirt. Christopher helped find a damp cloth to repair the damage. Then he fetched a new burger and found them a quiet corner to sit and eat. After that they started dating and Joanne spent every day on cloud nine.

She didn't mention her boyfriend because her mother would insist on meeting him and intuition told Joanne that wouldn't be a good thing. Her mum may have stopped her leaving home but Joanne felt she was still entitled to an independent adult life. Keeping Christopher secret was her way of safeguarding that. But her mother guessed what was going on.

'You've got a man,' she said one Sunday afternoon.

Joanne blushed, stared at the floor and said nothing. She wasn't good at lying and ignoring the statement was the easiest option.

'You're spending hours in the bathroom and your bedroom is a fog of perfume. And I found these in your knicker drawer.' She held up an unopened packet of condoms.

Mortified, Joanne fled to her bedroom and slammed the door.

'I'm almost twenty!' she called through the wood. 'You have no right to go through my things.'

'I was putting your washing away.'

That packet had been hidden, her mother had done more than put Joanne's washing away. And she was jumping to the wrong conclusion. She and Christopher weren't sleeping together. Joanne had overcome her embarrassment and bought those 'just in case'.

'I should be pleased you're taking precautions,' her mother called through the door. 'Accidents have life-long repercussions. That's something this family knows all about.'

Joanne didn't know what she meant by the last sentence but didn't give her mother the satisfaction of a reply.

Eventually Joanne had to come out of her room. For tea there was her favourite tuna sandwiches with chopped spring onions and salad cream plus a freshly baked coffee and walnut cake sat in the middle of the table.

'It's full of buttercream,' her mum said.

She was trying to make it up to Joanne without actually saying sorry. The gesture made Joanne feel guilty about her own behaviour. She should be nicer to her mum and let her into her life a bit more. Her mum never left the house. Apart from the television, Joanne was her only source of news from the outside world. It was cruel not to share things. But still, Joanne needed privacy. She was an adult now not a little girl.

'Christopher works at the bank,' she offered. 'He moved to our branch six months ago for a promotion to assistant manager.'

'Does he have his own house?'

'He's renting a flat at the moment but as soon as his mortgage application is accepted, he's going to buy something.' She was proud of having a boyfriend a few years older who could afford to buy property. Her mum was bound to approve of this too.

'So he'll be wanting to settle down then?' She was frowning as though this was a bad thing.

'I think so.' Joanne had her own hopes about what Christopher's 'settling-down' might involve.

'Invite him round next weekend. I'd like to meet him.'

There was no way of getting out of it and Christopher was enthusiastic. He suggested he and Joanne meet earlier in the afternoon before going to her mum's. They walked around the park hand-in-hand in the sunshine before sitting on a bench overlooking the lake. Two swans were gliding along the water. They came to a halt, facing each other and bent their necks in the way that swans do to make a perfect heart shape together.

Christopher squeezed her hand. 'Look at that,' he said. 'Swans mate for life.'

Then he went down on one knee in front of the bench and produced a sapphire solitaire ring. 'Joanne, please will you do me the honour of becoming my wife?'

At that moment the world stopped. Joanne's heart, her breathing, and the blinking of her eyelids all ceased. Secretly she'd hoped they'd get married but never expected it so soon.

'Say that again,' she asked him when her brain and body started to function again.

He gave her that toe-curling smile. 'Joanne, please will you do me the honour of becoming my wife?' His eyes were locked on hers; they were green pools of hope, love and honesty.

'I will!' Joanne squealed and flung her arms around his still kneeling figure.

He kissed her and they both wobbled over onto the tarmac in front of the bench. They sat there, in each other's arms, not caring what passers-by must think. Christopher stood up first, held out his hand and pulled her up. They reclaimed the bench with their arms entwined. Joanne wanted that moment of utter bliss to never end. She and Christopher had a future together. There would be a house and children, holidays and fun. They might have a honeymoon abroad and she'd fly in a plane for the first time. Her only sadness was her father wouldn't be there to walk her down the aisle.

Would her mum be well enough to come to the wedding? The thought flashed into her mind like a warning beacon and she banished it. Nothing was going to spoil this special day.

They arrived home for tea flushed, holding hands and fifteen minutes late.

Joanne's mum looked at them without a smile and then at her watch. 'The sandwiches might have gone a little dry,' she said.

Ignore her, Joanne told herself, don't let her spoil the day. 'Mum, this is Christopher. Christopher, this is my mother.'

Christopher held out his hand. 'I'm really sorry we're late, Mrs Sugden. But we have some news for you.' He glanced at Joanne. 'Special news.'

Her mum was looking annoyed. 'Can it keep until I've poured the tea? I don't want anything else spoiling.'

This icy welcome was unexpected. Her mum had suggested inviting Christopher to tea but now she was being the worst hostess ever. She and Christopher were placed at opposite ends of the dining table. Joanne's mother filled their cups and then passed the milk jug to Christopher.

'Help yourself to sandwiches. Those are ham and those are boiled egg.'

Joanne had been desperate to flash her left hand across the table but her mum had quashed her excitement as effectively as a bucket of cold water. For a while they made small talk and then Christopher threw Joanne a questioning look. She nodded at him, indicating he could make the announcement now.

'Mrs Sugden, we've only just met but Joanne and I have got to know each other well over the last few months.'

Her mother raised her eyebrows and Joanne knew she was thinking about the condoms.

'And, to my great pleasure, earlier this afternoon she agreed to marry me. We are engaged.'

A thrill ran through Joanne at the sound of those words. She grinned at her fiancé and placed her left hand with its sapphire, in front of her mother.

'Isn't it lovely? Christopher even got the right size.'

'Very nice. Help yourself to the sandwiches, I don't want them going to waste.'

The rest of the meal was awkward. Her mum didn't refer to the engagement. Instead she talked about next door's big ginger tom. It was in the habit of scaling the garden fence so it could terrorise the birds feeding. The bird table was her mum's pride and joy. She could manage to get that far out into the back garden each day to replenish it with the seed Joanne fetched from the garden centre.

'There are products to keep cats away. I could get you one,' Christopher suggested. 'Perhaps drop it in on my way home?'

Mrs Sugden pursed her lips. 'You think you'll be coming again?'

Christopher glanced at Joanne for rescue.

'Christopher's only trying to be helpful, Mum. If you don't want the cat stuff, that's fine.'

'Taking a daughter from a housebound woman isn't helpful. How am I supposed to manage when you two are wed and creating your own home with your bank subsidised mortgage?'

The penny dropped. Her mum was hostile to Christopher because she was going to lose her live-in errand runner.

There was nothing to be said in response. Joanne tried to talk about the weather and the swans they'd seen in the park. Christopher shared an anecdote about his grandmother's cat and the daily mouse it used to leave on the kitchen table. Joanne's mum took no part in the conversation. Christopher made his excuses to leave as soon as politeness would allow.

'Come back to the flat with me,' he said as they parted on the doorstep. 'Let's try and salvage some romance from our special day. And we've a wedding to talk about. I love you.'

Joanne shook her head. 'I love you too but I need to sort things out with Mum before I do anything else.'

When she went back into the dining room her mother was sitting with a framed photo of her late husband in her hand. There were tears in her eyes.

'He'd be so disappointed in you, Joanne. He'd never approve of you abandoning me to go swanning off to some posh house with an assistant bank manager. Blood is thicker than water. Family comes first. That's what your dad would say. I don't know how you can let him down this way.'

The photo was one of Joanne's favourites of her dad. His eyes were crinkly and smiley. He was wearing the chunky, navy blue pullover that always smelt of the seaside and holidays. She could imagine him stepping out of the photo and twirling a little girl version of her around and around. Her dad had always been proud of her and, even now, she still wanted him to be proud of what she did.

'Perhaps we could get a house big enough for you to live with us.' Joanne didn't want her mum to live with them but what was the alternative?

'You'd better find out what your precious Christopher thinks before making offers like that.'

The following evening Christopher took her out for an engagement meal. There was champagne on ice waiting at the table. It was the sort of restaurant where waiters take your coat and keep the table free of crumbs with a little brush. Definitely not the sort of place a young assistant bank manager could afford on a regular basis.

'I'll never get engaged again so I want to push the boat out,' he said.

There was a pianist playing gently and a candle on the table. Christopher produced a red rose. Everything should have been perfect, except it wasn't. Joanne still had to explain to him about her mother living with them. It was a great weight on her shoulders and she didn't have the right words. The waiter poured the champagne. They studied the menu and then ordered.

'To us!' Christopher raised his glass.

'To us,' Joanne echoed.

Then she explained about needing to get a house big enough to include her mum.

'No.'

She tried to explain that anxiety and agoraphobia were as real as a physical disability and that they'd hardly notice she was living with them. 'She could have her own TV in her own bedroom. We wouldn't have to be together all the time.'

'No. I can't live with a woman who showed no joy over her daughter's engagement.'

Joanne couldn't live with the knowledge that she'd let her father down. She couldn't live with his disappointed face in her head. Her relationship with Christopher fizzled and died. He moved to the next county to be assistant manager in a bigger branch. Joanne stayed at home with her mum.

Now, as she paused in the story to give Vanessa's pen time to catch up, Joanne's hand reached for the chain that hung around her neck. The links had been looped through a sapphire engagement ring.

'He didn't want his ring back?' Vanessa asked.

'I never offered it. I didn't see why I should be left with nothing. I didn't finish our relationship.' There was a sting of bitterness in her voice.

Just then two ladies took a seat at one of the other café tables.

'Would you excuse me?' Vanessa said.

CHAPTER FIFTEEN

Joanne was facing the counter but out of earshot. Oddly, Vanessa didn't look comfortable with her new customers. She waved them to a table and then appeared to back herself into one end of the kitchen, near the till. Then she made a phone call. A few moments later, the young woman who Joanne had seen upstairs in the museum hall, went rushing up to Vanessa with a big "I told you so" grin on her face. Then she bent down out of view.

Moments later, the young woman walked nonchalantly out of the café with a long parcel, wrapped in a tea towel, under her arm. She caught Joanne's eye and smiled. Embarrassed to have been caught staring, Joanne immediately returned her gaze to her album. Five minutes later, after serving the two ladies, Vanessa returned to Joanne.

'And then it was just you and your mum?' Vanessa resumed her questioning but looked a little unnerved by whatever had just happened behind the counter with the girl from upstairs.

Joanne nodded, trying to block out the thought of all those wasted years.

'So why have you decided to bring the album in now? And why donate the album and not your engagement ring

— surely Christopher broke your heart, not these pictures of your childhood?'

Joanne closed the album. 'When it was just me and Mum there was nothing to take pictures of. The rest of the pages are empty. And all these other pictures are lies. My whole upbringing was a lie.' Joanne's voice got louder; it was too much of a struggle to control her anger. 'Almost everyone else in those pictures knew the truth. I was the person it affected the most and I was kept in the dark. If I'd known I might have acted differently over university and Christopher. If I'd known I might have had a husband now and children or a proper career. What Mum said about blood being thicker than water wouldn't have mattered.'

Joanne realised the two ladies had turned their heads at her raised voice. She flushed and changed to an almost whisper.

After Christopher, Joanne became almost as much of a hermit as her mother. She had to go to work and do the shopping but she shunned all social contact. She couldn't risk falling in love and having her dreams smashed again. If she found new friends there would always be the fear that her mother would engineer a way to humiliate her in front of them or stop her from seeing them. Joanne spent her free time reading, watching TV and getting old before her time. She perfected her baking too.

'If social media had been a big thing back then, I might have become a baking vlogger or an Instagram star. Instead, our immediate neighbours testified that my Victoria sponges were getting lighter and the chocolate fudge cakes richer. I loved the trial and error process of creating new recipes. Adding nuts to the flapjack was a major disaster. The man next door spent ages trying and failing to saw through it with his breadknife before returning the solid block with a big thumbs down. But it didn't stop him from still wanting to be my guinea pig.'

Joanne was surprised to see Vanessa smile empathetically.

With age her mother became infirm and often ill. Joanne suggested she see the doctor but her agoraphobia was worse than the physical discomforts of her many illnesses and she refused to go. It would have been possible to arrange a house call but Joanne pretended that if her mother was really bad, she'd conquer her fear of going out or arrange the house call herself. It equated to turning a blind eye but Joanne felt this was justified on two counts. Firstly, after her behaviour over Christopher, she didn't owe her mother any kindness other than her presence in the house. This familial duty meant Joanne's life was on hold until her mother was dead — therefore the quicker she died the better. Secondly, if the doctor came there was the possibility they'd take her mother into hospital, at least for a short time. Such a respite from the woman's barbed comments and ungratefulness was like a mirage on the horizon. Joanne desperately wanted it. But once she'd had that taste of freedom, there was a danger she'd refuse to have her mother back. That would mean letting her dad down and having his disappointed face haunt her for years to come. She couldn't risk that. It was better to bury her head in the sand and let her mother slowly deteriorate — by refusing to go out that was the older woman's choice after all.

She'd died five years ago, after a long, miserable existence. Joanne had expected to feel euphoric. For a long time she'd imagined the fireworks and excitement of finally being free. It would be like a dog used to the confines of a flat suddenly being taken to the countryside and allowed to roam, race and rummage in the smells of rabbits and rats. It didn't turn out like that.

By that time Joanne was forty-eight. The friendships from her school days had long ago withered and died. At work, used to her flimsy excuses, colleagues had stopped inviting her on nights out decades earlier. Contact with Auntie Sylvia and Uncle Rodney had been virtually non-existent over the last ten years. Joanne's mother wouldn't visit them and forbade Joanne from inviting them.

'What's the point of going to all the trouble of cooking and cleaning for them?' she would say. 'At the end of the day they're only coming to gloat.'

'Gloat?'

'All we'll hear is what Kevin and Emma have been doing. About their wonderful careers and the fantastic grandchildren Kevin's wife has produced.'

'But you wouldn't let me—'

Her mother had put her hand up to silence Joanne before she could be reminded why her daughter didn't possess a degree, the key to Kevin and Emma's careers, and why she hadn't procreated.

'Even if you'd had children,' her mother said, 'it wouldn't have been the same.'

With hindsight Joanne should have immediately questioned that statement but she took it as part of the nature of the bitter old woman. Joanne had written to Sylvia every Christmas, on her aunt's birthday and after her own birthday, which Sylvia always remembered with a card and a small but carefully chosen present. Once it was a necklace, set with Joanne's birthstone and another time a pack of luxury hand creams. In her letters Sylvia always mentioned how sorry she was about the way things had turned out between the two families. Joanne knew the rift was of her mother's making.

One year, Sylvia phoned on her sister's birthday. Joanne's mother was aghast, shook her head and used exaggerated hand gestures to indicate Joanne should say she was too ill to come to the phone. Joanne followed orders and made reassuring noises to Sylvia, telling her there was no need to worry and the two of them were plodding along fine. Sylvia understood privacy on phone calls was difficult because her sister would hover in the hallway and listen. She didn't phone again.

All four of them came to the funeral, plus the partners of Kevin and Emma, making up half the total mourners. Joanne's and her mother's hermit lifestyle meant there were only a dozen people in the crematorium chapel. Take away

Sylvia's family and there would have been only the few neighbours who remembered the family from back when Joanne's dad was alive and everything was normal.

For a long time after her mother's death, Joanne sat at home and brooded on the wasted years of her twenties, thirties and most of her forties. Bitterness filled her like a foul-tasting bile. She began to hate her mother more in death than she had in life. She resented the duty she'd felt towards her. One day there was an article in the local paper about a new counselling service available to help people let go of the past and start afresh. Exhausted by the constant circle of black thoughts, Joanne decided to go along. Knowing her mother always sneered at counselling when it was discussed on TV, gave Joanne the delicious feeling of rebellion she'd missed as a dutiful teenager.

She couldn't be sure it was down to the counselling but Joanne started to pull herself together. It was corny but she began to understand the truth behind sayings such as, 'Life is not a rehearsal', 'Enjoy yourself, it's later than you think' and, 'We are masters of our own destiny'. She got a good haircut, renewed the contents of her make-up bag and modernised her wardrobe. She asked to go on the email list for nights out at work. At first, she was a square peg, on the outside of all the 'in' jokes and anecdotes of previous happenings when so-and-so had had too much to drink. But with perseverance, the evenings became easier and she began to relax. It was a sign that things were working out when the person buying a round remembered Joanne's usual was a gin and tonic and, in turn, Joanne needed less prompting about the order when it was her turn to lean on the bar and recite the group's requirements.

The local rambling club was advertising for members which gave her something to do at weekends. They were mostly retired, weather-beaten types who could walk for miles without a blister or aching muscle. Youth was on Joanne's side but a day on the hills with these oldies was a challenge. She joined a gym and her fitness and the enjoyment of the walks improved. Life was looking good, her confidence was building and, at last, she felt like a normal person.

Joanne ate the remnants of her lemon drizzle cake and then finished her tea.

'I don't really understand about the album,' Vanessa said. 'I can see that you didn't have the perfect mother but there were happy times. Why don't you want to keep the pictures?'

'It was a lie.' The words came out like a shot of venom and her face flushed. 'My whole life was a lie. A sham. I wasn't who I thought I was. But neither of my parents was brave enough to tell me. I think Dad would have but *she* stopped him.'

With her confidence back, Joanne wanted to make up for all the time she'd lost caring for her mother and being the dutiful daughter. Now she had chance to do things most free people take for granted. First on the list was a foreign holiday. She found a singles' holiday company that wasn't based around getting drunk and pairing people off. Joanne wasn't looking for sex or love, all she wanted was to experience a different culture. Thailand, South America and Australia all looked fantastic but she decided on something a bit tamer for her first foreign foray and chose a guided walking holiday in the Austrian Alps. With the deposit paid and the leave booked from work, the next thing was the passport application. After a few tries in the supermarket photo booth she mastered the solemn expression with hair well away from her face. Not the most flattering of pictures but who cared what the Austrian immigration officers thought? One of her neighbours was a teacher and countersigned the photos for Joanne.

'I can't believe this is the first passport you've ever had,' she said staring at Joanne as though she was from Mars. 'You've got a lot of time to make up!'

'Don't I know it!'

The passport application demanded her birth certificate. Her mother had kept all their important documents in a large sky blue metal tin, emblazoned with an old-fashioned "Cadbury's Roses Chocolates" logo. Red and pink blooms, interspersed with green leaves, stretched round its sides and the tin proclaimed it had once held 6lb of chocolates. It only just fitted on the top shelf of her mum's wardrobe. The uppermost documents in the tin were those Joanne had added recently: her mother's death certificate and her will. She took those out followed by the power of attorney form which she'd needed in order to do Mum's banking and official stuff. There was her dad's death certificate and his and her mum's birth certificates but nothing of Joanne's. She felt a flurry of panic; how was she going to get a passport without her birth certificate? She didn't have a driving licence — she and her mum never went anywhere, so what was the point? Her heart raced. Without proof of ID she was a non-entity. She didn't exist. She was an invisible, grey, virtually middle-aged woman who didn't get a second look in the street because no-one could see her. She was transparent and inconsequential.

Memories of opening a bank account hovered in a haze at the back of her mind. That must have needed a birth certificate. She'd had the Saturday job in the corner shop. Nothing clever, shelf-stacking, pricing-up cans of soup and packets of biscuits with a gun that had a life of its own and, occasionally, serving behind the counter with the boss at her shoulder to make sure she didn't have her hand in the till. A bank account wasn't necessary; she'd been paid in cash. She didn't even get a little envelope with a payslip. But her mum had insisted on the bank account.

'There's nothing to be gained by frittering that money,' she'd said. 'You'll regret spending it on make-up, clothes and fripperies. Get it in the bank — with your dad gone we need the means to survive in the future.'

The shop owner's miserly hourly rate of pay was unlikely to change their financial horizon but Joanne's mother always got her way. It was just before she stopped going out completely and she'd gone with Joanne to the bank, holding onto her arm as she always did when they were out. Joanne thought it was to stop her scarpering but with hindsight it was an early manifestation of her mother's anxiety. Once inside the bank, her mum's confidence returned. She did all the talking and document handling. Joanne signed where she was told. It was the same bank where she eventually went to work and there'd been no issue switching from that basic savings account to a current account and, a little later, adding a couple of higher interest accounts. Money laundering legislation was less stringent back then.

Once upon a time her mother had had the ID to open Joanne a bank account. She must officially exist. Proof of that existence must be inside this tin. If she went through the contents of the tin logically, she would find her birth certificate. She took everything out and spread it across the floor. There was an envelope. A plain brown envelope, unsealed and with no writing on it. Inside was her birth certificate. Only, it wasn't a birth certificate. It was an adoption certificate.

Joanne stopped mid-story, remembering the shock of discovering that piece of paper.

'What a terrible moment for you, love.' The compassion in Vanessa's eyes made Joanne want to cry.

'I . . .' She tried to ground herself in the reality of the café and not back in the past. 'Whenever I think about it, I go cold inside. The writing had been on the wall all my life but I didn't see it or maybe I refused to see it.'

'I'll get you some more tea and cake?'

Joanne nodded. She watched Vanessa go over to the counter and fill a fresh teapot from the gleaming coffee machine. Then the younger woman, from upstairs, who'd spoken to Vanessa earlier, returned. She still had the tea towel-covered object under her arm. Joanne fiddled with the front cover of the photo album aware of a low-voiced conversation between the two women. She wondered whether she'd rabbited on too long and this was Vanessa's way of diplomatically trying to get rid of her. But when the waitress returned with the fresh drink and a doughnut she seemed just as welcoming and interested as before. Joanne bit into the sugary sponge and then wiped her sticky fingers on a paper serviette.

'What did you do next?' Vanessa prompted.

Joanne had stared at the adoption certificate for several minutes before its full impact hit her. Then she ran to the bathroom and threw up. Afterwards she sat on the bathroom floor shivering with shock and replaying her life, from her earliest memories right up to that point of discovery. She remembered her mother's constant disappointment in her, contrasted with her father's unwavering love. She remembered the numerous times she'd asked why she had no brothers or sisters. Her mother always shook her head and changed the subject. Her father said Joanne brought so much joy there wasn't room for any other children.

After a few weird days of feeling as though she was in a parallel universe, Joanne got a grip on her emotions and completed the passport application. It felt as though she was doing it on behalf of a small girl who'd been torn away from her birth mother and placed with a hostile woman. All through her life she'd been a cuckoo in the nest and her mother had put up with her for the sake of her marriage. It was obvious now that her father had always wanted Joanne more than her mother did.

Austria was as perfect as she'd hoped: sunny weather, beautiful scenery and the company of like-minded people. Standing on one of the mountains she looked down and surveyed the valleys and villages. It was like the scenic layout for a toy train set. A child might pick up and rearrange a train set at will, having ultimate power over it, just as Joanne now finally had power over her life. At that moment she resolved to find her birth parents and discover her true history.

It took a while for everything to go through the system but finally she discovered the identity of her birth mother. Sylvia. The woman she'd always believed to be her aunt was actually her mother. The shock was greater than discovering the adoption but it explained so much. It explained her mother's jealousy of her sister, it explained how fond her aunt was of her as a youngster. It explained why her dad was always happy to encourage them to come to Joanne's milestone events and her mother wasn't.

When they met for the first time as mother and daughter, they both cried. Sylvia had come to Joanne's house and Joanne fetched a toilet roll to mop their tears and blow their noses. Sylvia explained what had happened in brief, stilted sentences.

'I was eighteen and about to be the first in our family to go to university. It was a one-night stand with a boy from another sixth form college. I barely knew him and never told him I was pregnant. My mum, your grandma, was devastated. I was Mum's beautiful little "accident" and came along in her mid-forties when she was least expecting it. I got spoilt rotten. By the time I fell pregnant your mum and dad had already been married fifteen years and no babies had arrived. Your grandma didn't want me saddled with a baby when I had the world at my feet but she didn't want to lose you either. She didn't want her flesh and blood to be given away outside the family. She wanted to be able to watch you grow up. I wasn't sure what I wanted. It was all such a shock. Never in a million years did I expect to fall pregnant. I seriously thought about aborting you.'

Joanne gave a little yelp. It felt like a knife being pushed into her heart. Neither her birth mother nor her adoptive mother had wanted her.

'I didn't know whether to tell you that or not.' Sylvia's voice was choked. 'But total honesty is important now. This family has hidden too many secrets. Since you were born, I have never once regretted carrying you to full-term. That too is the honest truth.'

Unable to speak, Joanne tore off more toilet roll and blew her nose. Sylvia dabbed at her eyes and gave Joanne a hug.

'We all came to an agreement about the adoption and it was approved by the authorities. I got the feeling that your mum was the least enthusiastic but your dad more than made up for it.'

Everyone had meant well at the time but Joanne still couldn't shake off her feelings of rejection. Aunty Sylvia had chosen to put her university ambitions before her newborn baby. Surely giving up the child you've carried for nine months must be the hardest thing in the world? No more secrets she'd said, so Joanne asked the question.

'It wasn't just my decision.' Sylvia paused, as though searching for the right words. 'I had to think of the family who would have to support me and little you. Mum, your grandma, was already retired. Don't forget she had me late in life. And Dad would only get the basic state pension. Where would the money come from? I knew you'd have a more comfortable life with my sister.'

Joanne nodded like she understood. She didn't understand really. Surely, if Sylvia had kept her, there would have been a way round all the problems? It was tempting to labour the point but she didn't want to create bad feeling between her and the only direct blood relative she had left. They had to pull something positive out of the darkness.

'I never forgot you were my daughter but I couldn't push in on your life,' Sylvia continued. 'It wouldn't have been fair to you or my sister or my own family. They don't know I'm your mother. Tonight, I'll tell Rodney the truth and then I'd like us two to have a proper relationship.'

Joanne gave her birth mother a huge hug. Sylvia didn't want the truth to be hidden any longer; Joanne was no longer going to be a dirty little secret.

'And that's my happy ending.' Joanne was blinking back the tears. She pushed the album over to Vanessa. 'The life in these pictures was a sham and I don't want to remember it. I've finally got a loving mum and the brother and sister I always wanted. And Rodney's accepted who I am without recriminations.'

'Thank you very much for sharing it.' Vanessa touched her hand. 'And I'm glad you've got a happy future.'

As she stood up to leave the café, Joanne's hand went again to the sapphire ring at her throat. 'Maybe one day I'll even find a man to love.'

CHAPTER SIXTEEN

'I have ingredients, I've got the video and tonight we are going to make a perfect red velvet cake!' Maxine's eyes were shining when she came into work one overcast Wednesday a week after Joanne's visit. 'Churning these out will save us so much money!'

I didn't share her enthusiasm but it excused me from spending time at home with Dave. And with the mouse caught and disposed of during Joanne's visit, there should be no rude interruption to today's baking. At five o'clock I locked the front doors and Maxine tripped happily down to the café. By the time I got there she had the scales, electric mixer and her tablet all set up. She handed me an apron and pressed the play button.

The face of an over-cheery young American man filled the screen. He looked wholesome, smiley and filled with positivity. An excess of positivity.

Then it all happened too quickly to keep up. First, he raced through the list of ingredients.

'Press stop!' I jabbed my finger towards the screen. 'What's "all-purpose flour" and he's not telling us how much we need of anything. How did you know what to buy?'

'I didn't have time to watch the video beforehand so I guessed it must be all the usual cake stuff plus red food colouring. And I was right wasn't I? I bought both kinds of flour because I wasn't sure.'

'So which is all purpose? Plain or self-raising?'

'I'll google it.' Maxine's finger raced over the tablet screen. 'Here we are — it's plain flour.'

'But he's not telling us how much.'

'So we click on this link underneath to get the recipe.'

Maxine appeared unfazed by this clicking here, there and everywhere to get information while at the same time converting it into the practical actions needed to produce the luscious, deep, moist cake that kept appearing on the screen in front of us as a finished product.

'A sieve!' Mr Cheesy Grin was finally talking about something I could relate to. I dimly recalled being told in school cookery classes that sieving the flour helped the cake rise.

'We don't have one.'

'We can do without. Don't sweat the small stuff — it's the overall method we're interested in.'

I suspected Maxine was wrong but we were too far in now to waste the rest of the ingredients for want of a sieve. She already had the flour and cocoa powder in a bowl and was breaking the first egg into a smaller dish.

'You do the whisking,' she commanded. 'With Mickey safely back in the wild there won't be the mess-up we had last time.'

'Stop the video! He's already finished that bit and we're missing the next part.'

Maxine paused our instructor but insisted we'd done everything up to that point. I wasn't convinced but we ploughed on regardless. Then he was showing us how to pour the red cake mixture into two tins ready for the oven. Maxine made sure they were equally filled.

Not that that did us much good.

As the cakes cooled and sank in their tins we realised that the use of a sieve did indeed help cakes rise. We also realised something else.

'Did you grease the tins?' I asked Maxine weakly.

Maxine shook her head slowly. 'You didn't by any chance?' I shook my head in return. 'We must have missed that bit,' she muttered.

My mother's voice rang in my ears afresh . . . *Never skimp on the greasing. If a cake won't come out of the tin, it's ruined.*

It was lucky that recovering lost cakes was my speciality. And also lucky that we had actually mastered the cream cheese frosting while the cake was in the oven. Having got used to the stopping and pausing of Mr America's commentary we had created something truly delicious. The frosting at least, was a triumph.

With the cake crumbs in a bowl — Maxine having scraped the cakes from the tin with a spoon — I retrieved the cupcake cases that sat at the back of the cupboard homing my initial, optimistic, baking purchases.

Combining the frosting with the crumbs and depositing them into the cake cases was a new one for me. But satisfying. Who could resist Red Velvet Mess Cup Cakes?

CHAPTER SEVENTEEN

June

While Dave had been absent the odd jobs around the house had built up. Preoccupied by the museum I'd ignored them. Now Dave had nearly got to the end of the list. He replaced a washer in the kitchen tap one morning at the beginning of summer.

'Thank you.' It was a relief to no longer have the irritating drip of water on stainless steel nor the worry of finding a reputable plumber. Without thinking I gave him an appreciative peck on his cheek.

He touched his skin and grinned at me. 'I think that means it's time.'

'What?'

'I've been back nearly two months. We're getting on well but still you don't believe I'll be faithful to you. I'm going to prove it.'

I looked at him questioningly.

'Your donors feel better after ridding themselves of the past. Now I'm going to do that so we can move forward together.'

I still didn't have a clue what he was talking about.

'Take this to the museum.' He handed me a short, cotton men's dressing gown. 'Gillian and I went away for a weekend to a little B&B in the Lakes. You thought I was at a conference in Preston. We booked en suite but there was a mix-up and the bathroom was down the landing. We had to buy the dressing gown and share it for going to the loo and shower. It was our first joint purchase and very significant at the time. It made me feel Gillian and I were a proper couple with a long-term future together. That was when I decided to leave you.'

'Oh?' I sat down heavily. How was this supposed to help us move forward? It was more of my 'happy' marriage slashed to pieces.

'You didn't deserve all the deceit that was going on. It would only be a matter of time before someone in the department cottoned on to me and Gillian and then told you. It was best I finished our marriage before that happened.'

'Stop it!' I didn't want any more bullets fired into the self-esteem I'd tried so hard to rebuild. How could I never have suspected what was going on? How could I have been so stupidly blind? I put my hands over my ears but Dave ploughed on, as though a full confession would absolve him of guilt.

I moved towards the kitchen door but he turned me around.

'This dressing gown is the last thing I have to remind me of her. That's why I want it in your museum. Gillian was a terrible mistake. I didn't appreciate what I had when I was married to you.'

He was holding the item out to me but I couldn't take it. Touching it would be like getting into a bed still smelling of my husband and his mistress. 'Bin it,' I said. 'But not in our bin. I can't have that . . . that thing in the museum, reminding me all the time.'

''nessa, I won't ever hurt you again. Surely this proves it?'

I turned away from Dave and his dressing gown and walked out of the kitchen, his words bouncing around my head. I understood why he thought offering the dressing gown to the museum would prove to me that Gillian was permanently in the past. But he didn't realise how it hurt to be reminded that my husband had been with another woman. I already believed she was in the past without this 'proof'. However, I wasn't sure that another woman wouldn't turn his head in the future. Nor was I sure he and I could ever be successful as a couple again.

The museum donors were opening my eyes to the bravery of others. It wasn't easy but they didn't settle for second best. And Dave now felt like second best. Just occasionally, when I was tired after a long day at work, I felt having Dave's support again could possibly be the right thing. But those dark days were becoming fewer.

At lunchtime, I was telling Maxine about the dressing gown incident, when Stephen arrived.

'It's not your day!' Maxine and I spoke in unplanned unison and then laughed.

Stephen frowned and held his hand up to silence us. 'Call it a bad day for memories. I need some calm.' His usual positivity had gone and I was reminded of the original Stephen telling the story of his red book. 'One of the girls where I'm working is just back from honeymoon with a great pile of wedding photos. She got married on what would have been mine and Trish's twenty-sixth wedding anniversary. And, would you believe it, they got married at the same Yorkshire church? Turns out she was brought up just outside my village.' He blew his nose and sat down. 'I'm not as on top of things as I thought. Do you mind if I eat my lunch here and pull myself together? Don't worry, I'll be gone again in thirty minutes.'

Maxine gave him a hug.

'Two steps forward and one step back. It's normal.' I patted him self-consciously on the shoulder. He reached his hand up and squeezed mine. I squeezed back, not sure if we were exchanging comfort or the communication of a deeper mutual feeling.

'On the plus side.' Stephen screwed up the foil wrapping of his home-made cheese sandwiches. 'I told them in the office about my anniversary and showed them that photo

I carry in my wallet. Six months ago I wouldn't have said a word except to make some excuse to get out of there. That's down to you, Vanessa, and this place.'

'Proof you are moving forward.' Was it pride in the museum or my infatuation with Stephen that made me blush as I spoke?

'Hear, hear,' said Maxine. 'It's weird but I always thought I'd feel worse if I told people about Daniel. But the other day at the antenatal clinic instead of pretending, as usual, to the girl next to me that this was my first baby, I told her about my son. I managed it without crying and it felt so much better than lying.'

Stephen and Maxine solemnly high-fived each other. The museum was helping me too but I wasn't yet ready to voice it out loud. Starting the business and helping others had given me the confidence to know that I could manage without Dave if I so chose.

When Stephen left and Maxine was on the museum desk, Polly and Malcolm paid another visit. Polly was walking slower and leaning more heavily on the stick. Still she held tightly to Malcolm. I settled Polly at a table and, covertly, looked for signs of bruising on her face, wrists and hands; the only parts of her skin not covered, even in the warm weather we were having. There was nothing obvious to see but the beige foundation on her cheek bones was heavy. Malcolm started his circuits of the café again but this time he was thumping the wall and shouting.

'I'm sorry.' Polly watched her husband with sad, shadowed eyes. 'We shouldn't have come but if I'd stayed at home, alone with him, for one minute more, something bad might have happened.'

'Something bad, love?'

'Me. I love him but I'm not always good with him. It's not him, it's me.' The old lady took a deep breath and gave me a thin smile. 'This café always feels like such a calm place and I just needed some of that calm. But we'd better go; he'll disturb the other customers.'

'It's alright.' I held Polly's hand; she was at the end of her tether and I couldn't let her go back to who knew what. 'There's no-one else in at the moment. Pot of tea and a big piece of Victoria sandwich?'

She nodded gratefully and asked for squash for her husband, producing a plastic cup with a spout, like toddlers use. Malcolm was persuaded to sit at the table and he twisted serviette after serviette in his fingers, slowly building a pile of long white sausages.

'I'll pay for them,' Polly said.

'Not necessary.'

'I wonder if he remembers having Victoria sandwich at Melissa's christening?' She glanced at Malcolm, cake crumbs on his lips and lost in his world of white wound tissue paper.

'Do you fancy telling me some more about you and Malcolm?'

CHAPTER EIGHTEEN

Polly

It had been a struggle to get to the museum this morning with Malcolm and her stick on the two buses. Her daughter, Melissa, kept telling her she should take taxis but that was an extravagance. Back in the day she'd have just caught the one bus and then walked from the city centre to here. That's what she and Malcolm did a few days after their engagement. The ring was slightly too big and they brought it back to the manufacturing jeweller to have it resized. Polly had packed some sandwiches and a scone each. They sat in Key Hill cemetery to eat them and then Malcolm showed her the grave of Joseph Chamberlain and Chamberlain's father.

'Alfred Bird's buried here as well,' he told her.

'The custard powder man?'

'Exactly.'

Malcolm had been full of interesting facts. That was one of the terrible things about his illness — all that knowledge apparently sucked from his brain.

Polly's mother made four Victoria sandwich cakes for the christening party when their daughter came along, as well as enough sandwiches and sausage rolls to feed an army.

Polly and Malcolm had saved the top layer of their wedding cake for the christening but they'd been married ten years before they were blessed with their daughter. It wasn't for want of trying but there must have been something wrong with one of them. Or maybe they weren't compatible in a baby-making way. Back then there weren't test-tube babies and such like, things were just left to nature and after five years Malcolm said they should relax, forget about babies and enjoy what they had. But every time Polly opened the pantry door, that special cake tin, decorated with pink and blue storks, stared her in the face. Malcolm sliced the cake up and took it to work. It was all eaten within a couple of days but still Polly couldn't forget about babies. She started looking into adoption and that's how Melissa came into their lives. Her mother was unmarried and, in those days, if you weren't wed you had to give the baby away. Polly felt sorry that some unknown young girl had had to part with her child but she was over the moon to at last have an infant to care for.

They were always honest with Melissa about where she came from and, when she was in her twenties, she went searching for her birth parents. At first Polly felt betrayed, as if they hadn't been good enough parents themselves, then she remembered they'd had the pleasure of raising Melissa. Her poor birth mother had missed out completely and deserved to at least know Melissa in adulthood. Melissa's birth father was never traced but her birth mother was now a big part of her life — it made them both happy. And happiness is all you want for your children.

Malcolm wasn't so accepting of Melissa's search for her parents because it coincided with Polly's diagnosis of breast cancer.

'It's like she's trying to find a replacement for you because she thinks you're going to die. She could at least have the decency to wait until you're in your grave,' he said, when Polly was in hospital following the mastectomy. His words were insensitive but she excused him because he was upset about both the women in his life.

'I'm not going to die,' Polly insisted, 'and Melissa has to do what's best for her. She didn't ask to be given away or to be adopted. We don't know what it feels like to be parachuted into a family that doesn't share your genes.'

'It's just not the right time to do it.'

'We can't let my cancer stop the life of a bright young thing like Melissa. It's not fair.'

Polly knew Malcolm didn't mean to be horrible. He was just being over-protective of her, like he'd always been. She wouldn't have made it through the chemotherapy without him. He negotiated flexible working so he could always be there to take her for treatment and he sat with her at home when she was sick. He cooked the meals, did the washing and cleaning. And all the time he treated Polly like she was still the beautiful young woman he'd married and not a bald hag with only one breast, mouth ulcers and a figure that had shrunk from curvy to skin and bone. When she felt comfortable enough to let him, he would kiss her with the same passion that he had on that park bench.

'I love you so much,' he would say and hold her tight.

With Malcolm's help and the bright breezy visits from Melissa, Polly beat the cancer into remission and it never came back. Eventually Malcolm accepted Melissa's contact with her mother but he refused to meet her. Polly went once because she wanted to thank her for the gift of Melissa. The woman was polite but it was obvious she was envious of the relationship Polly had with *her* child. Polly felt as though she was rubbing salt into a still open wound and never went again. After that, life went on in a routine normal manner. Melissa got married and had two sons.

When Malcolm first retired life was good. His pension was enough for them to live comfortably and enjoy days out and a couple of holidays each year. At first, they were adventurous with their travels. They went to New York and had a package tour to China. Malcolm liked going to new places. He would spend hours planning a sightseeing itinerary. Friends described to them their wonderful walking holiday in Madeira and Malcolm was keen to do the same thing. They booked almost a year in advance to be sure of getting the hotel their friends had recommended and flights that didn't mean taking off at the crack of dawn. Malcolm bought a book of Madeira walks, a map of the island and used his laptop to get all the information to plan their activities. A couple of months before they were due to go Polly started thinking about what to take with her.

'A holiday means new clothes,' she told Malcolm with a smile. 'Tell me what our itinerary is and I'll start buying.'

'I . . .' He hesitated, his face a mask of concentration as he tried to remember.

'Day one is a Sunday.' Polly tried to jog his memory. 'I think you talked about walking to that fishing village where Churchill painted his pictures. What's the place called?'

'It's in the folder.'

'Which is where?'

A flash of panic crossed his face and Polly started to worry. Throughout their marriage Malcolm had always been on the ball and at work he'd been nicknamed "Mr Organised". This was totally out of character for him. Until recently he'd never lost anything and seldom forgot names, dates or places.

'I'll get it.'

She could hear him above her in the spare bedroom where they kept the computer. He was opening cupboards, pulling out drawers and pacing backwards and forwards. Polly went into the kitchen to put the kettle on and there was the folder, on the kitchen table. He must have been looking at it only a few minutes earlier.

'Malcolm! It's here!'

He rushed downstairs. She'd never seen him look so relieved. The incident made Polly remember his other recent lapses of memory, things she'd put down to simply getting old. He'd forgotten their wedding anniversary for the first time. He'd set off to go to the dentist and returned home cross because when he arrived at the optician's there'd been no appointment on the computer for him. Polly hadn't known whether to say something about his growing forget-fulness or to bide her time. It might be nothing. Frightened of what she might discover, she'd bided her time.

She tried to excuse this Madeira episode as well but had to finally admit something was very wrong when they had their grandsons to stay overnight. She got out the old Snakes and Ladders board. It was a game they'd played ump-teen times with Melissa when she was a child but this time Malcolm just couldn't understand the rules. The boys roared with laughter when Malcolm climbed up snakes, slid down ladders and couldn't remember which colour counter was his. At first Polly thought he was doing it to amuse them but the confused expression on his face was genuine — he really didn't have any idea how to play.

When the boys had gone home, they talked it over and Malcolm admitted something was wrong and that he was scared. They held hands and Malcolm cried. It was the first time Polly had seen him cry since she was given the all clear from cancer. It broke her heart and she promised him they'd get through this together in the same way they'd got through her cancer. It was the least she could do for a man who'd looked after her so well.

'But there's no cure for dementia,' he said.

He was assuming the worst; they didn't yet have a defi-nite diagnosis but still there was nothing reassuring Polly could say in reply.

It took a couple of days to get an appointment at the local surgery and they ended up with a locum doctor they'd never seen before. Malcolm was on edge. He'd eaten very lit-tle breakfast and had spent the morning pacing the kitchen. In the hour before they left the house, he went to the toilet three times. The doctor was very understanding. Polly did most of the talking, with Malcolm only opening his mouth when asked a direct question.

'I think there is cause for concern,' the GP said gently at the end of the consultation. 'Malcolm, I'm going to refer you to the hospital for a proper diagnosis and treatment plan.'

It was bad news but Polly was relieved — at least Malcolm was going to get the attention he needed.

They gave him drugs but they didn't stop the disease slowly eating his personality and his ability to run his own life. Melissa helped her mother get power of attorney so she could manage the couple's financial affairs and make decisions about her husband's health treatment. It was a massive learning curve for Polly. She had to go from being a cosseted wife who worried about nothing except what to cook for tea, to learning how to pay all the bills, manage the bank accounts and how to find decent tradesmen to do the jobs that Malcolm could no longer manage, such as decorating, mowing the lawn and fixing dripping taps. After the second time he got lost driving home from Melissa's, Polly sold the car. Learning to drive was one thing she was too old for.

All of this, Polly could put up with. What destroyed her was the way Malcolm withered before her eyes. He was no longer the lovely man who had kissed her and proposed in the dark, six decades earlier. At times he thought Polly was his gaoler rather than his wife.

Melissa wanted to get social services involved. 'You could have a carer come in morning and evening to get Dad up and put him to bed,' she said. 'It would take some of the strain off. You know how he hates being washed and dressed.'

Polly didn't want that — she'd heard terrible tales and seen documentaries on TV about those so-called carers. Caring was the last thing they were. Half the time they didn't turn up and when they did, they were in and out in seconds and it was a different person every time. All that would've disorientated poor Malcolm even more. She battled on alone.

* * *

Polly finished her Victoria sandwich with tears in her eyes. I blinked hard to keep my own emotions in check. As I refreshed the tea in Polly's cup, Malcolm was on the move again, walking and chanting something indecipherable. Walking and chanting. In a world of his own.

'This is such a lovely place,' Polly said. 'I want all the lonely people to know it's here. To know you're here. It's a safety valve.'

'You say the loveliest things, thank you very much.' For a few minutes the seesaw balancing of the museum books, the baking disasters, the mouse, the constant cleaning of the café and kitchen and Stephen's dire warnings about the future didn't matter. I was filled with joy. Through Polly, I was seeing at first hand the good the museum was doing, the good *my* museum was doing. Money or anything else didn't come into the equation at all.

When it was time for them to leave, Malcolm allowed me to fasten his coat and Polly gave me a kiss.

At closing time, Stephen asked for a quick staff meeting. We had coffee and the remains of the Victoria sandwich to fuel us.

'Business update time.' Stephen's expression was sober. 'As I said eight weeks ago, at the end of April, with Maxine on the payroll, the museum only has until the end of October at the very latest, unless the tide turns. That tide has not yet even slowed.'

'No! Please don't make me get a proper job after the baby's born. I'd work for free, like Stephen, only we need the money . . .'

I squeezed Maxine's hand. 'Nobody expects you to work for free.'

'On the positive side,' Stephen continued, 'takings are rising slowly, month on month. I think that's due to Maxine's social media activities. She's wonderful — we've got over five thousand followers on Twitter now.'

I joined in with Stephen's little round of applause and Maxine blushed. But the cold fingers of fear were creeping around my heart. It wasn't fair that as well as helping people we had to do the impossible thing of making a profit.

'The potential of this place is huge,' Stephen said. 'So, I've been researching what other institutions do to drag people in. I was wondering about holding a singles' night. What do you two think?'

'A singles' night?' The concept didn't sound good to me. I didn't want drunken twenty-somethings cavorting amongst the exhibits.

'They hold them in other exhibition spaces. Birmingham Museum and Art Gallery has held them. We open late one evening specifically for people who are single. Guests look around the exhibits, mingle, chat and maybe strike up a friendship or more than friendship. You put on a buffet in the café — to be included in a higher than usual ticket price. It's a shame we're not licensed; glasses of wine would have been perfect but perhaps afterwards people might gel and go onto a pub together.'

'I don't want it to be sordid.'

'It won't be sordid. I've been to events like this and there's nothing more than the buzz of civilised chatter. We can have music playing and that space at the end of the museum could be a mini dance floor.'

'You've been to a singles' night?' Maxine looked at Stephen with incredulity. 'Did you get off with anyone?'

'Maxine!' Knowing Stephen's story, surely she could treat him with more respect?

'It's OK.' Stephen grinned. 'Just because some of us are older it doesn't mean we've lost all interest in the opposite sex' — his eyes locked on mine — 'does it, Vanessa?'

His eyes . . . I found myself tongue-tied. 'I . . . no.'

'To clarify, I didn't "get off" with anyone, Maxine, but I did chat to some interesting people.' Still his eyes didn't leave mine.

I hoped my relief that Stephen hadn't met anyone didn't show on my face. 'As long as it's civilised and not sordid, a singles' night sounds . . . possible.'

Stephen grinned and winked at me. 'You never know, even you and I might find new partners there!'

'You, perhaps, but not a reject like me.' The words were out before my brain had time to censor them.

'You're not a reject!' He was speaking as befits a man with polite manners.

'Don't mind me. You two flirt away. I'll just eat cake for the sake of the baby.'

'Let's set a date.' I tried to get the conversation back to business. It was so long since I'd been on the flirting scene, I wasn't sure I'd even recognise the signs.

'Last Saturday in August,' Maxine suggested. 'That gives us two months of publicity beforehand.'

'Rob and Nick's birthday.'

There was an awkward silence.

'Then we'll go for the following weekend,' I suggested.

'No. That day's fine. The boys are always in my thoughts without making shrines out of particular dates in the calendar. I didn't like it when Naomi wanted to fill those days with special events and I don't like it when those dates are avoided as well.'

'We'll need you on top form that evening, Stephen,' Maxine said gently.

'Agreed. It's near Maxine's due date so it may be just us two.'

'Don't worry, I intend to be there,' Maxine said quickly. 'This little one's going to hang on until September to be the oldest not the youngest in the school year.'

'I'll be OK. It's been seven years and each anniversary it gets a little bit easier,' Stephen said. 'I'll feel better, more normal, if you don't make special concessions for me. Don't worry, I won't blub all over the place.'

Maxine and I exchanged querying glances. Stephen sliced the air between us with a vertical hand. 'And don't cut me out or talk about me behind my back. Special treatment is not appreciated.'

'Last Saturday in August it is, then.'

* * *

A few days later Joanne returned to the museum, arriving before both Stephen and Maxine. She gave me a hug.

'I felt so much better after leaving the album here that I've decided to donate this as well.' She removed the chain and engagement ring from her neck. 'It's silly to keep wearing it all these years later. I don't want the money from selling it, I simply want other people to read my story and know they're not alone in their troubles.'

I took the ring in my palm and admired the sapphire. This was by far the most valuable donation we'd received and also the most beautiful.

'Thank you so much. I'll get a black velvet mount to display it on and I'll ask Stephen to put an extra shelf above your photograph album so that they're kept together.'

'Did I hear my name?' I felt his hand on my shoulder and turned quickly; his eyes were waiting for me.

'Joanne, this is Stephen. Stephen, Joanne.' My introductions were flustered.

We were stood by the glass case containing Joanne's photograph album. Every few days I opened the book at a different place, on the off chance that we got repeat visitors. Joanne and Stephen shook hands and he started asking her more about the album. With his attention she became alive and talkative. I was superfluous and went to lock the ring away and get started in the café. When I returned twenty minutes later, Stephen and Joanne were still talking. I stood within earshot.

'Would you come?' Stephen was showing her a mock-up of the flyer he and Maxine had designed for the singles' night. 'Assuming you're single and free on that date?'

Joanne blushed and then smiled at him. Ridding herself of her past had made her much more attractive than the beige mouse who'd told me her story. Stephen's arms were expansive and open as he faced her — not the man who'd had his arms folded across his chest as he told me his story only three months earlier. Two museum success stories for two people who deserved happiness.

'Will you be there?' she asked him. 'I'd need a friendly face to latch on to.'

'Absolutely.' He was charming her and a little seed of jealousy planted itself inside of me. I tried to uproot it before it could take hold. If I wanted a man, Dave was there for the taking.

'Yes, OK. I'll come along.'

A couple of minutes later, Stephen came over to me at the desk with a thumbs-up. 'We've got her approval.'

'That's good,' I said and then added lightly, 'You two seemed friendly.'

'Yes, she's nice. A bit shy so I'll keep an eye on her on the night. Make sure she enjoys herself and becomes an ambassador for the museum.'

Stephen was a free agent who could give his attention to whomever he wanted.

'Great.'

'What's the matter? You're frowning.'

'Nothing.' I busied myself with tidying the leaflets on the reception desk.

Stephen touched Joanne on the arm to get her attention as she passed the reception desk on her way out.

'Are you happy with the display of your photo album?' he asked. 'And with the ring going above it?'

'Yes. And home feels a lot better without relics from the past.' She'd taken her eyes off Stephen and was glancing across at me now. 'Thank you, Vanessa.'

I smiled and nodded at her, pretending everything was fine. Then I stepped forward and gave her a hug; I mustn't be churlish.

When she arrived for work a few minutes later, Maxine was full of apologies about her bus not turning up. 'And also,' she added, 'I forgot to tell you it's antenatal class this afternoon. Is it OK if I finish early? Adrian's picking me up so we can go together.'

'Absolutely,' I said. 'I remember antenatal classes — all that breathing and panting practice. Dave hated it. He said it was like being trapped in a room of breathless whales. Did you go with Trish, Stephen?'

The question was out before I could censor it. Maxine looked at me aghast and a flicker of panic crossed Stephen's face.

'Yes, I went,' he said eventually.

I struggled to think of a seamless subject change.

'I didn't like it either,' he continued suddenly. 'Because Trish was expecting twins the midwife was constantly highlighting what would be different for us and the likely complications. I always went home scared and worried. I remember having this stupid wish that we could give birth to one baby each so I'd know how she felt and she wouldn't have to have twice the suffering of all the other mums.'

His eyes looked too bright and I offered him the tissue box from the reception desk. He blew his nose.

'In the end there were no complications and both Nick and Rob were born naturally with only the help of gas and air. Trish was absolutely brilliant.' He took another tissue and turned away from us.

'Sounds like you were really supportive as a husband and father.' Maxine touched his shoulder. 'I'll send Adrian to you for lessons.'

Stephen faced us again. 'Thanks for asking me the question and not getting embarrassed. The more stuff is talked about, the easier it gets for me. I never realised before that that would happen.'

* * *

Dave was frying tuna steaks and mixing potato salad when I got home. I'd started looking forward to his cooking but today it failed to lift my spirits.

'Good day?' he asked.

'So, so.' Stephen and Joanne hitting it off had affected me more than I thought. Plus there was the bigger problem of visitor numbers failing to hit my business plan and spreadsheet projections. If the museum was snatched away, my whole world would come tumbling down. Dave and distant Liam would be all that remained and that wouldn't be enough any more.

'Want to talk about it?' Dave put a bowl of salad on the table.

I looked across at him and blinked away the prickling of tears. He reached for my hand and that little bit of kindness opened the floodgates. I couldn't tell him about Stephen and Joanne but the worsening state of the museum's precarious finances came out mixed with sobs and nose blowing.

'It's not about making big money. It's about helping people. But the place can't run on fresh air and Maxine needs a proper wage.'

Dave squeezed my hand.

'Sorry.' I blew my nose again. 'I hadn't realised how I'd bottled it all up.'

'I'm here for you. We always were good at supporting each other, weren't we? Remember when I got made redundant? It was a real kick in the teeth and I refused to get out of bed for three days. You bullied me in the nicest possible way and got me back on my feet.'

I remembered. I'd been livid that Dave had given up like that when he had a son and wife to support.

'And there were those awful months when your mother was ill. It was tough on you having to take her for treatment and watch her fade away. I did my best to be there for you. But maybe I didn't do it well enough?'

My turn to squeeze his hand in gratitude. 'You were great. You looked after Liam and did the cooking — but you weren't as good as this back then.' I gestured at my half-eaten tuna.

Later we watched television together. Side by side on the settee. Not touching. My feet were curled beneath me and I clutched a cushion. Not yet back to the feeling of our still-married days but maybe I could get there by learning to trust Dave again. There are few people you can sit with and not feel compelled to make conversation. Dave was one of those people. Maybe it wasn't so important that Stephen had hit it off with Joanne. At least it wasn't if I didn't think about it too hard.

CHAPTER NINETEEN

July
Pete

'I want to donate this tape to the museum — memories of an old girlfriend and all that.' Pete pushed a cassette tape over the museum reception desk and turned to leave.

'Please can you give us a little more detail, sir?' The man behind the desk caught Pete's arm. 'Anonymously, of course.'

'I don't think so.' Pete pushed the dark glasses firmly back up to the bridge of his nose — they were part disguise and part to hide any leaking emotion from his eyes.

A middle-aged woman appeared with a mug of tea and a scone. The man beamed when he saw her. She put them down on the reception desk and then smiled at Pete. 'Café's open and we've got a deal on cream teas if you're interested, love?'

'I . . .' He'd planned to be here for as short a time as possible and to give away the minimum amount of information.

'Donating to the museum and telling your story can be an emotional business,' the woman continued. 'A hot drink and something sweet often helps.'

She was right, he hadn't anticipated it but he did feel a little shaky now. At sixty-four years old and a man of experience, it was a feeling he wasn't used to. Giving away something that had been part of him for so long wasn't easy and he hadn't known they'd want the details behind his donation. Pete paused, unsure what to do. He blew his nose in an effort to clear the lump from his throat.

'We also have doughnuts, bread pudding and flapjack,' the woman was saying. 'It's nursery comfort food and really does make people feel better.'

'I . . .'

'Don't I know you from somewhere?'

'No.' In a minute she'd realise who he was and it would be all over the papers. He should go, emotion or no emotion. 'No, we've never met.'

'I'm sorry — my mistake.'

Then, without realising how it happened, Pete found himself being gently propelled to the museum stairs. The woman was chatting in a motherly kind of way, even though she was probably slightly younger than him. 'I want a cup of tea myself and a chance to take the weight off my feet. I'll sit down with you and you can tell me the story behind your cassette tape.'

Perhaps she'd sensed his tension and that's why she added, 'Don't worry, no names, no pack drill.'

She took him to a seat at the back of a café populated with Formica tables and plastic chairs. He took the plastic-coated menu card she offered.

'What do you fancy?'

He took a minute to read. 'Just a cappuccino, please and . . . bread pudding. I'll have bread pudding — I haven't had that for years. My gran used to make it when I was a kid.'

She brought tea for herself as well as his bread pudding and coffee. Then she sat down opposite him. 'Was it a compilation tape an old girlfriend made for you?'

'No, not a compilation,' he said. 'It's a long story. It doesn't matter, you can label it as a compilation.'

'The proper story would be better — for you and us.' She smiled at him encouragingly. 'It will help you leave with a lighter heart. I'm Vanessa. What's your name, love?'

'Pete.' He didn't offer his surname.

They were both silent for a time while he ate. She was right about the food and drink making him feel better.

'Pete, your story might help someone else in a similar situation.'

'It's nothing special — just long and maudlin.'

'Without the back story our exhibits mean nothing. We guarantee to keep everything totally anonymous.'

He sighed, she wasn't going to give up and the sugar rush seemed to have revived the public persona that he reserved for reporters and interviewers. 'OK.'

He went right back to the beginning to put everything in context. When he left university, forty-odd years ago, he was full of ambition — he wanted to do something with his life, leave his mark on the world. But not the charitable, helping other people sort of thing that Miss World contestants talked about. Pete wanted to see his name in lights. He wanted to make the big time. He wanted to be famous.

He ignored the milkround employers who were doing the university circuit to recruit the next generation of accountants, middle managers and penpushers. Instead he got a part-time job in a transport café on the outskirts of York where he'd studied. His wages just about paid the rent on one of the three bedsits above the café. All the bedsits shared the bathroom but Pete had his own makeshift kitchen with a sink. One of the residents was a wino who often banged on Pete's door in the middle of the night thinking it was his room. The third tenant was an elderly lady who spent her time manically cleaning the communal bathroom. Pete existed on a diet of fry-ups and builders' sweet tea from the café.

In the evenings he set up a band with a handful of other wannabes who he found by sticking notices up in pubs. There were four of them, plus two guitars and a second-hand set of drums. They mostly covered other people's pop stuff but Pete was writing his own songs too. He was the lead singer and took most of the musical decisions about what they would and wouldn't play. The others didn't always agree but Pete usually got his way on the basis that he'd created the band in the first place.

The café manager was taken with the idea of being linked with rock stars so he let the band practise in the café after hours. He probably hoped that when the band made the charts some of their glory would reflect on his establishment. There was usually an audience for rehearsals. Plenty of truckers parked up outside the café for the night and they'd wander in and give their opinion. They were the salt of the earth and knew how to call a spade a spade.

'Too puffy, you heap of big girls' blouses!' they'd shout if Pete tried to slip in a romantic ballad.

'It's got no bloody beat!' they'd yell when Pete experimented with one of his own songs.

Sometimes they were a pain but their straight talking toughened the band up for the heckling reality of pub and club audiences. It was hard getting a foothold in the local circuit so they were ecstatic when Bozzo, their drummer and self-appointed publicist, got the group its first gig.

'It's only the Miners' Arms,' he said, trying to quell their cheering, 'not Wembley Stadium.'

They danced around the greasy topped tables, waving their arms in the air like they'd made the number one spot on *Top of the Pops*. At last there was going to be money paid for their performance.

The gig was a disaster. The audience consisted of three old men and a whippet (yes, really). They all stayed for the first four numbers which were from the quieter end of the group's repertoire and one of the guys even managed to clap. The dog lay with his head under a chair the whole time. But when Pete upped the tempo and the atmosphere by breaking into something louder and livelier, the old guys shook their heads, pulled on their flat caps and left.

They got paid less than the cost of the petrol Shane had put in the beat-up old van to get them there. To say they were deflated was an understatement. Bozzo was all for disbanding. But Pete, Shane and Carl managed to dissuade him. Then Shane's brother took pity on them and booked the group for his wedding.

'You better not let us down,' the bride-to-be warned in a voice that said she didn't really want them there. 'And don't do your own stuff. I want songs that people will recognise. Stuff they can dance to.'

That meant creating a set covering all the old classics but it didn't matter — they'd get themselves in front of other couples who might be planning their own wedding. This was the band's big chance!

'No, I refuse to do "Oops Upside Your Head",' Bozzo said at the final rehearsal before the wedding. 'It's ridiculous everyone sitting down on the dance floor. It spoils the atmosphere.'

'Well said!' shouted the truckers who'd been singing along to the band's rendition of "Dancing Queen".

'It won't be in the set.' Pete tried to placate him. 'But we'll be taking requests and it'll more than likely come up — especially when people have had a few drinks. We have to practise it.'

They went down well at the wedding. The guests were psyched up to enjoy themselves and the dance floor was full all evening. Halfway through their spot it was buffet time and they were invited to join the guests and fill their plates. Bozzo, Shane and Carl went to get drinks and Pete found himself standing next to a young woman. They were both trying to balance a plate of finger food and a glass while eating sausage rolls and salad, standing up.

'This is like some challenge out of *The Krypton Factor*,' Pete said, as his plate tipped and greasy ready salted crisps cascaded down his only stage shirt. 'Why are there never enough seats at dos like this?'

She laughed and Pete realised she was pretty. Until the laugh she'd had a solemn face, as she concentrated on taking a bite from the sausage roll without spilling her wine. At first glance she appeared plain, ordinary — someone who didn't get looked at twice. But when she laughed her whole face lit up.

172

'There's space to sit on the floor over there.' She indicated with her head and then started to move her arm to point to where she meant and simultaneously they both realised that with both hands full of food and drink, she was trying to do the impossible.

They burst out laughing again.

'I don't really like buffet food anyway,' she said. 'It's all high fat and no vitamins. But I always feel compelled to pile my plate with sausage rolls, quiche and crisps. Then I have to eat it all or I hear my gran in my head asking — who's got eyes bigger than her stomach?'

'Your gran here then?'

'Yes. She's the bride's nan as well as mine — so you better watch yourself!'

Pete loved the way she giggled so easily. And the fact that it was him making her laugh. 'I'll eat what you don't,' Pete offered. 'I need a change from a continuous diet of all-day breakfasts.'

She was easy to talk to. Back in those days, girls weren't in awe of him. He could have a normal conversation without feeling he had to behave in an overly macho manner in order to live up to female expectations. It's hard to build a relationship when people have preconceived ideas about you. Even nowadays, as he headed towards his pension, he didn't always know who was genuine and who wasn't. He didn't know who was interested in the real him. Sometimes he didn't even know who the real him was.

Pete paused in his story, looked at Vanessa and fiddled with his cappuccino cup.

'Do you want to take the sunglasses off?' Vanessa suggested. 'I bet you can hardly see a thing in here. It must be like sitting in a coal mine.'

If he removed the glasses she would recognise him. He was surprised she hadn't guessed already from his voice and body language. Maybe she wasn't a TV watcher. But he couldn't take the risk.

'I've got a sight problem. The optician recommends keeping them on.' He regretted the lie as soon as it was out. Vanessa was looking at him with genuine compassion.

Pete tried to hide his discomfort by having a sip of coffee and another mouthful of bread pudding. Then, having got this far with the story, he carried on.

The girl at the wedding was called Sarah and she was a younger cousin of the bride. Pete was captivated by her and, just before the band got called to finish their set, he asked for her phone number. This was back in the good old days when people didn't have mobiles glued to their ears. Sarah sweet-talked an elderly relative of the groom into tearing a sheet of paper from the back of her diary and lending us a pen. Sarah wrote down her number, or rather her parents' number, because she was still living at home.

'Only until October,' she explained, 'and then I'm off to university.'

Typical of Pete's luck — he meets a beautiful girl and then learns their relationship is limited to three months. Even so, he deliberately left it a few days before calling Sarah. At twenty-two years old he should have grown out of the need to play it cool but he hadn't. Or maybe it was fear of rejection that held him back. Anyway, after what seemed like a reasonable interval, he used the payphone at the back of the café to call her.

She lived at the opposite end of town. Neither of them had any transport so they arranged to meet outside the town hall — when Pete made the suggestion, it sounded corny but he didn't want Sarah to have to walk into a pub by herself to meet him. They never stopped talking that first evening together. When the landlord shouted last orders and rang his bell Pete offered to walk her home. It was four miles out of his way but he was smitten and didn't want the evening to end.

'My house is just around this corner,' she said when they reached her estate. Then she stood quite still in a secluded part of the street. She seemed to be expecting something.

'Mum and Dad will be waiting up for me.' She moved closer to him.

Then the penny dropped — she wanted Pete to kiss her here rather than on her doorstep where her parents might be watching. Pete was only too happy to oblige. Their bodies fitted together naturally and, as their mouths gently got to know each other, Pete pulled her closer. Sensing her enjoyment and willingness, he let his hands trace her slim waist and pert behind. From the street light he could see the flush in her cheek as they pulled apart. Her eyes were wide and for a long time they just held hands and stared at each other in disbelief. It was as if they couldn't quite believe they'd found each other.

Silently Pete cursed the fact that she was going away to university. He couldn't bear the thought of losing the most perfect girl in the world so soon after he'd found her. He'd already experienced the freedom of being a student away from home. There'd be lots of people for Sarah to meet and, inevitably, a lot of them would be attractive males. He and she would become just another failed long-distance relationship. He didn't say any of this aloud — it was obvious Sarah liked him but he didn't know if her feelings ran as deep as his.

Sarah had lots of free time that summer between A levels and university and when Pete wasn't working in the café they spent most of it together. She came to the band's growing number of gigs. After that first wedding, word about the group's existence had got out and some small venues started approaching them instead of the other way around. Occasionally they got booked for another wedding and Sarah would use it as an excuse to get dressed up — she looked absolutely gorgeous in a skirt and heels. But mostly she wore jeans and a T-shirt as she acted as chief supporter in almost empty pubs and working men's clubs.

Pete was head over heels in love and he wanted to do something significant to let Sarah know exactly how he felt. Alone in his murky bedsit, he wrote "A Song for Sarah". He tried to capture in words and music the joy that lit up her face when she smiled and the exhilaration that filled his heart whenever he saw that smile directed at him. When he'd got the song as perfect as possible, he recorded it to a cassette tape, strumming the music on his guitar as he sang. In Pete's head this song would be the glue that bound them together.

Vanessa interrupted him, her face bright with anticipation. 'Is the tape still playable? Just so we could get a digital recording. Yours would be our first audio exhibit.'

'I don't think I want it to be heard.' He definitely didn't want it to be heard. Once people heard his voice, the story of him and Sarah would be all across the tabloids. He should've known he could never do anything as ordinary as donating to this odd museum.

'Could we at least have a copy of the lyrics?' Vanessa pushed.

'I don't know. I don't want some clever dick recording it and ruining all my feelings from that time. Some people have no respect for copyright. I brought that tape to the museum because I thought it would just sit in a cabinet with no-one knowing the detail of what was on it. Can't you just label it *"Wannabe pop star wrote a song for his girlfriend and she left him"*?'

'But your story will interest loads of people. These days everyone wants to be a pop star — think of *The Voice*, *The X Factor* and *Britain's Got Talent*.'

'I put on that form it has to be exhibited anonymously — otherwise that tape goes back home with me and I'll live with my heartbreak for a bit longer.' He spoke firmly, pushing his dark glasses closer to his face.

'Everything stays anonymous here,' Vanessa reassured him. 'If you let us use your song we still won't mention your real name.'

'That doesn't mean it would be unidentifiable. People may recognise my voice.' He paused and then conceded. 'You can have the lyrics but not play the tape.'

Pete gave Sarah the tape on 29 July 1981, the day Charles and Diana got married. The air was full of romance, people were in a party mood and the pubs packed. They stood at a crowded bar, pressed against each other by the volume of people.

'I love you, Sarah James,' Pete said, with his lips close to her ear.

It was the first time he'd said those three little words to any girl and he meant them. Perhaps it was too early in their relationship but he wanted her to know how serious he was about her. To him, she was, and would always be, the most wonderful girl in the world.

Sarah looked from Pete to the cassette tape he'd just given her and then gave him that unique sunshiny smile of hers. Pete waited for her to say those same three words back to him. All around them was noise, bustle and merrymaking but his ears were tuned solely to her voice and his eyes were watching her lips. She stared at him for a few seconds and then she pulled him towards her.

The passion in her kiss knocked Pete for six. His declaration of love seemed to have opened something within her. Never had she kissed him like that before. When they pulled apart he expected her to declare her love too. But she didn't say a word. Instead, she took his hand and led him outside into the warm evening. They sat on a bench in the park. It was getting dark but the playground was still full of yelling kids wearing red, white and blue T-shirts. They were high on the royal celebrations, street party food and summer holiday freedom. Ignoring the youngsters, Sarah turned her face to Pete and they kissed again. Her lips and tongue told him more than any verbal declaration of love. No-one had ever kissed him like that — either before or since. It was as though knowing that he loved her gave Sarah permission to let herself go.

'Shall we go back to my place?' Pete asked tentatively, feeling the moment had finally come. He gestured at the cassette tape. 'We can listen to the song together.'

Her eyes were quizzical, trying to read his face and get the meaning implied by the words. He knew what she was thinking. A couple of weeks earlier, over a bottle of wine in his bedsit, she'd admitted to being inexperienced with men and he'd felt pleased he might be the first to take her to bed. He could've talked her into it that night but he didn't want Sarah's first time to be fuelled by alcohol. He wanted her to remember it for all the right reasons. Now, like him, she must be thinking about that discussion and wondering if the time had come. Tonight, despite the party atmosphere across the country, she'd only been drinking lemonade and lime. Pete knew she'd be going into anything they did with her eyes open and without any undue persuasion. She'd be doing it because she loved him.

'I . . .' She was hesitant, despite the way she'd kissed so hungrily.

'I want us to do it before you go away to university,' Pete said. 'It will hold us together while we're apart.'

He didn't say he hoped she would enjoy it so much it might stop her going away.

'OK.' She was still staring into his face and he guessed she was nervous.

Back at the bedsit, Sarah went to the communal bathroom and for once Pete was grateful for the old lady's obsession with keeping it immaculate and sweet smelling. He did a whirlwind tidy up in his room, gathering dirty socks, a shirt and his scruffy jeans and dumping them in the bottom of the wardrobe. He turned off the big light and switched on the bedside lamp. As she came into the room he pressed a button on the cassette player. They sat holding hands as the melody of "A Song for Sarah" filled the room. Then she put her head on his shoulder.

'That was lovely,' she said as the final chords faded. 'Do I really mean that much to you?'

Pete nodded, emotion stealing his voice.

'That's the loveliest thing anyone has ever done for me,' she murmured and kissed him.

Embarrassed, he replaced her song with Fleetwood Mac's "Rumours" — it was one of Sarah's favourites.

'Have you got some . . . ?' Sarah's voice trailed off.

'Yes, I've got condoms. Are you sure you're happy about this?' The last thing he wanted was to create an unpleasant memory of coercion in Sarah's mind.

'Of course.'

He let his hand explore under her T-shirt and inside her bra. She tensed slightly and then relaxed. Gently he raised her arms and peeled her T-shirt upwards and off. He undid her bra and released her breasts.

'You are beautiful.' He meant every word of it as he stared at her curves.

He pulled her towards him, sensing her apprehension but she was totally willing and definitely aroused. That first night with Sarah was never equalled with anyone who came after her. It was more than about satisfying a physical need. It united them emotionally. Afterwards they lay on the bed for a long time, naked skin against naked skin. Pete had never felt so contented. He wanted this feeling to be a regular part of his life.

'You don't have to go to university,' he blurted out. 'You could move in with me and go to the college in town.'

He watched her eyes travel around the dingy bedsit and realised life with a struggling wannabe pop star might not be enough to entice her into giving up an exciting future to live in a dirty hovel like this.

'I'll decorate.' He'd never wielded a paintbrush in his life.

Sarah still didn't speak.

'I love you, Sarah. If you go away our relationship won't last — long distance ones never do. I saw it with my own university mates. The girlfriends they left behind were soon forgotten after a couple of parties and a few beers.'

'I sweated blood for my A levels. I can't just throw it all in. Besides, I'm not the type to jump into bed with some drunken student I've met at a party.' Her tone was angry and defensive at the same time. 'Just because I'm meeting new people doesn't mean I'll forget about you.'

'I didn't mean it like that. I just meant living in halls of residence you get to know people quickly. It's an artificial environment. Relationships speed up in a way they might not otherwise do.'

'It's late. I better get home — Mum and Dad will be wondering where I am.'

Pete felt kicked in the teeth by Sarah's dismissal of the subject. But he still cared about and wanted her.

'I'm sorry,' he said. 'I shouldn't have said that. I love you and want you to be happy. Take every opportunity you can.'

'I intend to.'

Although he could barely afford it, Pete called a taxi to take Sarah home. Then he lay on the sheets that still smelt of the most wonderful girl he'd ever met and selfishly hoped she wouldn't make the grade at A level.

This was the first time Pete had told the story of him and Sarah to anyone. Partly because it wasn't the sort of thing men shared with each other and partly because a man with his fame couldn't risk sharing such details with anyone, in case they resurfaced in the tabloids. Without thinking, he removed his dark glasses and rubbed his eyes. Then he caught Vanessa's expression and realised what he'd done. Her eyes were wide and her face showed shocked recognition.

'You're the surgeon! Charles Denver, in *Emergency Ambulance*.'

Pete jammed the glasses back on and looked around to see if anyone else had seen or heard. There were no other customers in the café. He relaxed slightly.

'I've watched it for years. You've been in it from the start, haven't you? Like Ken Barlow and *Coronation Street*?'

Pete nodded. The soap's storyline usually put him as the romantic lead in some tangled competition between nurses wanting to win his heart. As the years had rolled by it was the older, more senior staff who set their cap at him but none of them ever succeeded — Charles Denver used and discarded them like pairs of disposable surgical gloves.

'Don't worry. I won't tell anyone.'

He gave a small smile. 'I don't know why I'm paranoid. Even actors are allowed to have a past. But I don't want this plastered all over the gossip mags. Sarah was, and still is, special to me. If word gets out there'll be a witch hunt to find her.'

'If you're so worried, why did you come here at all?'

'She was my first true love, my only true love if I'm honest. I wanted it recorded in some way. I'm daft, aren't I?'

'Not at all. That's what the museum is all about.'

Pete took a mouthful of his cappuccino and then pulled a face. 'It's cold.'

'I'll fetch you another, on the house.'

CHAPTER TWENTY

Rose

On my way to make more coffee, Maxine beckoned me from the door of the café.

'There's a lady upstairs with a donation — she says it won't take long but she'd really like to speak to you. Something about bringing a message of hope and confidence to the museum.'

I dithered, not wanting Pete or me to lose track of his story. But his sunglasses were back on now and I reckoned he could probably do with a few moments to pull himself together. I nodded at Maxine to watch the café and went upstairs. A woman, my age and with my slightly dumpy stature, was seated alongside the reception desk.

'Hello, I'm Vanessa.' I pulled up a chair.

'Rose. I'd like to give two things to the museum — my name badge from when I was a library assistant with Birmingham City Council and this memory stick. It contains a video.'

My curiosity was piqued and I turned my notebook to a fresh page and wrote "Rose".

'A year ago I was made redundant. It was around the time the council went through every department and made massive cuts.'

'I know exactly how that feels.'

'It absolutely devastated me, even though I knew it wasn't personal. Books and reading and sharing that pleasure with other people had been my life ever since I left school. Reading a book gives you the chance to inhabit a life far more interesting than your own. Maybe I read too much and, because I was voraciously living all these other lives, I didn't bother building or maintaining my own life. I was your stereotypical librarian — a single woman living alone with only a cat for company. I'd kept hold of a couple of school friends for theatre and museum visits. Other than that, work was my life. It really did fulfil me to encourage families to read together, to put events on that got people through the door for the first time and to recommend books to those who only came to the library to use a computer. I didn't need anything else. My life was totally satisfying.'

Rose's eyes were shining with passion as she spoke and I waited for the hanky to come out and her lips to turn down as she talked about losing her job. But the unhappiness most donors showed didn't come.

'Now I know I was living in the shadows — even though they appeared quite bright at the time.'

After the redundancy, Rose had struggled with too much time on her hands. Most days she spent alone with her books. She became increasingly reluctant to go out and started ordering her shopping online and refusing the few invitations she received. One evening, Heather, her sister, lost her patience and forced Rose to let her in.

'You are going to make a new start,' Heather announced. 'Your confidence has gone and you're going to rebuild it. You are going to feel the fear and do it anyway.'

Rose insisted that all she wanted was to be left alone.

'Rubbish. There is a public speaking club that meets tonight and you are going. That will scare you into doing something with your life.'

Heather went through Rose's wardrobe and selected a smart blouse and a pair of trousers. When Heather was in battleship mode there was no arguing. Thirty minutes later Rose was being introduced to the president of the speaker's club and Heather made a swift exit. There were around twenty-five people in the room and Rose headed for the back but it was suggested she sit at the front because she'd be asked to speak soon. The thud of her heart drowned out the buzz of conversation in the room. Every part of her felt damp with nervous sweat. She was only vaguely aware of someone banging a gavel and starting the meeting. She thought she might pass out. To keep the blood flowing and herself conscious she stuck her head between her knees. Then, realising she looked silly, she sat up and made some little movements with her body instead. As she turned her head, she noticed a camera atop a tripod at the back of the room. She clenched her fists and tried not to throw up. Then they called her to the lectern, asked her to introduce herself and explain why she'd come. For a few seconds it didn't register with Rose that it was her they wanted. The second time they called her name she realised people were staring and that if she didn't move, things would get awkward.

At the front of the room, she gripped the edges of the wooden lectern. There was an air of expectancy. 'My name is Rose,' she began, 'and I got made redundant from the library.' The polite expressions of sympathy in the audience didn't make her feel any better. She tried to imagine the spectators naked but both her experience and her imagination were too limited. 'I've come here tonight because . . .' She paused. It was too difficult to make up a reason. 'Because my sister forced me.' A ripple of laughter rolled through the rows. She felt humiliated and then realised they were laughing with her rather than at her. The atmosphere in the room had relaxed. People were smiling at her and a little of the tension left Rose. 'She picked my outfit.' Rose gestured at her torso and legs. 'She brushed my hair and dumped my make-up bag in front of me.' She'd captured the audience's attention. They were coming on some sort of journey with her. 'She even sniffed my breath and gave me a mint to suck.' Now there was proper laughing and Rose felt as though she had power over these people. 'My sister dropped me off and ran away. I'm glad I stayed. Thank you.' She gave the audience a nod and there was loud applause as she returned to her seat.

'The applause was so loud that I thought some famous comedian must have gone up to the lectern after me.' Rose handed the memory stick to Vanessa. 'The video of that first speech is on here — I hope it will encourage others to dive in and try new things. Since then I haven't missed a Club meeting and I love it! Especially the impromptu sessions. And I now get paid for giving talks to groups about my life in libraries. I am so grateful to Heather but she still refuses to discover the confidence of public speaking herself.'

'That is such an inspiring story, Rose. Thank you for coming in. This will help show people that every cloud has a silver lining.'

I had a spring in my step as I went back to Pete in the café. People would love the positivity in Rose's story. Plus we had our first audio-visual display.

CHAPTER TWENTY-ONE

Once he was settled with his second coffee, Pete continued his story.

'I was selfish, wasn't I?' he said. 'I wanted Sarah to give up university solely for my benefit.'

'We don't judge anyone.'

He and Sarah didn't talk about her quitting university again but it was never far from Pete's mind. Mid-August and A level results day got nearer. Their relationship continued as before, with that added delightful element of sex. They never spent the whole night together; Sarah always went home to her parents. There'd be too many lectures and questions to be answered if she stayed over with Pete. Sometimes he walked her to the bus stop or if one of them was feeling flush she got a taxi. On gig nights or when the band had been practising, Shane drove her home in his van with Bozzo, who lived not far from Sarah.

Every night as she left, Pete hoped with all his heart that something would go wrong with her exams and she'd be forced to stay there with him. He didn't sleep well the night before the results came out. He wondered if he'd be able to wear a false smile the next day and tell her how pleased he was at her success. He doubted he was a good enough actor.

As she went to school to get the important envelope, Pete was serving egg, bacon and hot sweet tea to overweight truckers. She'd promised to let him know her grades as soon as she'd told her parents and he kept glancing at the café door, half dreading and half hoping that it would open and she'd walk in.

'You've missed the beans! I always have beans — you should know that by now.' One of the regulars made him jump by bellowing in his ear as Pete served his breakfast.

'Sorry!' Pete scuttled back into the kitchen to top up the plate with baked beans.

'I reckon you're in love, lad,' the trucker called after him.

Something like that, Pete thought.

The breakfast rush had finished and he was wiping the tables ready for lunch when the payphone at the back of the café rang. He stared at it, knowing it had to be Sarah. He couldn't talk to her. He wanted to run away and hide from her news.

'Answer that will you!' the boss shouted from the kitchen.

Pete wanted the ringing to stop before he got to the phone. He walked slowly. The noise didn't stop. Perhaps it wouldn't be her. 'Hello?'

'It's me, Pete.' Sarah's voice was bubbling over with enthusiasm and his heart sank.

How would he cope when she was gone? How would he cope knowing she was with all those testosterone-fuelled male students? There wasn't a hope in hell their relationship would survive.

'I got an A and two Bs!' Sarah was shouting down the phone. 'I'm so pleased. I never thought I'd get an A!'

'That's great.' He couldn't say anything else.

'Sound more pleased for me! I'll come round later. We're all going down the pub now to celebrate.'

'Enjoy yourself,' Pete said flatly and put the phone down.

This was the beginning of the end. Sarah would get carried away in her friends' excitement and go off to university. He'd be left behind and forgotten. He was the short-lived Christmas toy whose novelty had worn off.

'What's wrong with you? You've got a face as long as a wet weekend.' Kevin, the boss, was going around Pete's newly-wiped tables topping up the ketchup containers. 'What have you got to be down about when you've got that beautiful girlfriend popping round here all the time?'

'She won't be around here much longer. She's going to university.'

'Brains as well as beauty! Well, get off your backside, lad! Don't just sit back and let her go. Show her what she'll be missing. Cook a nice meal for her. Buy a bottle of wine and tell her how proud you are to be her boyfriend. Tell her about the great future you can have together. You can finish an hour early so you can get everything sorted.'

So that's what Pete did. His budget wouldn't stretch to steak, champagne and red roses but he made a reasonable spaghetti bolognese and bought some chrysanthemums and a bottle of cheap white wine. He had a bath and put on the new shirt he'd been saving for the band's next gig. Just before she arrived, he put the spaghetti on to cook.

'Wow!' said Sarah, when she saw the bedsit.

He'd cleared the usual pile of washing-up, set the scratched wooden table with paper napkins from the café and put Fleetwood Mac on the cassette player.

'I thought you deserved a celebration.'

She grinned up at him. 'Well I have been rather clever, haven't I?'

He pulled her close and kissed her, trying to show her the feelings she ignited in him. Her arms travelled down his back and tugged the shirt from his waistband. He responded in kind and let his fingers enjoy the softness of her skin. He guided her to the settee. Sarah nestled on his lap and then there was a sudden hissing from the cooker.

'The spaghetti!'

The moment was spoiled as Pete tipped Sarah off his knee and rushed to rescue the pasta pan that was spewing water on the gas ring and almost extinguishing the flame. Sarah laughed and poured the wine while Pete grated his last piece of cheddar. The spaghetti and the bolognese turned out fine. The whole evening was lovely and Pete almost forgot the sad event they were celebrating. Sarah reminded him when she was gathering her things to go.

'If I go to Sussex we won't be able to do this any more. It's too far to come home at weekends.'

Pete's heart suddenly had hope. Sarah had used the word 'if' instead of 'when'. Since their one conversation on the subject, on the day of the royal wedding, he hadn't openly mentioned the possibility of her not going to Sussex. This new use of the word 'if' was coming from Sarah, not him. At that point he should have been generous and said something reassuring about him visiting her down there occasionally or them having all the long holidays together. He'd been a university student and he knew what she'd be missing out on by not going. He should have encouraged her to go.

'I've got some thinking to do,' she said. 'I want to consider my options.'

'OK.' He didn't give an opinion. He would face the future guilt free if she decided to stay of her own accord. He wouldn't encourage or discourage. 'In the meantime, let's enjoy ourselves.'

Then he bent his head to kiss her lips. They were interrupted by a banging on the door.

'Wrong flat,' Pete shouted, assuming it was the wino from across the landing.

'It's me, Bozzo. I've come with congratulations for the lady.'

Reluctantly, Pete let him in.

'How sweet!' Sarah's face lit up when she saw the chocolates and flowers that Bozzo had brought. She hugged him tight and he looked bashful when she let him go.

'You deserve them,' he said. 'I wish I'd gone to university. You go and take all the opportunities you can.'

Pete didn't like the way he was fussing her. Sarah was Pete's girlfriend.

'Thanks for coming, Bozzo.' Pete indicated the still open door.

Sarah started putting her jacket on. 'Are you going home, Bozzo? Do you fancy sharing a taxi?'

They went off together, Bozzo carrying the box of chocolates and Sarah the bouquet. Pete felt like the abandoned toy again.

'I'm not going,' Sarah announced as soon as Pete opened the door to her the following evening. 'There's a book-keeping course at the college in town. It teaches everything you need to know to get a job and start earning. Or I could set up my own business. I might even branch out into managing up-and-coming bands! After all, you need someone to keep a proper eye on your books.'

Pete grinned at her in amazement.

'Well what do you think? Is that a great idea or what?'

'It's a wonderful idea!' He gave her a bear hug.

'There is just one problem.' She pulled away from him and pursed her lips in that odd way she had when she was nervous. 'My parents aren't going to be pleased. I don't want to tell them alone. Will you come with me?'

Pete didn't want to go with her. He'd never met her parents. They would hate him if they met him under these circumstances. He would get the blame for Sarah's decision.

'Yes. I'll come with you.'

'Great, I've already told Mum you'll be coming for lunch on Sunday.'

Her mum and dad went ballistic. Sarah made her announcement over the roast chicken, carrots and peas. The meal never got as far as the home-made strawberry trifle that was sitting on a doily on the sideboard. Her parents couldn't believe she was throwing away her future for Pete.

'Pete's going to be a pop star,' Sarah said. 'Once I'm qualified I'll do the band's accounts, publicise them, take bookings and all that sort of stuff. We're going to be a success!'

'You're both living in cloud cuckoo land. Sarah, you are throwing your life away,' her dad said and then he told

Pete in no uncertain terms that he was not welcome in his house again.

'What about the trifle and After Eights?' her mother whispered forlornly as Pete was almost pushed out the front door, leaving Sarah to face the rest of the afternoon on her own.

When the payphone rang in the café on Monday, Pete knew it would be Sarah. She'd be telling him her dad had made her see sense and their relationship was over. He ignored the phone and walked out of the café into the car park. A couple of lorries were pulling in for their mid-morning break and he listened to the truckers' football banter as they jumped from the cabs. He wished he had nothing on his mind other than the relative merits of Arsenal and Manchester United.

'Pete! Phone!' Kevin was annoyed at having to leave the kitchen to answer the call and then search outside for his assistant.

He'd left the receiver dangling towards the floor, twirling round and round on its curly flex.

'Hello,' Pete said.

'Dad's gone to work and Mum's at the shops. I've called a taxi. I'll be at yours shortly with all my stuff. Bozzo's helping me.'

'Oh!'

'You do still want me, don't you?'

'Of course, I do. I want you more than anything. You've taken me by surprise, that's all. Once the lunchtime rush is over I'll help you move in.' Then he looked around to make sure no-one was too close and lowered his voice. 'I love you, Sarah.'

'I love you too, Pete.'

She'd said it at last! He wanted to dance and sing. He wanted to tell the whole world that the beautiful, intelligent Sarah James loved him. Instead, he picked two squashed chips off the floor and went to butter bread for fish butties.

When Pete went up to the bedsit after his shift, Bozzo had already moved Sarah in and left. There was a "Welcome to Your New Home" card on the mantelpiece, which he'd signed: *To Sarah, with love from Carl, Shane and Bozzo.* Sarah had squashed Pete's stuff down one end of the single wardrobe and was trying to fit her clothes in the other end.

'We need somewhere bigger,' she said. 'There isn't room to swing a cat in here. As soon as I'm earning we'll get a proper flat.'

'Proper flats are expensive.' Pete put his arms around her and lifted her off her feet. 'All that matters is that we're together. Let's go to bed.'

They were still lying naked on top of the bedcovers, their bodies warmed by the late afternoon sunshine coming through the skylight, when there was a hammering at the door.

'Ignore it,' Pete said. 'The old wino across the landing forgets which flat is his.'

Sarah nuzzled into his neck and Pete marvelled that now they could be together forever. He wondered if he dared ask her to marry him. The banging came again.

'I know you're in there. Give me my daughter back!'

'It's my dad!' Sarah was off the bed in a flash and pulling on her jeans and T-shirt.

Pete stumbled into his trousers and then opened the door. It would have been obvious from their tousled hair what had been going on. Sarah's dad looked at Pete as if he was a rat the cat had dragged in.

'We're going home,' he announced to Sarah. 'Leave your stuff. I'll come and fetch it another time when things aren't so . . . emotional.'

Sarah went to Pete's side and reached for his hand. 'I'm going nowhere, Dad. I'm eighteen — you can't make me do anything I don't want. I love Pete and I'm staying here with him.'

The love word, she said the love word again! Pete couldn't stop the huge grin from plastering itself across his face.

'Why are you smirking?' Sarah's dad's top lip curled up. 'What you've persuaded my daughter to do isn't clever. It will end badly — mark my words! You are wasting her potential and her life.'

Then he left. Sarah was trembling.

'I am doing the right thing aren't I?' she asked.

'Of course, you are. We love each other. What can go wrong?'

For a while nothing went wrong. Each day, Pete worked in the café until mid-afternoon and then went to bed with Sarah for a couple of hours. Later she cooked tea with whatever leftovers Pete had managed to get from the café and then she went with the band to a gig or watched them practise in the empty café. After a while, Kevin gave her a few hours' work in the kitchen, which helped their finances.

'These afternoons will have to stop when my course starts next week,' Sarah said one day as she moved off the bed and prepared to shower before the evening's gig.

'There's always weekends,' Pete said lazily. 'And when we hit the big time we'll stay in four-poster beds in posh hotels. The world is our oyster.'

Sarah's book-keeping course started and Kevin re-jigged her hours in the café so she could keep earning. For a while they were living the dream — steady money, good company and the band was getting more gigs. There was still no response to any of the demo tapes Pete sent to record companies and radio stations but the wedding and birthday party circuit seemed to like them. They even made a profit on gigs and charged travelling expenses as an extra. Sarah took great delight in recording this in a notebook and stuffing receipts into a big brown envelope. She and Bozzo had worked out a routine between themselves for negotiating better rates from the band's regular venues.

Pete and Sarah were happy until the first week of December when Sarah's schoolmates reappeared from university for the Christmas holidays. She decided to hold a girly party to catch up with her closest girlfriends and, for the first time, she missed one of the band's gigs to do it.

'Can't you do the party another night?' Pete asked. 'You feel like part of the band now. You're our good luck talisman.'

'Don't be silly. You can manage without me and it means I get the bedsit to myself to entertain.'

When Pete got back from the gig, Sarah was sitting by herself at the scratched table with a cup of tea. She was wearing her thick winceyette pyjamas against the extreme cold of the room and looked forlorn.

'What's up? Didn't it go well?'

'Yes and no. I'm not sure I've done the right thing.'

'Why? What have you done?' Pete sat down and held her hand.

'I mean by not going to university. I wonder if I might be missing out by staying here.'

She cast her eyes around the dilapidated single room that they lived in. Pete noticed the peeling wallpaper, damp patch and threadbare carpet — all usually invisible to him. He never had got around to decorating the place.

'The girls were telling me about hall balls, societies, long talks into the night, the jokes they play on each other and lots more. Have we settled down too quick?'

'No way! You're the manager of an up-and-coming band — that's not settling down. It's more exciting than passively putting the world to rights over coffee at midnight.'

He wouldn't admit it to Sarah but Pete knew where she was coming from. He'd already done all those student things and got them out of his system. Poor Sarah was juggling shifts in a greasy spoon with disapproving parents whom she still dutifully phoned every Sunday night and a book-keeping course where most of the other students were either redundant middle-aged men starting their own businesses or matronly women looking to return to work after their kids had left home. Pete could see that the world Sarah's friends were describing would sound like heaven, especially to someone as intelligent as Sarah.

'Cheer up! You've got me — the most eligible bachelor in the world. What more could a beautiful girl want? Let's go to bed — it will all seem better in the morning.'

194

She gave him a dutiful small smile. He filled the hot water bottles and they layered their coats over the thin quilt. Pete hoped they could afford to move somewhere warmer before the next winter.

Pete's second cappuccino was now finished and when Vanessa asked if he'd like another, he nodded.

* * *

'I should've encouraged her to reapply for university at that point.' Pete cradled his third coffee. 'She might have continued our relationship then. But I didn't. I wanted to make the status quo work. I was like some perverse gaoler.'

As it got nearer to Christmas, Sarah became quieter and more withdrawn. The band was busy with gigs but Sarah came to fewer and fewer of them, preferring to see her old school friends instead. In bed she pleaded a headache instead of responding with delight when Pete squeezed her bottom or caressed her breast. A distance settled between them.

Pete wanted to make Christmas special for her so she'd snap out of this lethargy and be her old sparkly self. He borrowed some money from Bozzo and bought her a dress for Christmas. It was one she'd been admiring in the window of Topshop for weeks.

They had a special Christmas morning breakfast of scrambled eggs and scones with strawberry jam (café leftovers that wouldn't keep until after Christmas) and Pete gave Sarah his gift. She didn't even try it on.

'I was going to buy this in the sales next week. We can't afford the full price — we're behind on the rent this month.' She left it still half-wrapped on the table.

Then she shocked him by disappearing off to her parents' house for Christmas lunch, taking an overnight bag with her. Her dad collected her but he didn't come inside.

'I'm sorry, they didn't invite you.' She didn't look very sorry.

Pete was left to cook sausage and more eggs for himself. That was when he knew it was the end — what sort of girl-friend abandons her partner on Christmas Day with no prior warning? Not someone who feels they're in a long-term rela-tionship. She came back the day after Boxing Day with her father. This time he came in and helped her carry all her stuff out to the car. Then he left Sarah and Pete alone for a few minutes.

'I'm sorry it had to end like this,' she said. 'But I now realise you and the band are just chasing rainbows. You're no nearer to hitting the big time than when I met you six months ago.'

Her words were a slap across the face. 'These things take time. We could get our big break tomorrow.'

She shook her head. 'I'm tired of serving fry-ups to truckers who wolf-whistle when I bend over the table. Nor do I want to do the accounts for small-time businesses in back streets. And I'm fed up of applauding enthusiastically for a band that will never make it.'

'I thought you were enjoying our life together,' Pete said feebly.

'I was until my mates came home and I realised what I've been missing. If I don't go and get a degree now I'll waste my potential.'

'But we don't have to split up. We can still see each other on the odd weekend and in the holidays.'

'No, Pete. I want to leave without baggage. It's best we make a clean break now. I'm going travelling until the start of the next academic year. I'll pick up casual bar work or something along the way. Tell Kevin I'm sorry I didn't give any notice about quitting.'

A horn sounded impatiently outside. Sarah pecked Pete on the cheek and was gone. Pete opened the bottle of wine they'd been saving for Christmas night and which he'd then saved for when she came back from her parents. He didn't stop drinking until it was empty. Sarah didn't want him and she thought the band had no future. She'd ended his life in a couple of sentences. There was no reason to stay sober.

The rest of the band were shocked by Sarah's departure — they'd all become fond of her, like she was their sister. They carried on gigging but without Sarah it felt as though the spark had gone. Eventually they split up. Pete finished at the café and got a place at drama school. Carl and Shane stayed locally and Bozzo went south seeking something better. In the end they all lost touch.

Pete sat with his head in his hands. He'd let the third coffee go cold in front of him.

'She didn't take everything when she went,' Vanessa said. 'She left you the cassette tape?'

'No,' he mumbled. 'That's my copy. For a long time after she'd gone I imagined the two identical tapes were a bond between us — like the "half a sixpence" in that old song. While we both still had a copy of the tape, she might come back to me.'

'And now, after more than forty years, you realise she's not going to?'

'Yes.' His voice was heavy with emotion. 'I'll finish the story and you'll see why.'

A few years ago, after his last relationship broke up, Pete decided to track Sarah down. Her parents had long since moved so he had to use Facebook. He found her and they exchanged a couple of emails. She told him she was married with two grown-up sons.

'They're in a band,' she wrote, 'just like their dad was.'

The remark confused Pete but there was no way they could be his and he felt overwhelmed with jealousy. He'd been married twice and had other relationships but none had ever come close to how he felt about Sarah. At about the same time, Carl and Shane got in touch with Pete via *Emergency Ambulance's* Fan Club. They were having a joint 60th party and had tracked down Bozzo — Pete was the missing piece of the jigsaw.

Usually Pete was hesitant about meeting old acquaintances — often they turned out to be gold diggers jealous of his success, wanting money or a lift up the audition ladder via his contacts. But he knew the lads would be OK, so he went to the party. He arrived early. They'd set up drums and a guitar on the stage in the hired function room so the band could relive their 'glory' days. Pete was testing out the mic when Bozzo appeared twirling his old lucky drumsticks.

'We're not doing "Oops Upside Your Head", are we?' he asked with a smile.

Pete gave him a hug. 'How are things?'

'Great!' He paused and his face lost its grin. 'But I have to tell you something before we start partying. I don't know how to say this, Pete, and Sarah didn't want to tell you via Facebook and emails.'

Pete went cold inside. What bad news could there be about Sarah? Was she seriously ill? Why couldn't she tell him? Then he noticed a tall slim woman appear at the far end of the hall, flanked by two young men with floppy hair. Even from this distance and after almost four decades of absence, he recognised her.

'When the band split up, I decided to use my A levels. Sussex University was the only place that would take me,' Bozzo continued. 'I didn't engineer it — I swear! It just happened. I bumped into Sarah and the rest, as they say, is history.'

Pete didn't grasp what Bozzo was saying at first.

'We didn't dare tell you at the time and then you got famous and married,' his old band mate continued. 'There didn't seem any point telling you then.'

Sarah kissed him on both cheeks. Pete recognised her smell instantly. The perfume had changed but it was still unmistakably her. She was still beautiful — age had treated her well. As he returned the greeting he reached for her hands. For a few seconds they stood there touching. Something passed between them with that physical contact — a longing for a relationship that could never happen? The pain was too much and Pete let go first.

Then Sarah and Bozzo's sons dutifully shook Pete's hand. He wanted to rant, rave and fling accusations. Had there been anything between Sarah and Bozzo before they split up? Had Pete been cheated on? Was Bozzo a friend or a woman-stealer? But instead Pete went into polite 'famous actor off the TV making a public appearance' mode. His churning emotions were hidden as he played his part. He joined the band on stage, signed a few autographs for the guests who recognised him and came over to say how much they enjoyed *Emergency Ambulance*. Then he left as early as he could.

In the four years since that party, Pete had done nothing but mentally revisit the six months that he and Sarah were together. He was looking for signs there was something going on between Sarah and Bozzo back then. Constantly replaying everything was driving him mad. What happened when the pair travelled home together late at night after rehearsals? Why did Bozzo bother with the A Level congratulations gifts and new home card?

All this turmoil was the real reason Pete was handing over the tape. Until that party his relationship with Sarah was just a bittersweet memory, but now it was a nightmarish search for betrayal playing on a continuous loop.

Pete blew his nose, stood up and walked away. Then he came back, took a museum leaflet from the display stand and signed his autograph on it. He handed it to Vanessa.

'In exchange for the coffees and a listening ear,' he said. 'You never know, it might be worth something one day. But please, don't display it with the tape. For the sake of both me and Sarah that must remain anonymous. And, for the record, talking to you has made me feel better. Thank you.'

Five minutes later Pete was back in the café. 'I've just noticed the posters you've got in the foyer advertising the singles' night.'

'Come along. We can't guarantee you'll find love but hopefully there'll be like-minded people to chat to. Stephen's selling tickets upstairs.'

'I wasn't thinking of coming as a punter. I could come as the entertainment.' It was ages since Pete had done a gig and he suddenly fancied trying it again at a small venue that needed a leg up.

'That would be wonderful! Thank you.' Vanessa clapped her hands. 'I'll do some more posters with your name on. Maxine will get it out there on Twitter as well. You'll be a great crowd puller.'

'I'm a bit out of practise. Can't promise how good I'll be.' He could feel the beginning of apprehension and nerves. It made him shiver and meant he was doing the right thing. *Emergency Ambulance* had made him comfortable and complacent. It was time he got back to his roots and did something that made him feel scared, as though he was really living.

CHAPTER TWENTY-TWO

August

'That is lovely!' Maxine was holding up a light blue sleepsuit with a dark brown puppy's head emblazoned on the chest. 'I am going to have such fun dressing him up. Thank you, Vanessa.'

'No problem.' A rare afternoon of shopping had been a treat for me, while Maxine and Stephen held the fort at the museum.

On one side of Maxine was a growing pile of blue and silver wrapping paper and on the other, three more sleepsuits in various shades of blue, plus a little knitted hat and a cuddly toy sheep.

'I deliberately didn't choose a bear.' Buying things that wouldn't take Maxine back to the birth of her first child had been hard, especially since she'd told us the scan had indicated she was having another boy. In order for this new mum to survive emotionally, this experience had to be completely different from the first. 'Daniel's toy is safe here with me and your new little family has got a great future ahead.'

Maxine's hug was sudden, warm and long. When she pulled away, she looked across at Stephen who was holding out another present wrapped in baby paper. 'I'm not much of a fashionista,' he said, 'so I've gone down the educational route.'

She tore at the wrapping. 'Fab! A nursery rhyme book. Before, with Daniel, I never got the chance to sing and read to him but this time . . .' Maxine's voice choked and then she sobbed.

Stephen looked upset.

'It's not your fault,' I whispered. 'Let her cry. It's better that she gets rid of all that emotion here, with us, rather than carry it home into her new family.'

Maxine sat with her head on my shoulder until the weeping stopped. I stroked her hair. She'd become the daughter I never had and the daughter-in-law that didn't yet exist. When Maxine finally raised her head and blew her nose, Stephen looked towards me for his cue. I gave a nod. He went behind the café counter and emerged triumphantly.

'We made you a cake!'

'Made?' Maxine looked at me quizzically.

'Half-made. We bought the plain sponge but the top is all Stephen's work.'

The cake was covered with smooth blue ready-rolled icing and on top of that, in slightly crooked white lettering, was the message, *Good Luck! Come Back Soon!* Tears ran down Maxine's cheeks again but this time there was a smile on her face as well. 'This is one of the nicest things that anyone has ever done for me.' Then she caught my eye. 'One day we really will learn how to make a proper sponge cake.'

She opened her arms and gathered us both in a group hug; a demonstration of the affection which had grown between the three of us in a very short time. I was acutely aware of my left hand on Stephen's waist. The skin beneath his shirt radiated heat against my fingertips. What would it be like to pull that shirt from his waistband and touch the skin for real? I'd never find out. I forced my brain to switch from lust to the joy of our team camaraderie and good wishes for the mum-to-be.

'Phew, give me air!' Maxine stepped back from us, fanning her face with a hand. 'Having another human being inside you is like having a hot water bottle permanently stuck to your stomach.'

'Trish said something similar when she was carrying the twins. In the third trimester neither of us got much sleep because she was always hot and couldn't get comfortable.'

Maxine looked at me. Each time Stephen spoke about Trish and the boys it was a sign that he was healing. In us, had he found two people he felt totally at ease with? Or was this part of a more general recovery aided by the ethos of the museum? Either way, he was slowly moving forward. 'It's really lovely to hear you mention your family like that.' Maxine leaned forward and gave him a peck on the cheek. Stephen and I were still linked in the remnants of the hug and I expected him to move the hand that rested on my hip to kiss her back. But he left it there until I was forced to break away to help Maxine cut the cake.

She took a selfie of us with crumbs around our mouths and Stephen with the circle of blue icing on his nose that he'd put there to make us laugh.

'I'm gutted to be missing the singles' night,' she said. 'I wish I'd worked out the dates properly before suggesting the last Saturday in August. It must have been a case of hormonal pregnancy jelly brain.'

Then she was off into Adrian's waiting car, with two carrier bags of baby clothes, cake and our shouts of good luck.

'She wanted to stay right up until she went into labour,' I told Stephen as we cleared away in the café and got things ready for the morning. 'She thinks we can't do without her. We can't really but she needs at least a fortnight at home with her feet up before her due date. Both she and that baby deserve the best.'

'So how will you manage on the days when I'm not here?'

I'd been worrying about that but it was my problem, not Stephen's. 'I managed before either of you came along.'

'Vanessa, this place needs at least two staff, always. Otherwise people get fed up of waiting, be it at the desk upstairs or here in the café. And then they walk out and never come back. We can't afford to lose a single customer.'

'People cost money and they have to get the ethos of this place. And, as you keep telling me, we're going to be very lucky to survive beyond October so I can't take anyone else on. I was lucky with Maxine and you.'

'Stay lucky. My contract ends next week and I'm not yet committed anywhere else. I'll come in full-time.'

'And be paid in café leftovers?' I said sarcastically.

'Yes. If there are leftovers, I'll have them. Otherwise I'm yours for free until Maxine comes back. I've earned enough contracting to tide me over a couple of months.'

I didn't want him working for nothing. I didn't want to accept charity. The museum was a business and should be run as such. But he was right, I couldn't cope on my own.

'Thank you,' I said, trying to appear like a dignified business woman. 'That would be lovely. If you make a note of your hours then I'll make sure you get paid back in the future, when we're in profit.'

He shook his head. 'You and this place have given me enough already. No repayment needed.'

He'd taken a step closer, into my personal space. I suddenly had the ridiculous thought that he was going to kiss me. My body went tense. Did I want this? Yes. Business and pleasure, a bad mix? Probably, but this didn't feel like a business relationship. Dave hovered in my mind's eye. We'd been happy once. We'd created Liam together. But Dave didn't have Stephen's toe-curling effect on me. Dave was the comfy old slipper drawing me back. Stephen was the shiny new shoe that might take me somewhere better. Yes, I wanted this. My first kiss with another man since I met my husband. I was nervous but yes, I was ready.

Stephen placed his hands on my shoulders and cocked his head to one side. I looked up into his face.

'Trish would be proud of me now. She was always going on about "giving something back to society".'

Then Stephen reached for the sweeping brush and chased the last crumbs around the floor, along with the longings I'd hardly dare feel. Rejected was too small a word. I'd been the master of my own downfall. By opening the door for Stephen to talk about Trish I'd allowed him to fall back in love with her. He was happy with thoughts of his late wife rather than ready for a new relationship. I, and all my middle-aged failings, didn't stand a chance against his rose-tinted memories of a young, successful Trish.

'Was that the doorbell?' Stephen stopped sweeping.

I nodded and went upstairs. Visitors after closing time were rare.

'Joanne!'

'Hi Vanessa, sorry it's so late but I couldn't get here until after work.'

'No problem. It's lovely to see you.' Donors coming back to see us always gave me a thrill — it was the museum magic working at its best.

'Is Stephen here? I'd like a word about the singles' night.' Her eyes were shining.

'Follow me.' I didn't like her eagerness to see Stephen in particular.

'I'd like to help with the food at the singles' event,' she said to Stephen and then, as an afterthought, she glanced at me. 'My chocolate cakes go down well at work.'

'Chocolate cakes would be great,' he said. 'We're making sandwiches, stuff on sticks and simple salads but it would be lovely to have pudding as well.'

'Will six large ones be enough?' Joanne asked. 'They cut into about twelve pieces each.'

'Fantastic. Let me know the cost of the ingredients and we'll reimburse you.'

'No need. Leaving the album and engagement ring here has changed my life and I want to give something back. I can help serve food on the night or do whatever's needed . . . Better that than standing around like a lemon on my own.'

We both thanked her profusely. Stephen gave her a hug and saw her to the door. I tried to read his face when he came back to see whether the gesture had been anything other than friendliness but he gave nothing away.

'You knew we'd ordered gateaux from the caterers,' I said. 'And she might be a rubbish baker.'

'Doing the cakes will give Joanne a boost and we'll save money. As for being a rubbish baker — if chocolate butter-cream is involved, I'm sure it will be fine.'

Plus, maybe you fancy her a little bit, I wanted to add.

On the way home, I realised that my jealousy had made me miss an opportunity. Joanne might be able to teach me how to bake. I pushed aside my reservations about her intentions towards Stephen and texted her.

* * *

Joanne was sceptical about starting my baking career with deep and luscious chocolate cakes intended for paying customers.

'I'll still provide those,' she said. 'Let's start with bread pudding. It's already on your menu, fits your ethos of cake being soothing to the soul plus it needs no real skill.'

I tried not to be insulted by her last remark. Then Joanne got me tearing up bread, adding milk and squelching it alto-gether with my bare hands to break up the lumps and get everything well combined. I tipped in raisins, currants and sultanas plus a generous teaspoonful of mixed spice. Then there was more messy manual mixing.

'This doesn't feel like baking. It's like I'm back in infant school with soggy, home-made play dough.'

'It's building your confidence. Plus, you can add "home-made" to the menu description — that makes things sell better.'

I was getting a new respect for Joanne. It still surprised me how the people coming through the museum found the strength to put adversity behind them and find their own path in life.

'Thank you.' I opened my arms to hug her.

'No!' she cried, looking at my hands. She took a step back but not far enough to escape my embrace.

I realised too late why she didn't want me near her and now I was mortified. Streaks of pale, raw bread pudding glistened on the shoulders of her navy blouse and down the sleeves. We stared at each other. My still-sticky hands were in mid-air with nowhere to go. It would be against hygiene rules to put them back in the bowl but they were too messy to dangle by my sides.

Then Joanne grinned. She took my hands and rubbed them against my cheeks. Her grin turned into a laugh and the laugh became a guffaw. Her reaction was infectious. The two of us doubled over, shook and snorted until our stomachs hurt and we were exhausted.

'Sorry,' I said between taking deep breaths. 'Now we both look like we're in infant school.'

'Bags I be teacher again!'

We cleaned ourselves up and resumed the lesson. Joanne gave me a spoon to mix in the eggs and brown sugar. 'Just in case you're tempted to fling your arms about again!' she said.

To speed things up, Joanne greased and lined a square cake tin — or at least she said it was to speed things up — and I tipped in its precious cargo.

Joanne pointed to the bag of brown sugar. 'That is my secret ingredient. Sprinkle some on top to create a crunchy texture on the finished product.'

The bread pudding was a triumph.

CHAPTER TWENTY-THREE

'You look nice.'

Dave's voice from behind made me jump and I fumbled the clasp on my necklace. In the mirror I saw my ex-husband standing in the bedroom doorway, watching me try to make something decent of myself.

'I'm coming with you tonight.' He walked over to me. 'Do you want a hand with that?'

Without waiting for a reply, he took the clasp from my hands, which were reaching behind my neck, and secured the metal hook into the circular opening with one smooth movement.

'Thanks,' I said.

Dave was standing at my shoulder and through the mirror we looked like a proper couple posing for a photograph. He'd made an effort with his appearance too.

'You know it's a singles' night?' I said.

'I'm single. But I hope it's only a temporary state.' He put his hands on my shoulders and started to massage. 'There are mistakes I want to put right. The grass isn't always greener on the other side.' It was tempting to lean back into his strong hands; hands that had sorted out so many of life's problems in the past. I closed my eyes. He continued to ease the tension from my shoulders.

A car door slammed somewhere. Reality kicked in and I shook Dave off. 'This evening is work for me,' I warned. 'You'll be on your own. I'll be serving food, chatting and making sure everyone has a good time.'

'You'll be the hostess with the mostest and I'll be there to help you. We always were a great team, weren't we?'

'Please, don't come.' I didn't need the added stress of having Dave there. 'I won't have a spare minute.'

'It's bring a bottle, isn't it? There's white wine chilling in the fridge.'

Dave had always been like a steamroller when he wanted to do something.

* * *

Stephen was helping Pete unpack his equipment when we arrived. I nudged Dave into giving them a hand to set up the speakers and do the sound check. Pete was going to start as our DJ with some quiet, non-intrusive tracks, so people could chat and get their bearings. Then he'd sing some of his own stuff and a few cover versions when the party had got going. If there were enough guests to make a party. *Please, people, turn up after we've gone to all this trouble!*

I went down to the café. We'd closed early and Stephen, Joanne and I had spent the afternoon making sandwiches, filling vol au vent cases and sticking sausages, pineapple chunks and cheese on sticks. Now the feast needed arranging tastefully with some jugs of fruit juice and glasses for people who'd brought their own bottles. Stephen was right, we needed to investigate getting our own licence. It would look more professional if we served alcohol, plus there was money to be made from drink.

'Pudding's here!' Stephen and Joanne came into the café carrying two large cake tins apiece.

'Brilliant!' I fetched cake stands from behind the counter, trying to ignore Joanne looping her arm through Stephen's as they went back to fetch more tins from the taxi Joanne had waiting.

The chocolate cakes looked lovely; each comprising three layers of sponge, two layers of buttercream and a melted chocolate topping.

'Shall we cut them ready?' Joanne suggested. 'Nobody likes to be the first to break into a new cake.'

With the cakes displayed, Joanne went back upstairs with Stephen, casually linking his arm again. Music drifted down from the museum hall. I remembered my eighteenth birthday party and the terror that no-one would show. Growing older hadn't banished my chronic insecurity. I glanced at the café clock in the same corner-of-the-eye way I'd tried not to stare at the clock on our sitting-room sideboard. No-one ever came on time to a party, I told myself, it just wasn't done.

By our eight o'clock start time the only voices I could hear drifting down from the museum hall were those of Stephen, Pete and Dave. We'd sold few advance tickets and were relying on those organised people to bring friends and spread the word. I opened Dave's bottle of wine and poured a glass for Dutch courage. If this evening was a failure, the writing would be on the wall for the museum. October was only a couple of months away. Tonight a fairy godmother was needed to wave her magic wand and create a sparkly path from Birmingham city centre to the museum, for single people looking for an alternative to clubs and bars.

Then, over the noise of the music, was the sound of the museum front door opening and closing. I turned my brighter than usual lips up at the ends, put my shoulders back and went upstairs to meet and greet. It's amazing how you can put on a professional front when you're terrified inside.

'Good evening, I'm Vanessa, the museum manager. Welcome.'

'I'm Sophie.' Our first arrival was young and attractive. 'Oh dear, am I the first?'

'No problem. I'm on my own too.' Dave appeared from nowhere in his shining armour. 'Shall we explore this place together?' He gestured towards the display cases and Pete's musical set-up.

Sophie hesitated. At her age she'd have been expecting a better catch than Dave. Then she smiled. 'Sounds good.'

As they walked away, Dave had his hand in the small of Sophie's back. It was only a polite gesture but it made me realise how other women might fall for my ex-husband. He still had the ability to charm and flirt. Perhaps his affair shouldn't have come as a shock. If I'd been properly tuned into my husband, I'd have realised what was going on.

More people arrived singly and some in pairs or small groups. More women than men. The conversational buzz was increasing and the evening was going better than I'd hoped. The exhibits triggered discussion and little groups gathered in the café as well.

Joanne was spending a lot of time deep in conversation with Stephen. I tried to move towards them with the intent of breaking in. But people waylaid me with questions about the exhibits and I never reached my destination.

I spotted Tim from the local paper appear in the doorway and scan the room. He waved and came over to me, camera around his neck and notebook in hand.

'Sorry I'm late,' he said. 'I tried and failed to persuade Karen to come along with me. She's nervous about bringing her object in and I thought coming tonight might ease the awkwardness for her.'

'No problem. Whenever she's ready, she'll be very welcome.'

'I think the issue is that I'll be able to read the full story when it's here. She's worried it might jeopardise our relationship.'

'Then don't pressurise her to come.' There was no point in her raking up the past if it was going to destroy their future.

'I say it's better off her chest. I'll always love her, no matter what.'

I hoped Tim didn't come to regret his simplistic view. From the museum I'd learnt that those closest to us can hide the most shocking secrets.

Tim looked around the room through his camera lens. 'Now I'd better make some notes and take pictures. I'll do the biggest report that I can get past the editor — unfortunately he favours adverts over actual journalism.'

The party atmosphere was growing and Pete started to up the tempo by playing a few 80s tracks. People started foot tapping and swaying. When the first bars of "Don't You Want Me" by The Human League started, Dave threw me a look. His meaning was as obvious as if he'd shouted the question across the room to me. I shook my head. This was the very first track we'd danced to together and, unlike him, I didn't want to recreate that moment here on an empty dance floor. When Pete switched to the previous decade and Abba's "Dancing Queen", a couple of brave energetic souls took to the dance floor. The attraction of safety in numbers meant that several more soon joined them.

I meandered through the guests, my wine glass refilled, trying to gauge how they were feeling. Some of these people would be at a vulnerable point in their lives. They'd come because of an open invitation from me. They were my responsibility. The age range was broad, from late twenties to sixties. I tuned in and out of conversations. There were introductions, questions and polite laughter. Joanne was now on the edge of a mixed group. Stephen was next to Maxine's teddy bear exhibit talking to a man. Dave was in conversation with Pete. The apprehension in my stomach was almost gone. Stephen was right about a singles' event being good for the museum. It fitted our ethos about serving the community and gently pushing people onto the next stage of their lives. I liked that people might be making new friends because of us.

'Good evening ladies and gentlemen. Now it's time for some live music,' Pete announced and a murmur ran around the room. 'But first I need to introduce myself to you properly. You know me as surgeon Charles Denver from *Emergency*

Ambulance.' Pete was forced to pause as the audience clapped and cheered. He raised his hands and then lowered them, palms downward, to quieten the room.

'This place asks us to be open and honest about who we are and what we've done or experienced, in order that we can move on with our lives. Music was my first love. I am a failed pop star and have both good and bad memories of that stage in my life. Vanessa has helped me to get the bad memories into perspective and now I feel ready to challenge myself. And what better springboard to take life in a new direction than this unique museum?' More clapping followed. 'Now, a word from the creator of this wonderful place. Vanessa, come here please.'

I shook my head at him but he was beckoning me forward. My heart thumped and I started to feel clammy. Facing a class of thirty teenagers never bothered me but there were around seventy adults here. Strangers waiting to be entertained. Please don't ask me to make a speech. Please not.

Pete gave me a hug and a peck on the cheek. He raised my arm as if I were a championship boxer. 'This is the lovely lady who made all of this possible!' Everyone cheered. Then he handed me the microphone. I caught sight of Stephen to my left. He must have seen the panic in my face because he gave me a thumbs-up sign and a huge encouraging smile. I tried to take inspiration from Rose and her speakers' club experience. But like her, I struggled to mentally unclothe everyone. Except Dave. And imagining Dave naked didn't help. Then my eyes and my imagination flitted to Stephen. I suddenly felt even hotter. It was an effort to mentally replace his shirt, look away and refocus.

'Ladies and gentlemen, thank you very much for coming to this museum's first ever singles' night. I hope you're enjoying yourselves.' I was talking too fast and had no idea what I should say. 'Perhaps you'll make a new friend or two. Do please come back to our next event . . .' Now Stephen was giving me a double thumbs-up. I took another breath and continued, 'Then we hope to have alcohol for sale rather than asking you to bring your own.'

I handed the microphone back to Pete and barely heard him start his live set.

Stephen grabbed my hand as I tried to walk back into obscurity. 'Well done,' he said. 'Great minds — I was going to insist that we do these events every couple of months. Word will spread if people know it's a regular thing.' He kissed me on the cheek and we stared at each other awkwardly. We must have looked like two lovelorn teenagers, too awkward and naive to know what should come next.

Reluctantly I remembered I was the hostess. 'I need to check the buffet.' I dropped his hand and went downstairs, my palm still warm from his.

It was deserted in the café and much cooler. My cheeks were hot, whether from my impromptu speech or Stephen's cheek kiss, I didn't know. I tidied up, loaded the dishwasher with used glasses and tried to make myself feel normal. My thoughts were like the crumbs scattered across the floor. Stephen was hard to fathom. Was I imagining some connection between us that wasn't actually there? Was he still in love with his late wife? How did he feel about Joanne? Dave, on the other hand, had been wearing his heart on his sleeve. But I'd come too far to slip easily back into my old life. Striking out alone had become a kaleidoscope of adventure, sometimes scary and often joyful.

At eleven-thirty Pete started to slow things down by playing Whitney Houston's "I Will Always Love You". As the tune began both Dave and Stephen arrived in front of me.

'Will you—?'

'Would you—?'

I looked from one man to the other. They frowned at each other.

'Someone's spilled beer. Can we have a mop?' A guest was tapping Stephen on the shoulder. His eyes tried to speak to me. The message seemed urgent but I couldn't decipher it and he disappeared, like Cinderella leaving the ball at midnight.

Without waiting for a reply, Dave pulled me close. His smell was familiar. I was tired and automatically relaxed.

'It's too long since we danced like this,' he whispered.

I closed my eyes, my body against his. When the music finished, Dave guided me off the makeshift dance floor but kept his arms around me. The kiss took me by surprise. It was intimate and long. And enjoyable. Afterwards I felt disorientated. Then the main lights came on, destroying the mood. He still held my hand.

'Enjoy that did you?' Stephen was in front of us, frowning. 'Save more canoodling for at home later. I need a hand seeing people off the premises.'

Dave grinned at him and Stephen looked crosser. I should have gone to clear up the beer spillage — this was my business and Stephen shouldn't be doing my dirty work. He wasn't my Cinderella.

'Stephen, I'm sorry.' As I spoke, I realised I was apologising for dancing with and, especially, for kissing Dave. It was nothing to do with who cleared up the spillage. But there were people around us and I couldn't be explicit. Besides, Stephen might not see our relationship in that way. Maybe clearing up the beer was all he was narked about.

As people left, we stood side by side saying goodbye and handing out leaflets to the guests. Stephen caught Joanne by the hand as she went through the door. He said something, she smiled and stood to one side as he scribbled on a leaflet and handed it to her. I thought he said something about a phone number.

Then Dave was mithering about getting us a taxi. That's when I spotted the bewildered old lady standing on the pavement across the road from the museum. At first, I thought she was homeless and looking for somewhere to bed down; perhaps she used the doorway of the museum at night and we'd upset her routine. Only when she looked up did I recognise her. Polly. I glanced down the street, in both directions, but there was no sign of Malcolm.

I crossed the road. 'Polly! What are you doing here?'

Her eyes were red and she was holding a carrier bag. 'I brought you a donation.'

CHAPTER TWENTY-FOUR

Polly

Polly hadn't expected anybody to be at the museum. It was late. She'd put a short note in the bag with her donation to explain who it was from. Her plan was to post it through the museum letterbox. Or hang it on the door handle if the letterbox wasn't big enough. By the time it was found in the morning everything would be over. But the party had ruined her plan. With everyone leaving the building she hadn't been able to get near the letterbox and then that nice Vanessa had spotted her.

She was causing trouble arriving late at night like this but a small part of her felt relief at finding people still there. She didn't have to bear this alone any longer. Vanessa had exchanged sharp words with one man about a taxi and a few minutes later he'd got in a cab by himself. Then Vanessa had invited her to go into the museum café with her and a man that turned out to be Vanessa's colleague, Stephen. The kind pregnant girl wasn't there.

Polly hesitated in the café, leaning on her walking stick. She should go straight home. There was stuff to sort out and the house to put to rights.

'I'm causing you trouble after your nice party. I'll just leave this and go.' She offered the battered Tesco Bag for Life to Vanessa.

'No.' Vanessa ignored the bag and guided Polly to a chair. 'You don't go back out into the night without eating and drinking.'

Polly didn't have the energy to argue. She was tired and didn't know how to order a taxi to take her home. Her plan had been to ask the cab that brought her to wait but everything had gone awry when she realised there was an event on at the museum. The man called Stephen was already making tea and cutting a chocolate cake.

'It's on the house,' Vanessa said. 'We've had a busy night and need a sit down too.'

A cup of tea would make her feel better, more prepared to face what was to come. After what she'd done at home, she didn't think she could manage the chocolate cake. Her stomach was tight and anxious. But when Stephen put it in front of her, she realised she was actually hungry. The three of them had finished their cake and moved on to sipping tea when Vanessa peeked inside the carrier bag.

'Men's slippers. Are they Malcolm's?'

'They *were* Malcolm's.'

'Were?'

There was an awkward silence. Polly pulled the carrier bag back towards her and clutched it tightly. The café felt different at night-time or maybe it was because Vanessa was dressed up and wearing make-up. And Stephen was there, like a stranger. She wanted to come back in daytime when Vanessa would look comforting and kind and Stephen would be somewhere else. But tomorrow would be too late.

'More tea?' Stephen asked. Without waiting for an answer, he fetched the teapot and carton of milk from the counter and topped up all the cups.

'We'd love to have Malcolm's slippers as an exhibit, Polly, but why are you donating them? Doesn't he need them?'

'He's dead.' Polly blinked rapidly. There was no need for her to be sad. His death was for the best. And soon they'd be together again. Her and Malcolm. The proper Malcolm not the shell of a man who didn't recognise his own wife.

'Oh, love!' Vanessa placed her hand on top of Polly's. Polly noticed how thin and waxy her own skin was compared to the fuller hand of Vanessa. 'I am so sorry.'

'I want the good part of Malcolm to be remembered for ever. Even after I'm gone. At the end things were bad, terrible, but in his prime he was a good man, a very good man.' Her voice, already weak with age, trembled further. She tried to keep it strong for Malcolm's sake. 'That goodness deserves some recognition.'

'We'll make sure that happens.'

'I have to be getting back now.' Polly spoke rapidly. 'Thank you for the tea and cake. I've got some cleaning up to do.' She pushed the carrier bag towards Polly and put her hand on the table to lever herself up into a standing position. Then she remembered. 'Could you order me a taxi, please? I've got the money to pay.'

'Cleaning up? At this time of night?'

Polly felt her face crumple with unshed tears and she turned her head away from Vanessa and Stephen. 'Cleaning up,' she repeated. Her voice turned into a whisper. 'Cleaning up vomit. I . . . I killed Malcolm.'

'Killed him? When?' Vanessa's voice lost its comfortable tone.

'Tonight, this evening. It's all blurred.' Polly sank back down into the chair. Continuing with life was too much of an effort. She wanted it to end here and now.

In front of her, Vanessa was struggling with her facial expression. After displaying and then immediately trying to hide outright shock, she'd glanced at Stephen, frowned and then composed herself into sympathy and understanding. It was impossible to know whether this last expression was genuine.

'Tell me what happened, Polly, love. Where do you live?'

Even though Vanessa felt like a friend, she couldn't tell her that. She couldn't have an army of officials carting Malcolm away before she'd had chance to put him to rights and say a proper goodbye. And before she'd had chance to join him. 'The authorities will find out in due course.'

'You can't keep something like this a secret,' Stephen said. Polly wished he wasn't there. She was pleased to see Vanessa give him a look, as though telling him off for butting in.

An awkward silence hung over the table. Then Vanessa filled the void.

'No problem. There's no hurry for anybody else to know.' She touched Polly's hand. 'I'll get us another piece of cake and then you tell us more about Malcolm. From when we've talked before, I know he was a good man. But I could also see things were getting difficult for you.'

'Yes.' There was nothing to lose by telling them what life had been like recently.

Over the last couple of months, Polly had realised she couldn't go on caring for Malcolm. He was becoming aggressive more frequently. It wasn't his fault, he just didn't understand daily life any more or what was happening to him, as his brain functioned less and less well. Neither Malcolm nor she had any quality of life. There was only one solution — they must both pass away together so they'd arrive in heaven hand in hand and everything would be lovely again, like it used to be. Melissa would be upset when she realised what her mother had done but she'd still have her own family and her birth mother. We expect our parents to die before us and she'd get over it.

For them to pass over together, Polly couldn't leave anything to chance — she had to make sure that Malcolm was dead before she took an overdose herself. If he survived and she died, Melissa would've had him in a home with a click of her fingers, thinking it was for the best. And then Malcolm would be either ill-treated or ignored.

Earlier that evening, Polly crushed up all the sleeping pills she'd been hoarding. Half went in Malcolm's cocoa and half were saved for her to take afterwards. Polly was nervous and got them both ready for bed earlier than usual. Malcolm was calm and, unusually, seemed to be aware of who Polly was. They sat in bed, side by side, and he stroked her cheek with his finger tip like he used to before he got ill. He made little 'p' noises with his lips, as though he was trying to say her name. She squeezed his hand and he squeezed back. For a fleeting moment Polly wondered if he was about to make some miraculous recovery and she should pour his cocoa away. Then he turned from her, clutched the edge of the quilt and started working it in his hands, like he couldn't keep them still.

'Drink your cocoa, Malcolm.' She kissed his forehead and handed him his red plastic beaker with the spout lid.

She intended to stay awake and watch over him all night; she wanted to be consciously with him when he took his last breath. But she must have fallen asleep because Malcolm woke her at 10.15 p.m. He was being sick. It was too difficult to manoeuvre her husband out of bed and into the bathroom. Polly fetched a bowl but the worst was over. He laid back down and clutched the quilt. He seemed unaware of the smelly mess around him. She wiped his face and hands with a damp cloth. The pills wouldn't kill him now that half of them were no longer in his stomach. She wondered about giving him her half of the tablets as well but then she wouldn't be able to go to heaven with him. He smiled at her like a small child. Polly didn't think before her next action.

She took the pillow from her side of the bed, placed it over his face and pressed hard. She leaned on it with all her weight. His grunts were muffled, his hands waved and his legs kicked beneath the quilt. She thought he was going to push her off but the vomiting must have sapped his strength. Gradually the struggling stopped. Polly kept all her weight on the pillow for another ten minutes — she had to be sure he was dead. Then she removed the pillow. He looked peaceful and she knew she'd done the right thing. She kissed him, straightened the bedclothes and went downstairs. She planned to clean up the bed and Malcolm as best she could, make tea and take her share of the pills. Polly knew her stomach was strong and she'd keep the tablets down.

Then she thought about Vanessa and the museum. It was a way of getting Malcolm's life remembered. Despite how he had become in the end, Polly was immensely proud of her husband. He was a good man, a very good man, and it shouldn't have been necessary to end his life in such a humiliating way. She would be dead as well by the morning, therefore she had to take the slippers tonight. Polly abandoned making tea. Melissa had once given her the business card of a taxi firm, in case there was an emergency and Melissa couldn't be reached. It was too late for catching buses. Polly dialled the number for the first time.

* * *

The story was shocking and now Polly was gathering herself together, getting ready to leave. She was returning to her dead husband. She was going to kill herself and I didn't know how to stop her.

'Could you order a taxi for me, please?' Polly seemed to have found a new burst of energy and the ability to organise herself. 'There's a number on this bit of card but I haven't got a phone.'

'Hang on a minute, Polly, love,' I said. 'Let's talk some more.' From the corner of my eye I could see Stephen indicating the café counter with a directional nod of his head.

Polly opened her mouth in protest but, like a policeman on point duty, I held up my hand to stop her.

'We'll phone on our way out, from the reception desk upstairs,' Stephen said. 'But before we go, Vanessa and I need to tidy up and load these cups in the dishwasher. You stay sitting there and we'll be back with you in a minute.'

It was one in the morning but adrenalin was pumping through my body, drowning the tiredness I should be feeling. I hadn't anticipated a life or death drama in the museum. All the dramas should have been long since over and our visitors looking for a way to move forward, with hope. But now we had the sudden responsibility of stopping Polly's suicide and turning in a murderer to the police.

Stephen propelled me to the far corner of the kitchen area, the place where we stored the non-perishables like sugar, serviettes and amaretti biscuits.

'You've spoken to her before, a few times. Do you believe her?' he asked.

'I've met Malcolm as well. The last time was a while back. I didn't see him being violent but he wouldn't be easy for someone her age to look after. Yes, I believe her.'

'Shit.'

'We have to call the police. We can't let her go home to die. But I don't want her locked up either.' I pulled a serviette from a holder on the counter and blew my nose. Emotion threatened to overwhelm me. 'It was a mercy killing done out of love.'

'They'll take ages to arrive at this time of night.' He patted my arm. 'I'll drive her to the police station. Tell them the whole story and hope they'll be lenient.'

I nodded, grateful that I wouldn't have to be the one to turn her in. 'I'll wait here. You'll come back and tell me how you got on?'

'Yes.'

I watched him walk over to Polly. There was a long conversation that I couldn't hear and then Stephen came back to me.

'She's trying to bribe us into letting her go home and not calling the police.' He looked over his shoulder at Polly.

'What do you mean "bribe"?'

'Apparently, she's got £50,000 in savings accounts, spread across five different building societies. The pass books are in her handbag and she never goes anywhere without them. She says that one of us can go with her first thing in the morning and she'll draw out all the cash and hand it straight to us. All she asks is that we leave her with enough money to get home so that she can take her share of the pills.'

Things were becoming even more unreal. I looked across at her sitting in an old coat and looking like a bag lady. Polly caught my eye. She raised her hand and in it was an old-fashioned bank book.

'She looks like a pauper! We can't take her money and then let her take her own life.'

'I'm so glad you said that.'

'So, what do we do now?'

'I'm struggling to think straight,' Stephen said. 'It's gone one-thirty in the morning. I'm tired and this evening's been a turning point for me: I've finally realised what I'm ready for in life.' He paused, looked me straight in the eye and then continued. 'But it's likely to be snatched away by someone else before I find the courage to act. And now an old lady turns up and confesses to murder . . .'

I couldn't follow what he was saying. He was right; it had been a very long day and night. 'We've both had enough for one day. Let's lock up here and both go with her to the police station,' I said. 'She's an old lady and it was a mercy killing. They'll be lenient.'

Polly sobbed in the car. She sat with me on the back seat and I could do nothing to comfort her.

Dawn was breaking when we finished at the police station. We'd explained all that we could. Polly's daughter Melissa had been contacted and was on her way. A team had been sent to Polly's house. There was nothing more to be done by us. Stephen seemed to have been revived by several paper cups of police coffee and the return of daylight.

'Is it worth going home?' I asked. 'I should be getting up in half an hour for work.'

Stephen looked me up and down with a critical eye. 'You do look nice in that dress. But do you really want to face the public all day in last night's party wear? I'll drop you off at home. Have a shower, get changed and eat some breakfast.'

CHAPTER TWENTY-FIVE

I stood under the shower for a long time and tried to make sense of the previous day and night. The kiss with Dave had been a shock. He and I had slotted back together again effortlessly. But Dave had ended our marriage once and could do it again. Were his feelings genuine or was he after an easy route back to a convenient domestic arrangement? Was I after that too — given that Stephen and Joanne seemed about to become an item?

Polly's confession was an example of real true love. She'd nurtured and nursed Malcolm for as long as possible. Then, to stop them suffering the painful separation a specialist nursing home would bring, she'd gently ended his life and prepared to go with him. Would it have been better if she'd gone ahead with her plan without turning up at the museum? Or had that visit been a cry for help? No, she'd expected to find no-one there. It wasn't a cry for help; she really had wanted to die. And we'd scuppered her plans.

'Don't settle for second best,' my mother once said when I was talked into a double date. My friend had already bagged the handsome one and I was left trying to make conversation with his mate, who talked me through the history of the football league without pausing for breath. After that I'd followed

Mum's advice and become picky about men. Except now I was tempted to take the easy option, even though there was someone else who ignited every nerve in my body.

Stephen made me feel as though I was on the roller coaster of a crush on the best-looking boy in the school. Sometimes I felt I was in with a chance. Other times I felt I could never live up to what he'd had with Trish or what he was possibly building up to with Joanne. But being with Stephen made me excited about all the possibilities life can bring.

Towelling my hair, I tried to shake away the confusion and prepare for another day of coffee, cakes and museum donors.

'You're a naughty stop out.' Dave was eating cereal when I went in the kitchen to put the kettle on. 'Did you stay at Stephen's last night?' He grinned and winked at me but there was no mistaking the interrogation in his voice. Our kiss had meant something to him.

I could have retorted that was a case of the pot calling the kettle black. Or I could've explained about Polly. After a night without sleep and a mind that couldn't think straight, I didn't have the energy for either. 'On second thoughts I'll have breakfast at the museum.' I scooted out the door with a quick wave.

* * *

'Did you see the message from Maxine?' Stephen had already opened up and was behind the reception desk looking too bright-eyed, bushy-tailed and silver fox like for someone who'd had no sleep.

'What? I haven't had time to look at my phone.'

'She's had the baby, a couple of weeks early. There's a picture.' Stephen passed me his mobile.

The infant was an adorable little bundle wrapped in a pale blue blanket. I wanted to hold him in my arms and make cooing noises. Memories of Liam and our life as a family came flooding back. Dave had been a good dad. He never flinched at changing nappies, pushing the pram or reading stories. When Liam was in his teens, the pair had gone regularly to Blues matches. Football had been their special bond. Dave had supported Liam in everything he wanted to do, including emigrating to Canada, even though neither of us was really in favour of it. Had the gap left by Liam, precipitated Dave's affair? Had Liam been the only glue holding us together?

'*Michael. Born 10.15 p.m. Weight 7lb 6 oz. We'll be in hospital a couple of days. Please visit,*' I read aloud and then realised the significance of the time. '10.15 p.m. Michael was born as Malcolm died.'

Stephen nodded. 'The circle of life. Will we go this evening?'

'Yes and I'll be taking my melt-in-the-mouth bread pudding to show off.'

* * *

Joanne arrived just before we locked up for the day.

'Glad I caught you,' she said and then looked at Stephen. 'I really enjoyed last night. Can I collect my cake tins?'

'Come with me.' Stephen jumped in before I could say a word and I was left twiddling my thumbs on the reception desk. When they didn't return after a couple of minutes, I opened the door at the top of the stairwell and listened. Their voices were indistinct. Stephen said something and Joanne laughed. Then she spoke but her words were drowned by the clatter of tins. Why was it taking them so long? Suddenly they were coming back upstairs and I carefully let the door swing shut.

Joanne said goodbye to Stephen out in the lobby. He was grinning like a Cheshire cat when he came back through the door.

'For a quiet girl,' he said, 'she's got a wicked sense of humour.'

He didn't elaborate and I didn't ask.

* * *

Stephen drove us around the hospital car park twice before spotting a car pull out of a white painted rectangle. He reversed to take its place. We followed the arrows to the maternity department, me holding a flimsy white cardboard box holding four chunks of bread pudding and Stephen clutching a cellophane wrapped bouquet of pink carnations. We paused by the anti-bacterial gel dispenser to work the sticky clear film into our skin.

Maxine spotted us as soon as we entered the ward and waved. She was propped on pillows looking pale and tired but with a huge grin on her face. Adrian was sat on the bedside chair with the bundle from the photo in his arms.

'Well done, you!' Stephen gave Maxine's shoulder a gentle punch.

I bent over the bed and gave her a hug. 'I am so, so pleased for you.' I looked at Adrian. 'For both of you.' Then I was too choked to speak. My shoulders were moving with sobs that I didn't want to let out. This was a joyous occasion not a time for hippo-wallowing in the sadness of Maxine's earlier life. Stephen had found another chair from somewhere. He sat me down gently.

'Don't cry,' Maxine said. 'You've helped me face this moment without all those ghouls from the past tormenting me. Nothing that happened with Daniel can be undone but, thanks to you and the museum, I'm in a much better place now. Mum and Dad have already been to see me and Michael. They were lovely. Dad explained they were going to invest a small sum in Michael's name so that by the time he's eighteen it will be a useful amount to get him started at university or in whatever he chooses to do.'

'Do you want to hold him?' Adrian asked.

I nodded, still not trusting my voice to speak. Adrian gently placed the bundle in my arms.

'You need to make sure you support his head,' he explained.

I smiled. New parents were all the same; they forgot that other people had had babies and knew the basics of infant care. To all of us, our own babies are the most precious, unique thing in the world and we can't take the risk that the people with whom we entrust our treasure, don't know how to properly care for it.

Michael's eyes were shut. His lips were making the tiniest of movements. I ran my finger across his soft cheek. He opened both blue eyes and stared at me.

'You are so beautiful and perfect,' I whispered. 'I know you're going to make Mummy and Daddy so proud.' A tear fell from me onto his skin. I blotted it with my finger before anybody could see.

'Also' — Maxine was still talking about her parents — 'Dad said he's just done the same thing for Daniel. Only the amount he's invested is a bit more, to make up for the missed years of interest or whatever. When Daniel's eighteen, I'll trace him and there'll be a monetary gift from his maternal birth grandparents to help him on his way. Don't you think that was a lovely thing for them to do?'

I couldn't stop the tears any longer. 'I'm sorry. Stephen, would you take Michael?' I said.

Adrian stood up quickly before either of us could move. 'It's OK. Best if I manage the transfer.'

Maxine grinned at me knowingly. I smiled through the tears. Happy that she'd found a man so keen to protect his young.

'I used to hold one baby in the crook of each arm,' Stephen said. 'It feels odd just having one. Imagine — you two will only have half as much work as Trish and me. And you'll get twice as much sleep as we did. Having a baby is going to be a walk in the park for you!'

He was keeping it light but there was a slight tightness to his voice.

Michael stirred, waved clenched fists and began to mewl.

'Feeding time,' announced Adrian. 'I'll do the transfer again.'

'Do you want me to leave?' Stephen asked as Maxine began to unfasten the top of her nightdress.

'If you just want to look away while I get him to latch on that would be fine. That's the bit we're having trouble mastering, isn't it, my little one?'

I went to stand with Stephen at the end of the bed.

'OK?' I asked.

'I think I'm doing better than you.' He took my hand and squeezed it. There were unshed tears in his eyes. I squeezed back. His thumb rubbed against my skin. I didn't want to let go even though he only wanted comfort from thinking about the twins and Trish.

'OK, you can look now.'

We dropped hands and went back to our seats. Michael was settled contentedly at his mother's breast.

'So, what have I missed at the museum? I sense there's been a subtle change?'

'What?' I asked.

'In you two. You both look absolutely shattered. You look worse than I feel and I've just given birth and spent the night learning to breastfeed. *And* you're standing closer together. What's been going on?' Maxine sat forward eagerly, almost dislodging baby Michael from her breast. 'You haven't spent the night together, have you?!'

'No!' I leaned away from Stephen like I'd been scalded. 'But we didn't have any sleep.'

I let Stephen tell her and Adrian about the singles' night and the traumatic time with Polly.

'I don't know what to say.' Maxine handed Michael to Adrian who laid the milk-drunk infant in the plastic crib. 'That poor old soul. She's a lovely lady.'

We fell silent for a minute and then Maxine's gossipy enthusiasm came back at our expense. 'But you two would make a great couple, honestly. It's the way you look at each other.'

We looked at each other. And then away again quickly. But the eye contact had been made.

'She seriously smooched with Dave last night,' Stephen said, as though he wanted to underline the fact that he and I could never be a couple.

Maxine frowned. 'Was that a good idea?'

Three pairs of eyes were questioning me.

'I . . . well, he was there and a girl gets lonely.' I tried to fob them off lightly without revealing how confused I felt about everything. Thirty years of shared experience plus a son together had created a mighty strong link between Dave and me. There was no sainted ghost of Trish to compare myself to and no current competition. When Stephen had disappeared to clean up that beer, I didn't even consider saying no to Dave. With other couples taking to the dance floor it would've seemed petty. But at that point I hadn't known he would kiss me.

'Stephen is the better man,' Maxine pronounced.

He said nothing and I couldn't look in his direction. Stephen didn't want cast-offs. And he was still in love with Trish, who, if she'd lived, would've aged much better and been more successful than me at running her own business. And he had something budding with Joanne.

'We need to go. Early night and all that.' I stood up to escape further embarrassment and then suddenly remembered the little white boxes I'd plonked on Maxine's bedside cabinet. 'I almost forgot. I am now a master bread pudding baker. These will soon have you and baby Michael up to full strength.'

Maxine looked suitably impressed.

Stephen didn't start the engine when we got in the car. Instead, he took my hand and looked me in the eye. The tingle felt like my finger had been stuck in the cigarette lighter.

'Maxine was only after making a bit of gossip,' he said. 'She doesn't have a clue about our private lives. But putting her attempts at matchmaking to one side, you need to know that the museum and you, you especially, have enabled me to face the future and be my true self. You know about Trish and the boys but you don't drown me in pity and sad looks. Thank you for that.'

He removed his hand and started the ignition. I touched the skin where his hand had been and where I wished it still

was. He wanted to put Maxine's matchmaking to one side —
that was his way of telling me we were just friends.

* * *

Dave had the tea on when I walked into the kitchen. He gave
me a hug. Worn out after thirty-six hours without sleep, I
automatically put my arms around him too.

'Sorry,' he said. 'Sorry for the snide remark this morning.
I jumped to conclusions without giving you time to explain.'

I told him about Polly and spending the early hours at
the police station.

'That's dreadful. It just goes to show we should make
the most of life now.'

I wondered if that's what he'd thought when he went off
with his fancy woman. Seize the day! And don't worry what
harm you might be doing to others.

'I'll be honest with you. That kiss last night,' he said. 'Well,
it was obvious we both enjoyed it. So, when I saw Stephen drop
you off this morning, it felt like a kick in the teeth.'

I looked at the floor, unable to voice my confusion over
him and Stephen.

'I was thinking,' Dave continued. 'When Maxine's back
at work, why don't we leave the museum in the hands of her
and Stephen and jet off to Canada to see Liam? We'll be a
family again.'

'But we're divorced. How can we be a family?' I remembered what Liam had said to me a few months earlier and
wondered if they'd been speaking to each other.

'The holiday will give us time together. Time to heal
the rift. New surroundings so we're not reminded of what's
gone before. Liam being there will be a symbol of what we
created and what binds us together. People have been known
to remarry the same person.'

I sat down on the hard wood of a kitchen chair. My
ex-husband was giving me the opportunity to take him back.
I couldn't think straight. I needed to make an excuse.

'I'm living on a shoestring, barely taking any wage from the museum. A holiday isn't a priority.'

'The air fares are my treat. You deserve a break; that place is draining you, emotionally and financially. If I had the money, I'd take you first class and we'd stop over somewhere — make it a proper away from it all experience.'

'I wouldn't say no to first class but it'll have to wait for a lottery win.' I spoke flippantly, my brain was exhausted.

'A lottery win would mean you could give up the museum and become a lady of leisure.'

'No.' I was alert again. 'A lottery win would mean expansion of the museum, a pay rise for Maxine and a proper job for Stephen.'

Dave frowned. I ignored his disapproval. It was my museum. It was my life.

* * *

The following day a package arrived at the museum which reinforced my belief in what I was trying to achieve. It contained several vibrantly-coloured post cards from exotic destinations: Vietnam, Thailand, Australia, plus a letter and a well-thumbed glossy sales brochure for a development of new flats in Birmingham's Jewellery Quarter, just down the road from the museum. The letter was handwritten.

Dear Vanessa,

Please accept my good news story for the Little Museum of Hope. Three years ago I used all my savings, plus a generous contribution from my parents to put down a deposit on one of these flats and I took the largest mortgage the bank would allow. For eighteen months I struggled to make ends meet. It was a difficult existence. All I saw was the inside of my flat — I work from home and I couldn't afford to go out at night or to take a holiday or even the train fare to visit family. Then my sister got married and I missed two mortgage payments so that I could buy a suit, get the couple a present, travel to the wedding (held in Devon where my parents still live) and stay over with the wedding party at a hotel. After that, trying to pay the mortgage became a game of catch-up which I lost.

Nine months ago, I was forced to sell the flat at a loss. It should have been the worst time ever but it was the catalyst for happiness. I was able to pay back my parents, which took an enormous weight of guilt and shame from my shoulders. Most of my share of the deposit was gone but there was enough for a plane ticket and my first few nights in a hostel. I had to live with Mum and Dad while visas and paperwork got sorted out but the smell of freedom was like breathing pure oxygen.

Since I started travelling, I've met some fantastic people and worked as a cleaner, barman and waiter — and who knows what adventure is waiting around the next corner!

Losing that flat is the best thing that ever happened to me. I read about your museum in the Jewellery Quarter e-newsletter which I'm still subscribed to. It would be wonderful if you could display my story and show people that something which seems like a catastrophe at the time can not only have a silver lining but also a gold and platinum one too!

All the best,

Paul

I put the letter down and punched the air in triumph. It was messages of hope, like this one, that the museum really needed. This was a step nearer to the museum becoming somewhere that people could describe as their 'happy place'. It didn't matter that Dave couldn't grasp the concept behind Little Museum of Hope because more and more people were getting behind us. And that was enough for me.

CHAPTER TWENTY-SIX

September
Karen

Karen nearly walked straight back out when she saw how empty the museum café was. Even though it was lunchtime the place was deserted. Tears were threatening and she wanted somewhere noisy, with people to hide behind, not a place where her sobbing would be audible and obvious. But time was short and she'd promised Tim she'd come. Promised him she'd exorcise her past for the good of their future. He'd planned to be here too, for moral support, but his editor had sent him to a police incident on the M6, near Spaghetti. So, she was alone and, if truth be told, glad. Talking in front of him would have meant censoring herself, which defeated the object of coming.

A fabricated dentist's appointment had given her an extra-long lunch hour but fifteen minutes of that had been lost on the trek from her Colmore Row office to the Jewellery Quarter. Then she'd wasted more time walking up and down the street outside, totally failing to see the small signboard proclaiming "Little Museum of Hope". The reception person in the Pen Room Museum had finally pointed her in the right direction.

Now she wished she hadn't come. She could fake it. Take a selfie outside with the museum sign and then pretend to Tim the museum didn't think her donation and story were appropriate to display in a place visited by young people. Tim's jar of mud from Glastonbury was relatable but who would empathise with the terrible thing she'd done? There'd be no sudden celestial forgiveness in exchange for donating a worthless object to this odd museum. She should've thrown the obsolete phone in the bin ages ago and pretended that none of it ever happened. But it's not easy to live with a guilty conscience. Especially not when you see your victim in the office every day.

A table in the corner of the café was as hidden as she could get. Karen sat down and took a serviette from the stainless steel holder. She dabbed at the corners of her eyes, if tears ruined her make-up, she'd have no time to redo her face before going back to the office. A sudden beep and vibration from her handbag made her sigh. She wanted to ignore it but she was still on works' time. It was a text asking about the location of a client file. She responded and then pulled a second phone from her bag and placed it next to the first. There was less than a decade between their dates of manufacture but one was almost a mini-computer and the other would only cope with basic text and voice communication.

'Can I help you?'

The waitress made Karen jump.

'Tea? Coffee? Cake?'

There was no time for anything complicated. Something comfortingly sweet with an energy boost was what Karen needed. 'Coffee,' she said, 'and a piece of double chocolate gateau, please.'

The waitress brought a mug and a huge piece of cake. Uninvited, she sat down opposite Karen. It was an invasion of her personal space when she was feeling so fragile. Tim had said the lady at the museum was nice but she might not be so nice when she heard what Karen had done.

'Are you donating today, love?'

Karen nodded.

'Would you like to talk about it?' The waitress looked about ten years older than Karen herself and, despite the intrusive question, her voice was strangely comforting. 'It can help to know that someone at the museum is aware of the story behind the object you're donating.'

'It's not something I'm proud of.'

'We don't judge.'

Karen was unsure about confessing all to this woman. It didn't seem very official and museum-like.

'Let's start with your name, love. I'm Vanessa.'

'Karen.' She studied her coffee and chocolate cake and then looked up at Vanessa, wondering whether and how to start. Vanessa was rounded and soft, with hair that was going grey gracefully instead of snatching at youth from a bottle — a typical storybook grandmother who would make sure everything turned out alright in the end. Karen knew she'd never have that same content and caring aura. Whether she liked it or not, she would always project the harsh image of elbowing her way towards whatever she wanted, be that in her career or life generally. Few people knew she had the same insecure feelings as everyone else on the inside.

She took a bite of the chocolate sponge, being careful not to let the sweet buttercream fall in a messy dollop on the skirt of her grey business suit. The story of the mobile phone wasn't something she could tell her mother or her best friend. Tim knew the rough gist, not all the details. He should know, but she wasn't brave enough to say the words aloud and watch his expression. If he chose to find out, he could come here to read about it on his own and decide whether he still wanted to be with her.

An outsider, like Vanessa, would be the perfect listener. Tears were still not far away and there was a lump in her throat. Talking about it would release the emotion and she didn't want to go back to the office all red-faced and blotchy. Maybe she should leave now before crying made her face irreparable.

'Has a man treated you badly somewhere along the way? It's usually all their fault, isn't it?' It seemed Vanessa wasn't going to let her leave without getting to the bottom of the story.

Karen took a deep breath. 'You could say there were three of us in our relationship.' She fiddled with the older mobile. 'I'm not good at sharing and, in an unforgiveable burst of anger, I turned it all into a much worse mess. I've felt bad about it ever since and don't know how to make that bad feeling go away. I'm fed up of carrying the guilt around.'

Now she'd started talking, it felt as though a floodgate had opened and she didn't have the strength to push it shut again. Full disclosure was the only way forward.

Karen was thirty-eight and not in a relationship when the catalyst for future events was set in motion. There'd been men in the past, she'd even lived with one guy for eighteen months and that only ended because he wanted to get married and she wanted them to stay as they were. If only she'd walked down the aisle with him, none of this would've happened. But at the time she was riding the crest of a wave at work and the last thing she wanted was to become known merely as someone's wife and start producing babies. Lots of her university friends were doing that. Karen couldn't understand why they were abandoning the careers they'd striven for and then switching to part-time or second-best jobs. She swore she'd never do it. And she never had. Whether that had been the right decision she couldn't say and it was too late for second thoughts now.

When John Crewe joined the company as the new sales manager and her new boss, he made an immediate impact on her, both professionally and personally. He was given the desk opposite her.

'What are the coffee arrangements around here?' was his first question and she showed him their small kitchen with the dodgy microwave and the fridge, empty except for a four-pinter of milk, two out-of-date yoghurts and a couple of opaque lunchboxes, too full of green leaves to be a real person's meal.

He insisted on making all the coffee for their team for a week.

'I want to get it right,' he said, 'and not still be asking in a month's time who has the kitten mug and forgetting who takes sugar and who has sweeteners.'

John never asked anyone to do anything he wouldn't do himself, nor did he expect people to stay late to finish something, unless he also worked late. It was during occasional after-hours working that Karen got to know John better. He often talked proudly of his two teenaged daughters. Their photos, plus another of Fiona, his wife, were on his desk. Karen met Fiona a couple of times as she dropped or collected John from the office before his company car arrived. She was ordinary looking but sweet-natured and friendly.

A few months after joining the company, John celebrated his fortieth birthday and included his new colleagues in the invites to a party in a local hotel. Fiona was a flushed and sparkling hostess and, more than once, Karen noticed her and John communicate with only a glance. She'd never felt envious of a comfortably married couple before but suddenly there it was, starting to smoulder in her chest. She wanted to feel special to someone. Batting the uncomfortable emotion away, she joined her workmates on the dance floor and tried to lose herself in the music.

John shook hands with everyone as they left and Fiona thanked them for coming. Karen felt a firm squeeze on her hand. Did John keep hold for slightly longer than was necessary? Or was alcohol and wishful thinking affecting her judgement of time? Only a few years ago, John would have been the classic tall, dark, handsome hero but now his sprinkling of grey hairs and the creeping creases around his eyes gave him a classy, distinguished look. He had the broad-shouldered physique of a sportsman. That night, Karen didn't turn out the light until she knew sleep would claim her immediately; her brain didn't want time to dwell on how much she fancied her boss. Fancying your boss, especially one that was married, was an absolute no-no in Karen's mind.

On the Monday following the party, John brought a giant cake into work and he got the drinks in at lunchtime. A new intern started the same day. Just out of university, the young girl was nervous and unable to grasp how to display the team's sales figures in a spreadsheet. Anyone else would've passed the girl onto someone more junior to learn the ropes but Karen watched John explain everything with the utmost patience until the new girl was confident with her task. He then asked her to take the cake around the office with him so she got a chance to meet everyone. If people chose life partners in the same way that they chose horses, that is, for temperament as well as looks, Fiona had secured a man who ticked all the boxes. Again, Karen had had to squash feelings of envy.

She became uncomfortably aware of Vanessa watching her across the table. This confession was only going to get worse. Karen took a mouthful of chocolate gateau and closed her eyes. If she could turn back time to that point, she would have done things differently. Or, if she'd met Tim from the newspaper years earlier, things might have been different. She opened her eyes and watched Vanessa scribbling in a notebook. She played with the two mobile phones on the tabletop in front of her.

'I should have recognised the danger in having feelings for a colleague,' Karen told Vanessa. 'I should have resigned and looked for a new job. It wouldn't have been difficult; my skill set was very transferable.'

She watched Vanessa's face, waiting for words of judgement.

'Whatever you're about to tell me, I think you're incredibly brave to come here today,' the older woman said.

Karen gave a narrow smile; she didn't feel brave. She felt like a sinner going to confession without the reward of absolution or penance. She took another mouthful of coffee and a bite of chocolate cake and continued her story.

Karen didn't pounce on John or do anything overt to tempt him from his marriage. They worked closely together and their friendship developed naturally through shared small talk about their lives.

'Your Laura must be doing GCSEs this year,' Karen said to him once. 'How's it going? Is it stressful in your house now?'

'Tell me about it. She's moody and keeps telling us that life is much harder and more competitive for her than it ever was for me and her mother.'

Whenever John mentioned Fiona, Karen felt that stab of envy and tried to steer the conversation down another track.

'It'll all be over, come July, won't it?' she said.

'Yes, and I can't complain really. Both our girls are diamonds — apart from the odd messy bedroom they don't cause us any trouble. Laura represents the county at netball and Robyn is doing really well at the piano for a 13-year-old — she wants to do music at uni.'

'Wow! Two child geniuses — you must have good genes. And soon you'll be having all the boyfriend malarkey,' she said. 'I bet you'll be a typical father — no-one will ever be good enough for your daughters!'

He laughed and Karen told him how, as a 16-year-old, she'd tried to sneak boys from school up to her bedroom but no sooner had they got settled in for a pleasant snog than her mother would be banging on the door.

'Nothing was guaranteed to cool a young stud's ardour quicker than my mum's permed head poking around the door with the offer of jam sandwiches and milk in front of *Blue Peter*.'

He laughed and slid his office chair closer to her as he leant over to point out some figures on the computer screen. Their shoulders were touching and when either of them moved, their thighs brushed together as well. For Karen, the electricity was so strong, she thought sparks must be visible. John held his position but she had no idea whether he felt the same attraction. He carried on talking her through the numbers for the presentation later that day.

After a while he glanced from the screen to Karen's face and started to comment on the total of one of the spreadsheet columns but as his eyes locked on hers, he must have read her unspoken feelings. He stumbled over his words. Karen's heart thudded and she felt like a teenager again. The heat of a flush rose on her cheeks. This was the most embarrassing thing that had ever happened to her. John could be in no doubt now that she found him attractive. From his open body language and facial expression, he seemed to fancy her too. He was a happily married man for God's sake. They had to find a way back from this to a normal working relationship. It was possible. Lots of married men find other women attractive and never do anything about it because they love their wives.

As John mused over the conclusion for his presentation, his tongue skimmed his lips. Karen had to look the other way.

After he'd closed the spreadsheet, she offered to get them coffee, hoping that a break from his presence would enable her to switch off the hormones or whatever chemical it was shouting in her brain: 'Attractive man! Attractive man!' She went to the Ladies on her way to the kitchen and splashed her wrists with ice cold water.

Karen carried the mugs back to his desk. As he took his from her, emblazoned with "The World's Best Dad", their fingers touched. The resurging spark made Karen slop hot liquid over the rims of the mugs. John momentarily met her eye and then she was certain he felt the same way as her. She made a point of wheeling her chair away from his and prayed no-one else around them had noticed.

Acknowledging their attraction in this unspoken way didn't mean anything had to happen. Even faithful men can't always turn off the 'I fancy you' signals which are the result of thousands of years of evolution. Perhaps she'd casually suggest that she move to another desk, further away from John.

But she didn't have chance to put her relocation plans into action. When Karen got into work the next day there was an email waiting from John. Its contents surprised her. She looked up from her screen, John met her eye and pulled his chair over to her desk.

'Sorry about the short notice,' he said. 'I was going to go on my own to this conference but it would be good to get another opinion on the proceedings. What do you think? Can you put up with two nights in a hotel with me?'

'Do you want to rephrase that?' Karen forced herself to laugh. 'It sounds like you're propositioning me!'

'Sorry. That came out all wrong but you know what I mean. It's next week — can you make it?'

She had no plans that couldn't be changed but she hesitated. Being away together for two whole days might lead to a situation from which there would be no going back. Or it might purely be work.

'It would be good from your career development point of view.' He looked her in the eye and her stomach lurched.

'OK.' She wasn't sure what she was agreeing to.

On the first night of the conference, after the last speaker, she pleaded tiredness to John.

'Drinking with all these overweight men in suits doesn't do anything for me,' she said, 'and I need my beauty sleep.'

'I'll walk you back to your room.'

'There's no need, honestly.'

Their rooms were at opposite ends of the conference hotel, a result of Karen being a late addition to the booking, but John insisted on accompanying her anyway. He stood close as she fiddled with the credit card style key in the bedroom door lock. It might have been his close proximity or her general clumsiness but she couldn't get the thing to work.

'Let me help.' He placed his hand over hers and then gently applied pressure to push the card downwards.

There was a shot of electric tension as their skin touched. A tiny green light went on below the door lock and they went into the room. Karen pushed the key card into the electricity slot on the wall and turned to face him, standing between John and the main part of the bedroom.

'Thanks,' she said. 'I'll be fine now.'

He took a step towards her. The expectation between them was palpable.

'Maybe we should compare notes on this evening's speakers while it's still fresh in our minds,' he said. 'But say if you'd prefer me to leave.'

He was giving her a way out. She could be his conscience and send him away. Or she could forget he was married — looking out for Fiona wasn't her responsibility. They'd both had wine during the evening, maybe it clouded their judgement.

'A nightcap and a debrief won't hurt,' she said.

'There's just one problem.' John followed her past the bathroom door and plonked himself on the bed. 'This hotel doesn't have minibars. I think they want us spending our money downstairs.'

'What about coffee?' She pointed at the kettle and bowl of instant sachets. 'Or room service?'

'I'll order a bottle of red.' He picked up the phone. 'That's what you were drinking with the meal, isn't it?'

While they waited for the wine, John used his mobile to call home.

'They'll be expecting me to ring at this time,' he said apologetically.

Listening to him catching up on his family's day was awkward. Perhaps she should tell him to leave. She went and stood by the window with her back to him. The heavy beige curtains were still open and the lights of the city were laid out below like a free illuminations show. Karen had never slept with a married man before. It was wrong but there was an immense tug of physical attraction coursing through her body. She hadn't had a relationship with anyone for several months and the knowledge that John found her attractive was a powerful aphrodisiac.

'I gave the bar a miss,' he was saying to his wife. 'I'm whacked out. I'm going to watch the news and then go to bed.'

Karen turned to face him as he ended the call. She wondered how often he'd lied to Fiona. She wanted this to be the first time. She wanted to be something special to him.

Room service knocked and placed the wine and two glasses on the dark wood table that acted as a desk in the bedroom. John poured. Karen kicked her shoes off and they sat side by side at the head end of the bed sipping the rich ruby liquid.

'What did you think of the new sales strategy our European director wants to implement?' John asked.

'He seems to think he's selling baked beans where one-size fits all.' Karen fell in with the shoptalk. 'Bespoke software services need a completely different and more tailored approach.'

John outlined how he thought they might make the director's new strategy work in their regional office. The alcohol, on top of what she'd had at dinner, relaxed Karen and mellowed her inhibitions. She felt John's hand on her thigh. She chose not to move it. Being in the strange hotel room made her feel like an actress in a film. She didn't feel like Karen from the Sales Technical Support team; she felt she was playing a part. John put his wine glass down on the bedside cabinet and removed her drink to the same place.

'We don't want any spills on this virgin white bed linen,' he said.

'I don't think it's going to stay virgin much longer.' Her voice was almost a whisper and her whole body hummed at the thought of what was about to happen.

Their mouths met and John's arms were around her. For several minutes they kissed and ran their fingers over each other's faces.

Then John pulled away from her abruptly. 'Should we be doing this?'

Reality surged in. 'It's your choice.' She didn't add that he'd made the first move. Her heart thudded with both the dreadful fear he was about to walk out on her and the wonderful anticipation of what would happen if he stayed. 'You're the one who's married.'

She desperately wanted him to stay but sensed he was slipping away from her and back to sweet Fiona.

'It's not that you're unattractive.' He shuffled off the bed. 'You're very attractive. But all I can see in my head is Fiona's distraught face. I want to do it and I don't want to, all at the same time.'

There was nothing Karen could say. Tears of humiliation were pricking. She was the cheap floozy unable to compete with the fragrant wife.

'I need time to get used to the idea of being unfaithful.' He was talking to the floor while he located his shoes.

Karen watched him put his shoes back on, rebutton his shirt and tuck it into his trousers. For a few lovely moments she'd been able to run her fingers through his chest hair, feeling wanted, attractive and feminine. Now none of that applied; she'd been part-used and discarded like the little bottles of shower gel in the bathroom. She'd never be able to face him at work again.

'Sorry but I've really messed up,' he muttered. 'I shouldn't have come into your room.'

She couldn't speak as he peered out the door — checking no-one was looking before he made his escape. Anger and humiliation stopped Karen sleeping. Eventually her thoughts settled and she realised her feeling of rejection was worse because she was already a little in love with John. A tiny part of her wanted them to grow old together, content in each other's company.

Sitting here in the museum café with Vanessa's eyes on her made Karen's cheeks burn at the memory of her stupidity. Maybe Vanessa had already labelled her as a husband thief. 'That's as far as I want to go,' she said.

'There's no hurry. Would ten minutes on your own help? I've got to nip upstairs and check something anyway.'

'Yes. Thanks.'

* * *

I'd left Stephen setting up our first audio-visual display using the public-speaking video on Rose's memory stick. It had been sitting in a cupboard while we worked out the best way of using it.

'It's working,' Stephen said as I reached his side. 'Press that button.'

I pressed and a small black screen came to life showing the backs of several rows of people. A man in a suit, wearing a chain of office, introduced the meeting and explained the agenda. His voice boomed around the museum hall. 'Too loud!' I covered my ears.

Stephen turned it down. 'Do you think headphones would be a good idea? So, it doesn't distract other visitors? Or are there health and safety issues after COVID?'

'Headphones would be good and we can provide cleaning wipes.'

Stephen restarted the video and we watched the awkward silence before Rose walked up to the lectern. She clutched the edges of its slanted top and looked like a rabbit caught in the headlights. I remembered the terror of my few mumbled sentences at the singles' event. Her first words were too quiet to hear and a woman on the left-hand-side at the back put her hand to her ear and leant forward in an exaggerated manner. Rose got the message and raised her voice.

She had been right about the appreciative applause at the end. As it died away the screen went black again.

'That girl should be doing stand-up,' I said. 'And she was so right about her story being inspiring. We never know what we are capable of until we try. I think we should have that emblazoned on the wall in here.'

'We never know what we are capable of until we try,' Stephen repeated slowly. 'I like that.'

CHAPTER TWENTY-SEVEN

Karen gave Vanessa a small smile as she walked back into the café.

'Was that it with John?' the waitress asked as she took her seat at the table again.

Karen shook her head. With hindsight, she should've waited for someone single and wonderful, like Tim, to turn up. But at that point she was careering towards forty and it looked like that might never happen. Sometimes you have to grab what you can, when you can. Karen took another mouthful of gateau and coffee and continued the story.

She joined John at breakfast the next morning. He didn't wave her over or anything — she just dumped herself on him. They were going to have to work together, therefore they'd better get over the embarrassment of last night and relearn how to be platonic colleagues.

'Good morning,' she said brightly.

John nodded at her. He looked terrible, as though he hadn't slept a wink all night.

'I managed to stick the cork back in the wine,' she said. 'But perhaps I should just pour it away — I don't like drinking alone and we have to go home tomorrow.'

John fiddled with a plastic marmalade sachet, pulling at the tab to open it — even though he already had two slices of toast smothered in the golden spread in front of him.

'Let me,' she said. One short, sharp pull and the lid came off.

'Yes, pour it away.' He stood up, ignoring the freshly opened marmalade, and walked off.

His attitude felt like an unjust punishment for something that had never happened and had been at his instigation. John wasn't being fair. Karen swapped her empty plate with his, still laden with marmalade-heavy brown toast. Then she asked the waitress to bring some fresh coffee. She hadn't slept well either and needed something to sustain her through the day.

There was a big dinner that evening with awards and prizes for the best salesmen. Karen didn't qualify because she supplied technical support to the sales team rather than actually selling. She went on sales visits to advise on the bespoke changes that clients requested to the company's software packages.

John, on the other hand, was a master at charming orders out of cash-pressed customers and at the awards ceremony he was presented with a long weekend theatre break in London. Jealousy churned inside Karen at the thought of John and Fiona enjoying it together, their daughters safe at home with their grandparents. Meanwhile she'd know that he'd fancied her but not quite enough and she'd be back to sprucing up her dating website profile. Or maybe after last night's experience she'd give up men for good.

John was seated a few places down the dinner table from her and, of course, Karen had been watching him. He'd drunk nothing but water throughout the meal — he was obviously determined not to give into temptation that night. As soon as was decently possible, Karen left the party and went up to her room without speaking to John. He'd avoided her all day, so there was no point trying to be friendly to him. Thank goodness they'd come to the conference in separate cars — a couple of hours cooped up together on the journey home would've been hellish.

Karen's pride was hurt and never again would she trust the body language, or even the spoken language, of a male. She picked up last night's wine, pulled the cork out and carried it into the bathroom. She paused before pouring it away. If she drank it she might get some sleep tonight instead of constantly replaying what had happened on the bed with John and wondering if it had been her fault. But the habit of drinking alone was a slippery slope; once started it might never stop. She raised the bottle above the sink and began to tilt it.

'Oh, what the hell!' she shouted at the mirror and filled a bathroom tumbler with the rich liquid.

She was halfway down the glass and munching on the mini pack of shortbreads from the hospitality tray when there was a single, sharp knock at the door.

'Wrong room!' she shouted. It had to be. John was the only person in the hotel who knew her and there was no reason for him to come looking for her now. Besides, she'd taken off her business suit to relax with some trashy television and had no intention of answering the door to a stranger in her bra and pants.

'It's me.'

The shock of his voice made her choke on the last bit of biscuit. She didn't want to speak to him. She didn't need formally telling she was rejected; it would be less humiliating if they both continued pretending last night never happened. Perhaps he was at the door to suggest she leave the company to avoid awkward scenes at work and so the temptation for him to stray from his marriage was put well out of his way. If so, he could go to hell; this situation was not of her making.

'Don't worry. You can go to bed safe in the knowledge that I won't breathe a word about last night.' She stood next to the door and raised her voice so he'd be able to hear through the wood. 'We can both pretend it never happened.'

'Let me in!' He knocked again.

She paused, her hand on the door knob.

'Quickly, before someone sees me out here and word gets back to the office.'

He was only worried about his own reputation — why hadn't he just phoned her room to get whatever he needed off his chest?

Karen didn't want her reputation tarnished either, by someone seeing and hearing John shouting through her door. No doubt two and two would be put together to make five. She grabbed her skirt and blouse from the back of the arm-chair and pulled them on. She probably looked a total mess but she didn't care.

John almost fell inside when she opened the door.

'Karen, we have to talk about last night.' He frowned at the drop of red wine remaining in her glass.

'I purposefully kept a clear head,' he said reproachfully. 'I've never been unfaithful to Fiona before. This is a massive thing for me and I'm betraying the trust of three important people.'

She turned her back on him and threw herself face down on the bed. She didn't know why she was crying. It wasn't like there'd been time for them to get attached to each other. Nothing was broken that couldn't be mended. She was over-reacting. You couldn't be in love with someone who'd humiliated you in the way John had.

'You're a married man and last night was a silly mistake,' she mumbled to the pillow. 'Go now, don't make it worse.'

A strong arm gripped her shoulder. John rolled her over and she was staring up into his face. Concern, confusion and something else were etched into his half-frown. His eyes looked directly into hers and she recognised something else: passion. He wanted her. He kissed her, a deep, long and desperate kiss. He really wanted her.

'I can't betray them all for a one-night stand,' he said pulling away. 'In all my life I've never had a one-night stand.'

Karen couldn't bear the way John was blowing hot and cold like this.

'I have to know you're in it for the long run,' he continued.

'What?'

'If we do this, I don't want it to be a dirty little one-night stand. I want there to be some emotion in it. I want there to be a future to it — even though it will have to stay secret.'

Karen felt as though she was riding a roller coaster. Now her heart soared at the thought of John wanting a serious relationship and not just a fling. 'Of course I'm in it for the long run — do you think I'm some kind of whore?'

'I didn't mean it like that.'

He kissed her again. As his tongue probed deeper, his hands were finding their way inside her blouse. They separated for a few seconds and removed their clothes. Then lust took over. There was no clumsy awkwardness, it really did feel like they were made for each other. Sex with John was one of the best experiences she'd ever had.

Afterwards she lay in his arms and he stroked her hair, occasionally leaning over to kiss her gently on the lips.

'I'm so glad I did this stone-cold sober, Karen,' he said.

She was glad too. He'd been influenced by nothing except his true feelings for her. She felt loved, feminine and attractive. What came next for them, she didn't know. He was the married one; it had to be his call how they played things going forward. She was not going to play the part of the mistress desperate for any nuggets of time her lover could spare from his family. After a while John got up and fetched the second tumbler from the bathroom and shared out the remains of the wine.

He put the glasses on the bedside cabinets and bent to kiss her again. He tasted sweet. Then his mobile burst into song and his face lost its lazy postcoital grin. The over-cheerful trilling had been like a cold wind blowing through the room.

Even though the museum café was warm, Karen shivered at the memory. Using a fork, she broke the remains of her chocolate cake into small pieces and chased them around her plate.

'Do you want to carry on?' Vanessa asked.

Karen shook her head.

'He gave you this, didn't he?' Vanessa pointed to the older mobile on the table between them.

'He returned it to me. Originally it was my gift to him.'

'Is that your donation to the museum?'

Karen nodded.

'I know it's difficult but please finish your story, Karen, if you can. It would be a shame to leave the mobile without the museum having the full facts. Everything is displayed anonymously so no-one will ever know who you are.'

'Unless John sees it. Or his wife.'

'They know the story already.'

'Or Tim. He knows I'm ashamed of an office affair but he doesn't know exactly how it ended. He doesn't know how very badly I behaved.'

'I think you want him to know, don't you, love?'

Karen nodded and blinked back the tears. 'I want a relationship that's totally honest. When I was with John I was constantly having to watch what I said.'

The touch of Vanessa's hand across the table felt reassuring and Karen continued with her narrative.

After the conference she and John saw each other regularly outside of work. John told his wife he was holding sales team meetings over a pint and a sandwich in the pub. In reality, he went round to Karen's place and they did what people do when they're having an affair. Karen looked forward to this physical closeness and also to the simple pleasure of having someone she loved in her flat. She frequented recipe websites to find something new to cook for him each time. She bought new bed linen and two expensive crystal wine goblets. She even tried to persuade John to go shopping with her for a new settee.

'You spend so much time here,' she said one evening as they lay bare skin next to bare skin. 'It's only right you should have a say in the furnishings.'

He tilted her chin upwards with his finger and she looked into tender, loving eyes. 'We can't go out in public, love. Fiona has loads of gossipy friends — we'd be spotted and reported on the bush telegraph.'

Karen nodded. She didn't cry until he'd left and then she beat her pillow with the frustration of having to always be the invisible woman.

'It's awful not being able to at least phone you,' she said to him the next time. 'I understand the kids need you but sometimes, especially when you're with them all weekend, I just want to hear your voice.'

'Fiona sometimes uses my mobile,' he said, 'when hers is lost or she's forgotten to charge it. I can't risk her finding calls or texts from you. And the girls might answer the landline.'

So Karen bought him a second phone.

'Keep this one hidden,' she told him. 'It will be my life-line to you. It can be on silent if you want — just check it regularly and then use it to call me back.'

It worked and Karen felt less isolated. John called her each day at weekends and during holiday times. She never asked how he excused himself to make these calls — the less she knew about his home life the easier it was to bear. The phone conversations didn't replace his longed-for physical presence but they did make her feel less like a cheap floozy wanted only for her body.

Despite their close proximity at work they were careful to keep everything on a businesslike footing. During lunchtime drinks with colleagues they kept at opposite ends of the group. But occasionally John would catch Karen's eye and her heart would lift with the secret they shared. One Thursday there was a lunchtime pub session to give a male colleague a wedding send-off and not all the gifts purchased with the whip-round were tasteful. The saucepan set and gravy boat were from the official wedding list but the groom blushed when he unwrapped the final present. Someone forced his arm into the air so that everyone could see the cover of *A Honeymoon Instruction Manual*, illustrated with stick figures of a man and a woman.

'We don't want you to be all fingers and thumbs on your wedding night!' shouted someone, starting a tidal wave of similar remarks.

'We want you to feel that we're right there with you, urging you along!'

'Don't want you to fall at the first hurdle!'

'I'll borrow it when you come back!' John called.

Karen's head swivelled towards him, her body suddenly tense. What was he going to say next?

'It might teach an old dog some new tricks,' he continued.

He caught her eye, grinned and winked. She felt better — he was only joking with the lads, as far as she was concerned he had no need of a sex instruction manual.

John spoke again, looking away from her. 'It's our twentieth anniversary next month. Fiona's parents are having the kids *and* paying for our second honeymoon, cruising the Caribbean. With all those hours at sea we'll be able to put that book to good use!'

The jealousy reared up in Karen. John should have told *her* this news first not broadcast it to the world. She was supposed to be important to him. Then it hit her in the face: she could never replace Fiona in the pecking order. Or get anywhere close to it. The cement of twenty years' shared history was too strong. This reality was like a tank, thundering over her heart and crushing it. Despite all the emotional energy, hopes and dreams she'd ploughed into their relationship, she'd never be good enough to usurp Fiona.

Karen walked out of the pub leaving John guffawing with the rest of them at rude jokes about male private parts. She walked in circles around the city centre until lunch was over. She wanted to go home, curl into a ball and cry but they'd notice if she wasn't back at the office. Why hadn't John explained to her first about this second honeymoon? In the pub he'd looked as though he was excited about this time alone with his wife. It was obvious John didn't share the emotional connection she felt for him. She was just his sex toy to satisfy his libido.

Anger overwhelmed her and all she could think of was revenge. She wouldn't be his dirty little secret any more. This was the end. It was time to clear the air so that all three of them in this relationship knew the score.

She wasn't thinking rationally. She wasn't thinking cause and effect. She wasn't thinking of anyone except herself and how she could damage the person who'd used her. Karen was the proverbial woman scorned. She scrolled through her mobile for his home phone number. She'd had to beg him for it — saying it was only for an absolute emergency and that she would be the model of discretion. She'd never used it but this was an emergency and she had no intention of being discreet.

A young girl answered after just two rings. It must be half-term or something for her to be at home in the middle of the day.

'Mum!' she yelled when Karen asked to speak to Fiona. 'It's for yoo-hoo!'

'Hello?'

'Hello.'

'Who is this?'

John's wife obviously didn't recognise Karen's voice from the few times they'd met. Karen imagined her standing in the hallway of their four-bedroomed detached house (she'd driven past a couple of times just to see what it looked like) or perhaps she was in the kitchen using a cordless phone while she mused about what her husband might like for dinner. Either way, Karen guessed she'd be neatly dressed in jeans and a feminine blouse — bought with their joint credit card.

Karen remained silent, wanting Fiona to suffer.

'I don't buy over the phone and I don't take part in surveys.' The voice had become tetchy.

'I'm not selling anything. I'm going to give you some free information.' Karen sensed Fiona was about to put the phone down so she hurried on without thinking how this would damage at least three other lives as well as John's. 'Your husband has been having an affair — with me. But don't worry, I'm about to end it so he will be all yours again. Try asking him if he enjoyed the final night of the last sales conference he went on.'

Then Karen hung up. She felt better. The tension and anger which had descended so suddenly in the pub had gone.

And she felt as though she'd been released from chains. The fact that her rage vanished so quickly made her realise she hadn't cared for John as much as she thought. Had she only imagined herself in love because being physically desired made her feel good? When she thought about it, being with John had made her feel both less and more lonely at the same time. Perhaps it was a good thing they were finished. Theirs had been a relationship based on deception and, like a castle built on sand, it would never have lasted.

John didn't return to the office after lunch. The others said his wife called him home for a domestic emergency.

Karen pushed the old phone towards Vanessa. 'Please take it up to the museum for me. I suddenly feel exhausted and I've got to get back to work.'

'Don't go yet,' Vanessa said. 'You said this was his phone. How did you get it back? Did you and John continue to work together?'

Karen looked at her watch; she could manage a few more minutes.

She'd expected John to call that night, after she'd betrayed him, but he didn't. He was late to the office the next day and looked terrible. He was unshaven and wearing the same clothes he'd had on the previous day.

'I hope you know what you've done,' he hissed when they were alone in the kitchen. 'Why did you do it? I thought we had something good between us. I thought we cared about each other.'

'You showed me no care at all when you told the whole office about your wonderful, sex-filled second honeymoon before you explained it to me,' she hissed back.

'That was between me and Fiona — nothing to do with you.'

'You just said you cared about me! If you cared about me I should have been told immediately the cruise idea was suggested.'

John's mouth opened but no words came out. His face registered incredulity. 'My wife and family life doesn't

256

involve you. I never, ever, said I would leave Fiona and the girls. What we had was good but you must have known my family always came first.' He shoved 'their' phone into Karen's hand. 'I won't be needing this any more.'

Karen took the phone home and dumped it on the kitchen work surface. Putting it straight in the bin seemed too final. After that, she and John only spoke when it was absolutely unavoidable in the office, otherwise they communicated work stuff via curt emails.

John deteriorated. She discovered via their colleagues that his wife had thrown him out and that his daughters refused to see him. No-one else knew why and he wouldn't say. He behaved honourably in that way at least. Karen learned he didn't have the finances to rent a flat and was sleeping on a succession of floors and sofas. At first she thought it served him right but, as it continued into a second month, she began to feel guilty. Surely, when Fiona felt he'd been punished enough she would take him back. But she didn't.

Now Karen deeply regretted that phone call to Fiona. She should've simply spoken to John and ended their affair quietly. Neither he nor his family deserved to have their world brought crashing down like this. The old mobile phone became Karen's hair shirt. Seeing it every day was a self-imposed punishment for the terrible thing she'd done to that family. She felt the guilt even more when she started dating Tim and knew John had no-one.

Karen desperately wanted to put things right for John. She went, unannounced, to see his wife. Fiona wouldn't let her in but Karen pleaded. Fiona looked haggard and too thin. Karen painted herself blacker than black and John whiter than white. She pretended that the whole affair had been instigated by her and that John had just been a pawn in Karen's evil machinations. She emphasised that John had felt no emotional connection to her. When she'd finished her speech both she and Fiona were in tears. But still she wouldn't take him back.

'He betrayed his family. It doesn't matter who was the instigator. He's a grown man and he took the decision to sleep with you. And he carried on sleeping with you for months and months.'

Fiona continued to make sure John got what she thought he deserved and Karen still struggled with the guilt she felt for ending the affair so catastrophically in a moment of anger. Karen sat back in her chair. She felt exhausted but also like a weight had been lifted.

Vanessa went behind the counter for a minute and then put another cup of hot, sweet milky coffee in front of Karen. 'On the house. Drink it before you rush back to work. It will help.'

'Tim was right. This place does have something special about it. It's not an immediate and complete cure for my angst, more like a gentle reassuring nudge to a better future.'

Vanessa smiled.

* * *

Karen felt wobbly when she left the café. Tim would go and read her 'confession'. He might hate her for allowing a moment of anger to destroy a family. But if he still wanted her, their relationship would be strengthened. If he didn't, it would be for the best. She was done with secrets. She wanted to be her whole, true self with her life partner. Telling her story had been more difficult than she'd imagined but now she wanted to do something even harder; she wanted to make peace between herself and John Crewe. How to do that, she wasn't sure. Even though some years had passed and they still worked in the same office, he never looked her in the eye. She didn't blame him for blanking her. If he persisted, she would, instead, give her time to a worthwhile charity involving children or families, and make amends that way.

CHAPTER TWENTY-EIGHT

A week or so after Polly's devastating confession in the museum, her story hit the headlines. The press didn't get it from us. I spotted it in the newspapers on the way to work. Most of the front pages were exclaiming over the latest utterance of the president of the United States but a couple the tabloids mentioned Polly towards the bottom of their front cover.

"*Murderer Gives Away Victim's Slippers*"

"*Elderly Lady in Mercy Killing*"

In the newsagents I picked up the nearest paper and it confirmed the police had found Polly's husband dead in bed. It made me sad. Very sad. Despite all the indications to the contrary, I'd wanted a happy ending. I wondered if Polly had told them about using the pillow as well as the sleeping tablets or would forensic tests reveal that? The Little Museum of Hope was mentioned in detail and in a positive light. It was free advertising for us, from an awful situation. I felt guilty.

'The prompt action of Stephen Bond and Vanessa Jones saved the old lady's life,' the paper said. 'Donating to or visiting their unusual museum helps to mend broken hearts. It's a social service for the lovelorn.'

When I arrived at the museum, Stephen already had copies of a couple of the other papers. I put my glasses on to read the stories in detail.

'They've charged her with murder. That's terrible, I didn't think they'd do it. She's too old.'

'It's horrible but being old doesn't put you above the law,' Stephen said. 'Look at the charges of historical child abuse and the war crime trials.'

'But this was a mercy killing. There was nothing wicked about it.'

'They'll go easy on her. When the judge has all the facts. At least she can't kill herself now and that's what we wanted, wasn't it?'

I must have looked upset because Stephen came closer, lifted my chin with his finger and looked into my eyes with genuine concern. 'Cheer up,' he said. 'She's got bail. We'll be able to visit her and see how she is.'

That day was our busiest ever and several people came up to the desk and asked if they could see Malcolm's slippers and read the full story in Polly's own words. Stephen told them we hadn't yet put the slippers on display.

'Because of the publicity around her case it's impossible for us to display them anonymously,' I heard him explain at least four times. 'We need to get explicit written permission from Polly that she is happy for them still to be shown in the museum.'

We'd decided this tactic between us. It seemed the only fair way forward.

'We've sold out of cake for the first time ever,' I told Stephen when we closed up at the end of the day. 'And only two scones left. In different circumstances I'd call it a celebration. Here, one scone each.'

I handed him a plate with a scone chopped in half and topped with cream and jam. 'Do you think today was a one-off? Or do I increase the order with the bakery and talk Joanne into more baking lessons so that my output isn't limited to bread pudding?'

Stephen had a pink, creamy smear on his top lip. I fought the temptation to remove it with my finger, settling instead for a gesture at my own lip to tell him it was there. He grinned, mirrored my movements and caught the smear.

'Leave it until Friday,' he said. 'And then increase the order for Saturday if visitor numbers are still up. Today's news will be tomorrow's chip wrappers. And Joanne has already told me she's happy to give you more lessons whenever you want them.'

The following day the phone turned red hot. More of the papers, news websites and TV channels were running Polly's story. The first time I received a demand for an exclusive interview about Polly, I was too shocked to say anything other than, 'No!' and slam the phone down. Neither Stephen nor I wanted her sad story bounced around the newsstands.

Over the next couple of days, reporters started wandering round the museum incognito, asking seemingly innocuous questions about the exhibits and then catching us off guard by suddenly mentioning Polly. The ticket money from these leeches was welcome but we learned to recognise them from the way they looked into every corner of the exhibition hall, as though expecting to stumble over Malcolm's slippers. When their questions began, we stuck solely to the story of the museum and its purpose. Stephen pinned up a notice prohibiting photography. The less material these hacks had for their papers the better.

'We should give one paper an exclusive and then the rest will have to stop bothering us,' Stephen said eventually.

'We should talk to Melissa. Find out what she and Polly think — and how much of the story they are happy to go public with. But if we're giving an exclusive then it should go to Tim from the local paper. He's supported us all the way.'

We visited Polly at Melissa's house that evening. Melissa's husband was out with the boys at football practice and so the two women were alone. Melissa served us mugs of tea and chocolate digestive biscuits. Polly looked older, sadder and frailer. I felt as though we should apologise for keeping her alive but the words would sound in bad taste.

Stephen sat next to her on the settee and took her hand.

'I guess you've seen the papers?' My voice sounded too bright.

Stephen gauged the mood better. 'Your actions were truly humane, Polly, and done in the name of love,' he said in a gentle tone. 'So far the papers have majored on sensationalism which is totally out of place. Reporters are at the museum every day wanting more. We've refused. But this interest won't die down until they get a story.'

All of us were looking at Polly.

'I don't want Malcolm's story on a page next to some girl who's got her top off. He isn't, wasn't that kind of man.' Her voice was quiet but determined.

Stephen was now holding both her hands. 'Our thoughts exactly,' he said. 'We'd like to give an exclusive to Tim, a reporter from the local free newspaper. He wrote about the museum when it first opened and really understood what Vanessa was trying to do. Following on from that, his girlfriend, Karen, recently donated an object to the museum as well.'

'Tim will make a really good job of it,' I added. 'There'd be no sensationalism and we'd be doing him a good turn. Think how much this would help his career.'

'That's another positive you can leave behind, Mum.' Melissa looked from her mother to us and then back again. 'We've been talking about all the positives that Mum and Dad have both done in their lives. Of course, in my opinion, adopting me and imbuing me with unconditional love, was the very best thing. And they enabled me to pass that on to the next generation.'

As if on cue, a car door slammed outside and two boys in football kit raced into the lounge. They stopped abruptly when they saw strangers.

'Hello boys. How was the match?' In the blink of an eye, Stephen switched from the gentle tones needed by the bereaved to matey men's football talk. Fleetingly I wondered if he saw in these two boys something of Nick and Rob. If he did, he didn't show it; he still held one of Polly's hands.

'Yes, to that reporter,' Polly whispered to me in a barely audible voice. 'But I don't want to talk to him and I don't want the rest of the family hassled either. Melissa will give you some photos he can use. Make sure they're good ones — even at my age a lady still has some vanity.'

Melissa pulled me to one side as we were about to leave. 'Obviously I'm in favour of your reporter but given that' — she glanced over at her mother and lowered her voice — 'there will be a trial, I need to get the OK from Mum's solicitor first. Can I text you later?'

'Of course. We don't want to rock the boat.'

Melissa was as good as her word and, an hour later, texted the go ahead for the article.

Tim came to the museum the next morning, early before the public arrived. His excitement at being given the exclusive was obvious. 'When I told him where I was going, Phil, my editor, wanted to come too. "Don't you trust me to get it right?" I asked him. "I deserve this scoop. When you couldn't be bothered to write about the museum opening, you sent me instead. I did them proud and this is my reward." You should've seen his face — he was jealous as hell.' Tim was setting up his camera. 'I thought we'd have a general shot of the museum interior because I understand what you said about Polly wanting the ethos of this place to be centrepiece for the article, even if what happened to her is the catalyst for me being here.'

Stephen threw me a glance and I nodded back. This is exactly what we wanted, the focus on us, not Polly. After the photos, the three of us went into the café.

'Bread pudding?' I offered, always keen to show off my own creation.

Tim put a digital recording device on the table and asked us questions about Polly and Malcolm. Then he sat back and savoured his cake while we talked about the various other donations we'd had.

'Your girlfriend, Karen,' Stephen said, 'that was a story with a real message to take away.'

Tim put his hand up to call a halt and switched off the device. 'I'm not including that one. I haven't read the full story of what she told you yet, but whatever, it's too close to home, even with the use of a false name.' We nodded our understanding and then Tim's voice dropped a little. 'I think coming here did help her. She's been less uptight over the last few days, more focused on the future and giving something back to society. She's found this charity. Basically, adults offer their time to a disadvantaged youngster. Every week or every fortnight they take the kid out somewhere nice or do some activity that the child wouldn't otherwise get the chance to do. It might be going swimming, baking a cake or anything. Karen's going through the selection procedure. She said it's her way of making up for the two young lives she damaged. I'm not sure whether I'm ready to know the truth about how she did that damage or not.'

'Only read it when you feel ready,' I said gently. 'But what she's doing now is great! I feel so proud of the effect our little museum is having.'

'*Your* museum,' Stephen corrected.

'But it feels like . . .' Stephen was so dedicated to the museum that I sometimes forgot he had no financial interest in it all. To the business and to me, he was so much more than just a volunteer.

'There's something between you two, isn't there?' Tim said.

Stephen and I looked at each other. His eyes wouldn't leave mine. I couldn't turn my head and my stomach flipped over. 'No,' we said together.

Tim's expression was disbelieving. 'It's the way you glance at each other, like now, and seem to know what the other will say. Mark my words, before very long you'll be sending out the wedding invites.'

'Polly's given permission for a photo of Malcolm's slippers.' I changed the subject. 'I've got them here. Is the light all right for the camera or do you want to go upstairs?'

He got the message and the conversation returned to Polly and the museum. Tim took some pictures of the slippers. We finished the interview as the first visitors walked into the café. I went to serve them, still dwelling on what Tim had said about Stephen and me. My business manager was constantly making me feel like a teenager with a crush but at my age and with my baggage, there was more at stake than the possibility of being dumped after a couple of weeks. I thought about Dave and his suggestion of visiting Liam together. Karen's story had underlined the importance of keeping families whole and not letting one error of judgement spoil all that had been built in the past. But a relationship couldn't be maintained long-term for the sake of the children. Dave didn't make my stomach flip. But did Stephen have room in his heart for anyone but Trish? Did Joanne come into the frame?

Tim didn't leave the museum straight after the interview. As I was upstairs, pinning up the notice for the day's café special offer, I noticed him at the display cabinet containing Karen's old mobile phone. Karen had said he only knew part of the story, not exactly how low an outburst of temper had taken her. It would be Tim's decision whether to read the full story and his choice about what happened next. I went towards him. Karen had been so honest with us, the least I could do was stick up for her. Tim looked shaken. He'd sat down on the wooden bench just behind the display, his camera bag and rucksack between his feet. He rested his elbows on his thighs and his chin in his hands.

'All right?' I asked.

'I don't know. His poor daughters, having their family wrecked like that.'

Please don't let him end the relationship because she was brave enough to share her story and move on. Please don't let the museum be the cause of them both losing this chance at love.

'What Karen did was wrong,' I said, 'but she's a different person now.'

'Please don't give me your judgement. You don't really know either of us or the dynamics of our relationship. I need to make up my own mind.'

His words felt like a slap in the face, an accusation of poking my nose in where it wasn't wanted. 'OK. I'm sorry.'

Tim was still sitting there an hour later when I came back into the museum hall with Stephen's morning coffee. 'Has Tim said anything to you?' I asked.

Stephen shook his head.

By lunchtime he was gone and we were none the wiser about his intentions. If their relationship came to an end because of the museum then I'd have to seriously rethink what we were about.

'I had a text from Joanne,' Stephen said casually as we tidied up at the end of the day. 'A group of them that met at the singles' night are going out for a drink. She's invited me along.'

'That's nice.' I stared hard at the dishcloth I was wringing out. 'I hope it works out for you both.'

'What?'

'I hope it's a good night.'

'I'm still fairly new to the area so I thought it would be good to meet some new people. I can talk about the museum. No objections?'

'No. Why would I? You don't need my permission to go out with people.' There was a catch in my voice. I turned the tap on to hide it. It made life simpler knowing that Stephen was interested in Joanne not me. I wasn't sure what she had to offer that I didn't, but that was romantic chemistry for you. I fumbled for an internal switch that could turn off my feelings for Stephen.

* * *

Tim wrote a well-balanced article on Polly and the museum. He also included resumes of some of the other donations but without mention of Karen's. Following on from this, we did good business, with lots of locals calling in. During four days we took the same money as we'd taken during the previous four weeks.

'It still doesn't seem right,' I said to Stephen, 'to be making money out of someone else's misfortune.'

'We're not. The slippers aren't on display. Look upon it as a gift of free advertising. We could never afford an advert on the front page of a newspaper. And it's not only us. It's been great for the whole area. The Pen Room say it's their busiest week ever and all the tours at The Museum of the Jewellery Quarter have been fully booked.'

'Does this buy us any extra time?' It was the question I didn't want to ask in case Stephen slammed down the shutters on us. 'It's September now. You said October was our limit. Has Maxine got a job to come back to?'

A shadow passed over Stephen's face. 'No change. The recent extra income helps balance July and August which were poor because the hot weather tempted people to the seaside instead of into cities.'

I ordered more cakes for Saturday only. The weekend was busy but then we became old news and numbers went down again. They settled at slightly above our pre-Polly days. Still not enough to make the museum a long-term viable proposition. Unless something happened soon, I would lose my investment and there would be no job for Maxine, and Stephen would have to volunteer elsewhere. And that joy and pride I felt every time a donor left with a new spring in their step would be gone. That last thought and the prospect of forfeiting our three musketeers' camaraderie upset me far more than the possibility of losing money. The museum had taught me that happiness had far more to do with personal relationships than money.

Stephen didn't offer a report on his drinks' night with Joanne and the other singletons. I didn't ask. His private life was none of my business. Instead, I pushed aside my jealous thoughts about Joanne and asked her to teach me how to make scones — one of our bestsellers.

'I'd love another baking date,' she said. 'The secret to scones is to use icy cold butter. I'll talk you through it step-by-step when we're together.'

CHAPTER TWENTY-NINE

October

Six weeks after Michael's birth, Maxine brought him into the museum. The little mite was again cocooned in blue blankets but this time in his car seat on wheels. His eyes were closed with dark lashes resting on chubby cheeks and his lips making little sucking motions. I wanted to scoop him up, hold him close and breathe in that sweet milky smell of baby.

'Go ahead.' Maxine read my thoughts. 'But if you wake him, it's your job to get him back off to sleep again.'

I didn't need telling twice. We'd installed a couple of armchairs in the museum for people who just wanted to sit and reflect. I sat in one of these cradling Michael. With newborn Liam, life had been a constant round of feeding, changing, anxiety about whether I was doing it right and trying to make him sleep. When he did sleep, I charged around the house trying to get as much done as possible in that short slot of freedom or I slept myself. Someone else's baby was an excuse to be idle and simply enjoy holding and watching a sleeping infant.

Gradually, even with his eyes closed, Michael must have sensed it wasn't his mother cuddling him and he began to whimper and then to grizzle.

Stephen arrived alongside me with the pram and gestured towards it.

'Always worked for me when Trish needed help getting the boys off to sleep.'

I placed Michael gently back in his cocoon and Stephen pushed him around and around the glass cases.

'Much, much easier than manoeuvring a double buggy,' he declared as he wheeled the sleeping baby back to his mother.

'I bet you were a great dad,' Maxine said.

'Probably no better than anyone else. But I did my best . . .' Stephen's voice tailed off and he stared at the floor.

He was in need of a hug but I didn't want it misconstrued the wrong way: a clingy, unwanted romantic interest trying to usurp Joanne or an offer of the pity he'd signalled a long time ago he didn't want. I made no move towards him. It was as though a glass screen had come down between us. Instead, I bent over the pram and rearranged blankets and traced the baby soft skin with my finger.

A phone ringing made us all jump. Stephen patted his pockets and then cut the noise.

'Joanne!' he said and then lowered his voice, took a step away and turned his back on us. 'I'd love to . . . Yes . . . That would be great.'

It was good he had a girlfriend, I told myself firmly. He deserved to find happiness after everything he'd been through and all the unpaid hours he'd put in at the museum. And Joanne deserved the love of a good man.

'Dave's been in touch with me,' Maxine announced when Stephen had finished his sotto voce conversation.

'My Dave?'

'Yes.' Maxine was smiling. 'He wants to buy air tickets for you and him to fly to Canada for a holiday with Liam. He wanted to know when I'd be back at work so that Stephen and I could hold the fort while you were away. But I guess you know this already?'

'We'd mentioned it in passing.' I'd expected us to discuss it further before taking the decision to book tickets. This felt like Dave directing my life and I didn't like it.

'I'll hold the fort for as long as you like,' Stephen said. 'Family's important. It'll be lovely for all three of you to be together again.' He paused. 'If the museum's still in business.'

'What!' Maxine looked from me to Stephen and back again. 'What do you mean if it's still in business?'

I glared at my business manager. 'Don't worry, Maxine. Things looked a bit dodgy during the hot summer but, since the publicity over Polly, business has picked up.'

Maxine frowned as though she didn't trust what I was saying but she didn't push it. 'I'd be happy to hold the fort too.' She glanced at Stephen. 'Being home alone is driving me up the wall. As long as you don't mind me bringing Michael in and parking him in the corner? I want to be out of the house but I don't want to leave him with other people yet.'

Stephen nodded.

'I'll tell Dave to go ahead and book.' Maxine got her phone out.

I sat down in the armchair again. Everyone was too eager to get rid of me. I was being pushed out of my own museum. Seeing Liam again would be fantastic and watching him and Dave renew their relationship would be lovely. I should be grateful for the support of all these people around me. So why did I feel empty? Joanne and Stephen. While I went off to Canada, they were going to become an item and I was jealous. Stephen didn't want me so I didn't want him to have anyone else. I turned my head away from my musketeers, gave my cheeks a hard slap, made my lips smile and then stood up to face the world.

'I'll open up downstairs,' I said, stepping back into my professional role. 'Maxine, if you're happy to stick around with baby Michael today, please can you help out up here?'

Alone in the café I took some time to breathe and pull myself together. I was going to see my son! We would be a sort-of-family in a way that we hadn't been since we waved Liam off at the airport with his giant rucksack. Family ties were the ones that lasted over the years. Becoming a couple with Dave wasn't compulsory to make this trip. The museum had shown me I could cope without the man who had brazenly rejected me. When we came back from Canada, I would tell Dave we had to sell the house and start afresh in our own little shoebox flats. Life was for moving forward not recreating the past.

Feeling more composed, I carried coffee upstairs for Maxine and Stephen. After taking her mug, Maxine pointed between the display cabinets. Tim was again staring at Karen's story and the old mobile phone.

'This is my fault,' I said. 'I can't let it end badly.' Maxine pulled on my arm but I ignored her and strode down the exhibition hall. Before I reached him, Tim had pulled out his phone.

'Karen?'

'Please, Tim.' I went right up to him, invading his personal space and privacy. 'She's a much better woman now. If you finish with her it's like you're both jumping off a cliff for no reason.'

'I'm not—'

'She loves you and you love her. You don't have to love the person she was before. The past is gone.' I grabbed at his phone so he couldn't make both their lives implode.

Tim glared at me, snatched his phone, walked several paces away and turned his back. He didn't go far enough. I could still hear. 'Karen.' His voice was gentle. 'I'm at the museum. I've read the whole story. It's the second time I've been here and studied the whole thing. I've been thinking about us.'

There was a long pause. Impossible to tell if Karen was talking or if Tim was trying to find the words for bad news. I closed my eyes and crossed my fingers.

'Karen, be quiet, please. I need to ask you something. Will you marry me?'

Flabbergasted didn't cover it. Was Karen as shocked as me? Tim turned around, phone still at his ear. I'd never seen a grin as happy.

'She said yes!' He hugged me and I could hear little excited squeals from his mobile.

'Congratulations!' I shouted to Karen. 'I know you'll both be very happy.'

Tim bounced out of the museum, stopping briefly at the reception desk to make Stephen and Maxine cheer at his news.

Tim's proposal put a smile on my lips for the rest of the morning. The museum was having the effect I wanted and, come hell or high water, I would find a way to keep it going. Stephen said October. A month was a long time in business.

CHAPTER THIRTY

A few days later, Melissa came into the café. I watched for Polly following but there was no-one. Melissa came straight up to the counter, instead of finding a seat. Her face was carefully made-up but the tiredness around her eyes couldn't be hidden.

'It's good to see you,' I said. 'How's your mum doing?'

'Can we talk?' She gestured over to the empty tables. 'Is Stephen around? He ought to hear this as well.'

I phoned upstairs for him to come down, then I made tea, buttered three of my own, museum-baked scones and carried the tray over to the table that Melissa had selected.

'I wanted you to know before it hit the papers,' Melissa started as soon as I'd transferred the floral crockery from the tray to the table. 'Mum died yesterday morning. It was natural causes.'

I glanced at Stephen. He looked as shocked as me.

'Oh, Melissa.' I reached across the table and put my hand on hers. This was especially bad coming so soon after she'd lost her dad. 'I'm sorry, love.'

'I don't know what to say,' Stephen said. 'Is there anything we can do? Either personally or as the museum?'

Melissa shook her head. We sat in silence for a couple of minutes. Then Melissa sniffed and pulled her hand from mine in order to find her handkerchief. I poured the tea.

'There's something else you need to know.' Melissa blew her nose. 'Mum changed her will a couple of weeks ago. She added this museum as a beneficiary.'

'What?' Stephen and I spoke in unison and then stared at each other again.

'She told me how honourable you'd been by refusing the £50,000 she offered. At the time she was angry but eventually realised you'd done the right thing and then she worried she'd caused offence by making the offer . . .' Melissa paused before continuing, 'So, this place is now £50,000 better off. Mum wanted to make sure the museum could continue its work — she believed in its ability to help people through their sadness.'

'Oh!' My hand went to my mouth.

'Wow!' Stephen's voice was almost a whisper.

'I'm sure you can put it to good use.'

'But what about you, Melissa?' Stephen said. 'Surely that money should go to you?'

'Don't worry about me. I get the house, which, after what happened there, will go straight on the market. And, towards the end, my parents were very frugal. With Dad the way he was they couldn't go out much anyway and Mum refused to splash out on new clothes. Sometimes I'd go around there and the two of them would be dressed like tramps. There are other savings and investments for me. Besides, I'm hardly poverty-stricken.' Melissa indicated her well-cut jacket and trousers. There was a designer name stamped into the dark hide of her leather handbag.

'I don't know what to say except thank you. I don't know whether Polly realised the museum was in financial difficulty but that amount of money will really help us.'

'Yes, thank you very much.' Stephen echoed my sentiment. 'Melissa, your mother was a good woman and she obviously loved your father deeply.'

'Would you like your father's slippers back?' I said. They were still sitting in the locked cupboard beneath the reception desk upstairs. 'It's impossible for us to display them anonymously now and they're probably of sentimental value to you.'

'No, keep them and display them with the full story. Perhaps you could put a collecting box alongside for one of the dementia charities? People need to know how the illness devastates people's lives.'

'Thank you.' Again, Stephen and I spoke in unison. He glanced at me and, even though we weren't touching, that electricity was there again, linking us together. I looked away. This middle-aged infatuation would disappear once I started seeing him and Joanne together.

'The solicitors will be in touch in due course to arrange payment of the money but I thought you'd like to know in advance — in case you wanted to make plans.'

'Thank you so much.'

We both saw Melissa to the door of the museum. As soon as she was out of sight, Stephen drew me into a great big hug.

'The three musketeers ride again!' I squealed when I'd struggled free.

'Into the new year!' Stephen said. 'The museum can go well into the new year. That gives us time to get the singles' night established in people's diaries, plan a proper Valentine's event and get a membership programme going.'

'And we could get a sign-writer to do us a proper "Little Museum of Hope" sign for above the front door. Several visitors have commented about how difficult we are to find — who knows how many just give up and go somewhere else instead?'

'Good idea!' Stephen gave me a double thumbs up.

'Is it bad of me to feel that something really good has come from Malcolm and Polly's deaths? Something that makes me feel happy?'

'No. It's what Polly would've wanted.'

We were in the museum hall breaking the news to Maxine, when Dave walked in.

'What's going on?' He was looking at Maxine high-fiving Stephen and then giving a little twirl.

'The museum is safe!' Maxine explained about the money.

'Wow!' Dave said. 'You'll be able to give yourself a pay rise, 'nessa, and we could have a romantic few days in Paris before flying on to Canada. What about a candlelit meal on one of those boats on the Seine? We could upgrade to first class and have champagne. You said you wouldn't turn down first-class flights.'

No-one spoke. The atmosphere had suddenly chilled but Dave didn't notice. He took hold of my hand and kissed it theatrically. 'This museum's all about mending broken hearts and that's what it's done for you and me. Maxine gave me the go-ahead to book tickets and I've been in touch with Liam to arrange dates. He can't wait to see us both. This money will ensure we can really enjoy ourselves. It will be a fresh start.'

Still no-one said anything. Dave looked from me to Stephen to Maxine. 'What's wrong? I'm sure 'nessa will make sure you two each get a little bonus. She does own this place, you know.'

Stephen and Maxine stared at me. I felt for Dave standing in the embarrassing hole he'd just dug himself. Despite all the conversations we'd had, he still hadn't grasped the ethos of the museum and what the place meant to me.

'Dave,' I said slowly. 'This money wasn't left to me as an individual. It was left to the museum to ensure it can continue to exist and help people. You know it struggles to make ends meet. You know the business has a constant overdraft. The money isn't for spending on personal holidays.'

'You own the business and therefore you can take out of the business any money you see fit. Don't you want us to go together to see Liam? I thought family came first with you.'

'Of course, I want to see Liam. I want to spend time with him just as much as Maxine wants to be with baby

Michael. But I can't use Polly's money to turn the trip into a luxury junket.'

Dave shook his head as though he genuinely couldn't understand what I was saying. 'You're the sole proprietor. You can do what you like with the money. Mending your own family is more important than making strangers feel better. Maxine is just staff and Stephen's only a *volunteer.*'

There was shock on the faces of my musketeers.

'If this money isn't used solely for the business, *as Polly wanted*' — I emphasised the last three words — 'the museum will close. Lots of unhappy people won't be helped. Maxine will be unemployed and Stephen and I . . .' Despite his new relationship with Joanne, the thought of no longer working with Stephen was so bad I couldn't finish the sentence.

'I can't be around someone unwilling to share their good fortune with their family,' Dave said.

'I think this is a private argument.' Stephen gestured to Maxine to move away.

I tried to give Stephen a grateful look but he'd already turned and busied himself with the computer. Maxine picked up a duster and headed over to the display cases. Dave and I went down to the café.

'I can't be around someone who wants to go against the wishes of a dead old lady. Polly wanted her money to help other people like herself. I too want those people to be helped to move on and live the best life they can. It can't be done without money.'

'There are cheaper ways of employing people. A sixteen-year-old at weekends would cost far less than Maxine, in terms of minimum wage.' He paused and then added more gently, 'You won't even need a business when we're married again. I'm still earning and there'll be a pension when I retire. Wasn't the museum just an antidote to loneliness?'

I clenched my fists to stop myself strangling him. When Dave abandoned me for Gillian my life fell apart. He robbed me of my self-confidence, leaving me weak and pathetic. I blamed his affair on my failings as a wife. The future became a long, dark tunnel with no pinprick of light. But a lot had happened since then. Now I could see Dave for the man that he was: always wanting more than he was entitled to, whether it be another woman, the woman he'd once discarded or an old woman's money on which he had no claim. Out of all the wrongs he'd done me, the latter was the final straw.

'I can't live with someone who won't share their good fortune.' Dave seemed unaware that the knives he was using on me were now blunt. 'And, if you won't share, I think it's my turn to have the marital home to myself.'

He expected me to back-pedal and capitulate but he was playing into my hands. 'Selling up and splitting the proceeds is the fair way forward,' I said. Now the light at the end of the tunnel was almost blinding. I relished the thought of a baggageless new start, wherever that might be, even if it meant camping out in the museum. It was time to start unpicking that last matted spaghetti lump of our marriage.

'Have it your way but you'll regret it when this place crashes and burns. £50,000 won't make it last forever.' Dave turned and walked out. He didn't bother to catch the front door of the museum and it slammed shut behind him. I felt exhilarated, weak, brave and scared all at once. Something more final and defining than the divorce had happened.

I made it up the stairs to the museum hall and then crumpled onto the hard chair behind the reception desk.

'Atta girl!' Maxine gave me a friendly punch on the shoulder. 'You are totally in the right. In life you have to move forwards not backwards.'

'You were listening?'

'No choice. You left the café door open and your voices were so loud.'

'Café,' Stephen mouthed at Maxine and gestured downwards.

She gave a mock salute, unclipped Michael's seat from its wheels and disappeared, leaving the empty pram frame next to the reception desk. Stephen pulled a second plastic chair alongside mine.

'That was tough. How do you feel?'

'Mortified to have my dirty linen washed in public.' I tried to grin, sit up and appear light-hearted.

'No, really,' Stephen pressed. 'How do you feel about Canada, Liam and what he said about the house? He's right about you owning the museum and therefore Polly's money being yours to use how you see fit. Using it to mend your broken family could be the sort of good Polly was hoping to do. I know you were looking forward to the three of you being together again.'

'No, Polly didn't intend it for personal use.'

'But you deserve some happiness in return for all the people you've helped.'

'The concept of the museum helped them, not me personally. Just like the museum's helped me as well. I'm a better person now and I can finally see Dave for the toad that he is.'

'Don't you want to visit your son?'

'I'm still going to see Liam. On my own, flying economy and without a stop in Paris.' After everything that had happened, the pull of the mother-child bond was a physical tug on my heart and a lump in my throat. 'He's probably the only person left who really loves me.'

'So, you don't want Dave back as your husband?'

'No. I thought I might but I was looking for the easy way. Being back with Dave would've been like following a well-trodden path. Comfortable until we got to the part where it all went wrong last time. And after his outburst just now, I know we would have got to that part very soon.'

'What about mixing business with pleasure? Would that work?' He paused for a moment and then spoke hesitantly. 'After what happened at the singles' night, I couldn't say anything until I knew I wasn't upsetting things between you and Dave.'

'What?' He was confusing me and I looked into his face for clarification. His eyes were soft and deep. He took my hand. My stomach flipped over. I removed my gaze from him. He was teasing. What about Joanne? This wasn't fair. This couldn't be how Stephen operated.

'Us?' he said.

'Joanne?'

'What?'

'You went out with her. She phoned you just now.'

Stephen threw his head back and laughed. 'I do believe you're jealous!'

I pulled my hand away. 'I'm not jumping from Dave's frying pan into your fire.'

'She invited me along with a group of people who met at the singles' night. They wanted to have some official input into making it a regular event. The call was a follow-up.'

'And you didn't tell me because?'

'You've been overloaded with stuff on your mind. I'm supposed to be your business manager and I was simply looking into new business opportunities.'

'Us? You said us. What did you mean?'

'This.' He leaned over and kissed me on the lips. It was long, slow, tender and, quite simply, the best thing ever. It demanded that my eyes close, my toes curl and the real-life surroundings fade away. It was far, far lovelier than any kiss from Dave.

A round of applause made me pull away.

'At last!' Maxine was stood in front of us with the baby carrier over one arm. 'I thought you two would never come to your senses and realise you were made for each other. Even before you acted like two lovebirds at the hospital, I knew you were a perfect match. Now, Joanne is on the phone querying whether you're still on for the chocolate cake baking lesson tomorrow? And she says I can join in too!'

'Tell Joanne, "Yes".' My voice was shaky after what had just happened. Then Stephen's arm was around my shoulders pulling me close again. I snuggled deep into the place where I belonged.

'But tonight, we will both be otherwise engaged,' he announced and kissed me again.

I had finally found my life's passion.

THE END

THE CHOC LIT STORY

Established in 2009, Choc Lit is an independent, award-winning publisher dedicated to creating a delicious selection of quality women's fiction.

We have won 18 awards, including Publisher of the Year and the Romantic Novel of the Year, and have been short-listed for countless others.

All our novels are selected by genuine readers. We are proud to publish talented first-time authors, as well as established writers whose books we love introducing to a new generation of readers.

In 2023, we became a Joffe Books company. Best known for publishing a wide range of commercial fiction, Joffe Books has its roots in women's fiction. Today it is one of the largest independent publishers in the UK.

We love to hear from you, so please email us about absolutely anything bookish at

choc-lit@joffebooks.com

If you want to receive free books every Friday and hear about all our new releases, join our mailing list here.

www.choc-lit.com